Succ
An Urban Fantasy / Paranormal Romance

By B.R. Kingsolver

~~~

Published by B.R. Kingsolver at Create Space

~~~

Copyright 2012 B.R. Kingsolver

brkingsolver.com

~~~

Cover art by Mia Darien

Miadarien.com

~~~~

Look for the further adventures of Brenna
O'Donnell in Book 3 of the Telepathic Clans Saga.

Succubus Rising,
An Urban Fantasy / Paranormal Romance

~~~~

i

Praise for *The Succubus Gift*, Book 1 of the Telepathic Clans:

The novel itself is expertly written and an utter joy to read. The characters are all delightful. There were times while I was reading this that I laughed out loud, and other times when I held my breath in anticipation of what might occur. 4.5/5 stars – Night Owl Reviews

This book had it all; lots of action, romance, suspense and humor. Loaded with intrigue and drama ... 5/5 quills – Mel's Book Blog

Let me just start by saying WOW, because this book completely blew my expectations out of the water and then some. The initial synopsis plot struck me as interesting, but it didn't prepare me for the utterly heart stopping onslaught of sex, violence and paranormal abilities ... a great unique addition to the paranormal/urban fantasy genre and I'd definitely recommend this to fans of the genre! It had everything I could ask for, love, sex, violence, witty banter, supernatural abilities. I am so excited to see what Kingsolver does next! 5/5 HOT steaming cups - Tea and Text

Well written, a story that kept me turning the pages and wanting to know more... I can't give a higher rating save to add that you really should buy this book and follow this series... I would never have missed this for the world... A full five out of five pitchforks. - Succubus.net

~~~

Dedication

To Valentina and the kids. It's all for you.

~~~

ACKNOWLEDGEMENTS

Valentina, for your encouragement, reading my first efforts, creating my website, and so much more. Mia Darien for the cover art, edits, comments and suggestions. Jane and Jackie for putting up with me and giving me invaluable feedback and editing help. Hennessee Andrews for reading, editing, and help with the delicate scenes. JQ Trotter and Delancey Stewart for edits, comments and suggestions. To all of you, a sincere thank you.

~~~

Table of Contents

Pronunciation Guide to Names

Some of the names in this book have been Anglicized, for others:

Aine: aw-nya – delight or pleasure

Aislinn: awsh-leen – dream or vision

Aoife: eef-ya – beautiful or radiant

Beltane: bel-tane – May Day, the beginning of the summer season, a springtime festival of optimism

Brenna: bran-na – raven, often referring to hair

Caylin: kay-lin – slender, fair

Irina: ee-ree-na – Russian form of Irene

Mairead: mah-rayd – Gaelic form of Margaret

Morrighan: mor-ri-gan – Celtic goddess

Poitin: po-teen – Irish moonshine

Rhiannon: ree-an-on – Welsh for maiden

Samhain: so-ween – The harvest festival, now called Halloween

Seamus: shay-mus – the supplanter

Sean: shawn – Gaelic form of John

Sinead: shi-nayd – Irish version of Jeanne

Siobhan: shee-vawn – Variation of Jeanne

Slainte: slayn-cheh – 'Health' in Gaelic, a toast

Tuatha De Danann: tu-a-tha de dan-an – The people of the Goddess Danu - The original pre-Celtic inhabitants of Ireland

~~~

A full list and description of the Telepathic Gifts appears at the end of the book.

~~~

Forward

Brenna Morgan had always considered herself a 'good girl.' Her experiences with men and sex were limited, and not very encouraging. It wasn't that she didn't enjoy sex. Quite to the contrary, she enjoyed it immensely, but the same thing would happen every time she went to bed with a man. They made love and then he rolled over and went to sleep while she was still in the midst of her orgasm. She wouldn't hear from him for at least a week or two afterward.

Convinced something was wrong with her, she spent her time alone and never allowed herself to hope for a relationship. She threw herself into her studies, finishing her PhD in Neuroscience at twenty-two. As a telepath, she hoped that studying the brain and how it worked might shed some light on her abilities. In the deepest recesses of her mind, she hoped someday to find another telepath.

Orphaned at eight, she was lost to her family, who thought she had died in the plane crash that killed her parents. Bounced from one foster home to another, always hiding her telepathic abilities, she earned scholarships to a prestigious university. She worked whatever jobs she had to, going hungry and living frugally, so she could graduate without debt.

After all this, it was a shock when she tripped over her cousin one evening. At the time, all she knew was that he was another telepath. As she was welcomed into the O'Donnell Clan by the grandfather and aunt she'd never known, the revelation that an entire telepathic society lived hidden in society's shadows turned her life upside down.

An even bigger shock was discovering she was possibly the strongest telepath in history. No one in history had ever inherited more than fifteen Gifts, but she had all twenty-five. One of those Gifts completely changed her self-perception. She had the Kashani Gift, commonly called the Succubus Gift. Her spectacular physical beauty combined with certain physiological and mental traits to make her different from normal women.

While she had an enhanced ability to attract and pleasure men, the downside was that she drained three quarters of a man's life energy when he climaxed inside her. It wasn't something she could control or prevent. It made morning sex with any man impossible. One and done, then he had to sleep for two or three days and spend days of recuperation to recharge his energy.

Any attempt at a relationship was difficult, to say the least.

She would have despaired if not for tall, handsome Collin Doyle, a powerful telepath himself. He knew what she was, but professed to be in love with her. He told her he didn't care if she slept with other men and even after she took him to bed and drained him, he showed her his mind and convinced her.

Naturally, this homecoming wasn't enough chaos in her life. She soon learned that telepaths from rival Clans were hunting succubi, torturing and killing them. When the succubus Cindy Nelson, her mentor, was captured, Brenna volunteered herself as bait. An elaborate mental construct, like a stage set, was implanted in her mind. With a physical makeover, she was transformed into the predatory redheaded succubus Samantha.

Things didn't go as planned. Brenna ended up being captured and locked in a basement with a monster named Manfred Gless. Gless was a strong telepath with the O'Donnell Gift of mental-shield-shattering Domination that gave him the ability to control people. But Brenna also had this Gift and proved to be stronger. She captured his mind, killed his associates and escaped, but not before being brutalized herself.

Cindy was grievously injured but survived due to the Talents of the Clan's Healers.

While the characteristics of the Succubus Gift seemed evil when she first learned of them, the Clan's history and mythology told a different story. Long before the Romans, the Clans ruled Europe. They worshiped the Mother Goddess, and their priestly class, the Druids, were succubi. The energy drain was an offering to the Goddess through Her priestesses. As she learned about the Gifts, it was easy to see how her ancestors were seen as witches and sorcerers. It was easy to understand why the Clans created myths to hide themselves.

~~~

Succubus Unleashed

<u>Chapter 1</u>

*You have to have the kind of body
that doesn't need a girdle in order
to get to pose in one. - Carolyn
Kenmore*

They noticed him when he walked in. Six feet tall and
very good looking, he stopped just inside the door to let his
eyes adjust. Walking to the bar, he ordered a beer and
turned to survey the room, his eyes stopping when he saw
them watching him. A smile spread across his face.

Sitting in a booth across the room, they scanned his
mind, as they did with every man who caught their
attention.

"Ick," Rebecca said, her mouth crooking in an
expression of distaste.

"Prey," Brenna said with a bright smile.

He was arrogant, conceited, misogynistic, and self-
centered. Brenna was sure she could come up with an
unflattering word to match every letter in the alphabet to
describe him. The bulge in his pants, of which he was so
proud, wasn't really that great, but did promise a fulfilling
encounter.

Rebecca chuckled, taking a long pull at her beer. "I'll
look for someone a little more palatable while you're
gone."

"Try to find one with a friend," Brenna replied. "I
don't plan on spending much time on him."

Exerting Influence, Brenna smiled seductively when
she caught his eyes. Soon he drifted over to their table.

"Are you going to ask me to dance?" Brenna purred,
looking at him through lowered eyelashes.

He nodded. She waited.

"Oh. Do you want to dance?"

1

"Sure. I thought you'd never ask," she smiled, kicking her Glam up a couple of notches.

He wasn't a bad dancer, and when the band played a slow song next, she flowed into his arms. Dribbling pheromones until his eyes glazed and his erection pressing against her stomach was rock hard, she blurred the minds of everyone around them. No one noticed when she broke away. Taking him by the hand, she led him to a dark corner near the restrooms.

Unzipping his pants, she freed his erection and lifting her skirt, fitted him into her. She sighed as he slid into her, filling her. Her back against the wall, she put her arms around his neck and wrapped her legs around his waist. A soft puff of pheromones ensured his cooperation. She leaned back to enjoy the ride.

His life energy flowed into her when he climaxed, triggering a delicious orgasm. As he began to wilt, she put her feet back on the floor. She stood for a few moments reveling in his energy flowing through her, shuddering with pleasure, and watched him slump to the floor unconscious. Adjusting her clothes, she went into the restroom to freshen up, a smile tugging at her lips as she brushed a stray hair back. With one last approving look in the mirror, she headed back to her table.

Two young men awaited her with Rebecca. A quick mental scan told her they were nice guys. Tom and Dave invited them to a party and paid their tab on the way out. Rebecca exerted a bit of influence to ensure they left the waitress a nice tip.

Six months earlier, such behavior would have appalled Brenna Morgan.

~~~

Brenna had been told her parents were wealthy. Until her recuperation from the injuries suffered when she was captured by the succubi hunters, she hadn't found time to get together with her Aunt Callie to get the details.

2

O'Donnell Group was a multinational forty billion dollar corporation owned by the Clan. It only employed telepaths. The official corporate headquarters was in Washington, DC, but the actual center of operations was located in a hidden valley in West Virginia. The sprawling manor house was connected to a modern three-story office building where over a thousand people worked.

"You said to come see you and we'd take care of the financial garbage. Well, I'm bored, so I guess even finances will be an improvement," Brenna said from the door of her Aunt Callie's office in West Virginia.

Callie laughed. "You caught me at a good time. I have everything finished, and your name change from Morgan back to O'Donnell will be finalized in a week or two. Let's take this to my parlor, order some tea and biscuits, and go through it."

Callista O'Donnell Wilkins was the President of O'Donnell Group, the Clan's business interests. She had been Brenna's mother's best friend and now served as surrogate mother, mentor, and friend to her niece.

Callie sat several fat files down on the end of the table, and opened one as a woman from the kitchen came in and set a tray with a pot of tea and a plate of cookies on the other end. Callie thanked her and Brenna poured tea for both of them.

"Okay, let's start with an overview." Callie pointed to a sheet of paper. "I would call this a balance sheet, but since you don't have any debts, there's nothing to balance.

"Your major assets are O'Donnell Group stock, O'Donnell Development stock, a hoard of gold your father bought in the seventies, your mother's estate in Ireland, your father's estate in Ireland, investments and other holdings, which include stocks, bonds, real estate such as the Baltimore house, and cash.

"The Clan and O'Donnell Group used a number of land parcels your father owned through O'Donnell

3

Development to build some office buildings and shopping centers, and we owe you rent for that land. We had to recover the profit from O'Donnell Development and your dividend payments from O'Donnell Group for the past fifteen years. Your other grandfather was able to tally up the profits from your mother's horse stables, and those went into the mix."

The list had Brenna's head spinning.

Callie continued. "Basically, your father held five thousand shares of O'Donnell Group as his birth gift. You also have two hundred shares as your own birth gift, giving you five thousand two hundred shares total. The stock isn't publicly traded, and Seamus owns seventy-five percent, so this is really only money on paper, understand?"

Brenna nodded, already a bit lost.

"The Group's assets are currently valued at about forty billion dollars, so your share is worth about two hundred million. The annual dividend has been running a thousand dollars a year, so the dividend you'll receive in January will be around five million."

Brenna sat straighter, looking at the paper. "Five million dollars?"

"That's before tax, of course. Now, you own all the stock in O'Donnell Development, and we've determined its value is about two hundred eighty million. Your income figured on twenty-five percent of the profits will come to about seven million this year."

"Seven million dollars?"

"Yes, that's right. Before taxes of course."

"Of course."

Callie, lost in her explanation, didn't notice Brenna was now paying very close attention, her eyes big as saucers.

"The gold your father bought back in 1975 has appreciated substantially, but provides no income. It's readily disposable however. The market value is currently about one hundred twenty million.

"Your mother had the house in Ireland and substantial investments of her own when she married your father. Likewise, your father's personal investments and the castle and estate in Ireland are valued at forty million. Then there were their joint assets after they married."

"Castle?"

"Yes, when Seamus made his first life change, he left the family estate to your father. That includes two thousand acres and the castle that was the traditional O'Donnell Clan seat.

Callie tapped the paper with her pencil. "All told, the assets total eight hundred thirty-eight million dollars and your income this year will be almost twenty-one million. I figure after taxes you'll net around thirteen to fifteen million. Seventy-five million of your assets are in cash and short-term notes."

She turned to look at Brenna, and realized she should have taken things a little slower. The young woman was staring at her, eyes wide, face pale, clenching the arms of her chair as if the building was being shaken by an earthquake.

Speaking slowly, Brenna asked, "I have seventy-five million dollars in cash?" Callie nodded. "My income this year will be thirteen million dollars?" Again Callie nodded. "My net worth is twice that of the Queen of England?"

"Well, yes, approximately."

"Holy shit."

"I told you it was real wealth. That's why it's taken so long to put it all together. It's complicated."

"Callie, why did you order tea instead of whiskey?"

Callie laughed. "Should I ask for a bottle to be sent in?"

"No, don't bother." A bottle of Midleton's appeared on the table with a shot glass, teleported from Brenna's room

5

upstairs. She leaned forward and poured the glass full, tossed it down, and sat back in her chair.

"I think this news is as disturbing as being told I'm a succubus."

Taking a deep breath, she poured whiskey in the glass again and downed it, then looked at Callie, "Oh, I'm sorry, how rude. Would you like some?"

It started with a soft chuckle and built to a whole-hearted belly laugh. "I wish you could see your face," Callie sputtered, "it's priceless."

Brenna stared at her then looked around the room. The West Virginia manor house was almost twice as large as the White House, nestled in a private twelve thousand acre valley. "How much is Seamus worth?" she barely whispered the question.

Seamus O'Donnell, Brenna's grandfather, had come to the United States in 1890 with about a third of the three thousand members of the O'Donnell Clan. The Clan now had over forty thousand members, more than half in the U.S., and was the strongest telepathic Clan in the world.

"Let's put it this way, if the financial magazines knew he existed, they wouldn't be calling that software guy the richest man in the world. Although, to be fair, Seamus had a century's head start on him."

"And all of that will go to you as the heir when he dies?"

Callie sobered, "Yes, unless the Clan decides someone else is better qualified. The challenge is to maintain his legacy and take us into the next century. So far, no one has impressed us that much. Your father was far more qualified than I am. I ended up designated by default when he died and I really don't want it."

She studied Brenna. "Seamus probably will continue to run things for the next thirty or forty years, though he may decide to step down while he still has his health. I think this thing with Cindy has shaken him. She might actually be able to talk him into the children she wants, and spending more time with her."

Callie chuckled, "Now that you know you're a multi-millionaire, what's the first thing you're going to do?"

Brenna thought about it, then brightened. "Go shopping, with you and Rebecca and Irina." Excitement crept into her voice. "Let's go to New York and buy clothes and have a week on the town. How does that sound? Siobhan, too. And we'll get a list and her sizes and get some stuff for Cindy, so she'll have some new clothes when she gets better. I mean, aren't we going into the winter social season? That's what someone told me. Aren't there going to be balls and parties and Thanksgiving and Christmas and New Year and all that?"

"Is that all you want to do," Callie laughed, "buy new clothes?"

Brenna blushed. "You know what I wear. Nothing fits."

Callie had to admit that was true. Nothing off the rack would fit a body with Brenna's outrageous curves. The girl had spent her life wearing whatever she could find, clothing that sometimes came close to fitting.

Smiling softly, Callie nodded. "Anything else?"

"I own a company with architects and building engineers?"

"Yes, one of the best."

"Who do I contact there to get something built?"

"Jack Calhoun is the president. What do you want to build?" Callie asked cautiously.

"An indoor swimming pool, or at least enclose the pool you have so we can use it during the winter."

Relieved, Callie smiled, "Yes, contact Jack. I'll get you his phone number and email address. You might also consider making an appointment with him to introduce yourself as his new boss. Seamus is resigning as chairman of that company, so you'll be assuming the position."

7

"I will?" Confusion reasserted itself. "Is that how it's done? Callie, I haven't had a single business class. I'm a scientist. I don't know squat about running a business, or investing or stocks or anything." She sat back in her chair, and Callie could see her considering the implications of her newfound wealth.

"Callie, you and Seamus will help me, won't you? You won't abandon me?"

Callie's eyes got a little blurry, "No, Brenna, we won't abandon you. Any help or advice you need, we'll be here for you."

"Good, thank you. Oh, and you'll figure out what I owe you for rent and stuff?"

"Huh?"

"I've been living here and in Baltimore rent free, eating your food, getting free security services, transportation, all that stuff. If I have my own money, then I should be paying my fair share, not leeching off everyone else. This little jaunt I'm proposing to New York will require a fairly large security force, won't it? It's my personal travel, not business. So figure out if you want to bill me on a pay as you go basis, or a flat monthly fee. Set up a special account you can draw on."

"Brenna, members of the O'Donnell family don't pay for their living expenses, Seamus does. And security isn't something you pay for either. All of our family and the top executives are assigned a security force."

"And you pay me rent for the Baltimore house, rent for the land you developed, and all kinds of other stuff? Fair is fair, Callie. I don't expect people to support me in this extravagant lifestyle for free, especially when I'm not contributing and have money. I've been supporting myself since I was sixteen years old, and I'm not going to start taking charity now that I'm rich. That doesn't make any sense."

~~~

8

Collin Doyle was the Clan's Director of Security. In his mid-thirties, he was young for such an important position. Tall, devastatingly handsome with a reputation as a ladies' man, he and Brenna had been drawn to each other from the first moment they met.

Their relationship had been strained since the time of Cindy's kidnapping, when an ill-conceived jest had angered Brenna. They hadn't slept together since, although she had gone to see him as Samantha, the persona she assumed under a mental construct in an effort to trap the succubus hunters. She'd made love to him in a fierce, predatory way that she'd never done before, riding him to exhaustion and draining him.

After she escaped from her captors, he'd been loving and tender, cradling her like a child and making her feel safe. Until he held her that day, she hadn't truly felt safe since her parents' deaths.

Collin was lying in bed reading when there was a knock on the door. "Come in," he called.

The door opened and Brenna walked in, crawled up on the bed and sat facing him cross-legged. "Can we talk?"

"Sure, we haven't done much of that lately."

"Collin, can you please try not to say things that piss me off? Especially in public?"

"Brenna, I meant that as a joke."

"Yeah, I figured that out. It wasn't very funny, though. Yes, I'm young, but to say that I'm barely out of diapers in front of a bunch of people … it was demeaning. I know when I came here people thought it was funny that someone with the O'Neill super shielding Gift didn't even know something as simple as filtering, but honey, you need a filter between your brain and your mouth."

He chuckled softly, "Kallen said almost exactly the same thing that day. I apologize."

"Accepted, although I've already forgiven you. You know, sometimes I want to kill you, and other times … that day at the gas station, you didn't fuss, or bitch at me, you gave me exactly what I needed. You were strong and caring and everything that I love about you. Do you know why Samantha came to see you that day before she went to New York?"

"I have to admit, that's puzzled me."

"Rebecca warned me that if I assumed that role, had a construct implanted in my mind that turned me into a fully-functioning succubus, it would change me. She told me I would either become a succubus or be sick to my stomach afterward at what I'd done as Samantha. Well, as soon as they triggered the construct, I knew which one it would be. Even though I was someone else, I've never felt as comfortable with myself as I did at that moment. I knew the first man I was with would get the ride of his life, the best that I had ever given anyone. At that moment, you were the only one I wanted."

Brenna shook her head. "You know I wasn't sure if I could handle being a succubus. But when I played one as bait, I felt as though all the pieces had finally fallen into place."

A soft smile touched her lips. "Sometimes I want to kill you, and other times, I hope you'll be with me until I die. When I escaped those monsters, you gave me exactly what I needed. You didn't nag or be weird."

She leaned toward him, capturing him with her eyes. "I know I need one man in my life, a special man, one who will love me no matter what. I'll give that man all of me and make him glad I did. I hope it will be you."

Reaching out, she touched his cheek and drew her hand down his bare chest. "Cindy and Siobhan have told me how lonely they are. I've been lonely all my life, and I don't want to be lonely for the rest of it. My mother found a secret, a way to keep the man she loved, a way to defeat the loneliness, and I think the way she did it was to always give the man she loved her best."

Collin captured her hand, holding it over his heart. His eyes misted, the look on his face one of tenderness and yearning.

Taking a deep breath, she said, "I want you to move in with me. I can't change what I am. I can't promise you sexual fidelity, but I can promise I'll always give you me at my best, in bed or out."

He raised an eyebrow, "The best of your anger, too?"

She chuckled, "I'm good at a lot of things, and I do have a temper. I'm good at being exasperated at you, too. At least you can't complain you didn't know what you were getting into."

"I've never been good at relationships, it always falls apart."

"Because you can't keep it in your pants?" He nodded. "I'm not asking you to be a saint while I sleep around, Collin. I just want to be your first choice. If we're in the same town, I want you in my bed, if we're not, then as long as you're honest with me, and with your other women, I'm okay. I don't want my showing up on your doorstep to be a surprise to anyone."

"When do you need an answer?"

"If you're not in my bed tonight, I'll have my answer." She leaned forward and kissed him deeply and passionately, then stood and walked to the door.

~~~

Chapter 2

Whoever said money can't buy
happiness simply didn't know
where to go shopping. - Bo Derek

Rebecca Healy was a wilder, someone who had grown up outside a Clan, not knowing why she could read minds or knowing there were others like her. With fifteen Gifts, she had the potential to be one of the strongest telepaths in the world.

Rebecca opened the door, strode into Brenna's room, and sat with a bounce on the bed. "Hey, sleepyhead, wake up. You're going to be late for breakfast."

Collin raised his head from beneath the covers. "Damn, Healy, don't you know how to knock?" A giggle filtered up from somewhere around his chest.

"Oops. Sorry." She jumped up and headed for the door.

"Collin's moving in," she heard Brenna say as she shut the door behind her. She stepped back into the room.

"Are you both completely clueless?" Rebecca asked with a grin.

"I guess so," Collin said with a smile.

"Well, I guess that's a good foundation for a relationship. When you finish, perhaps you can let me in on the little road trip Callie mentioned this morning."

"Oh." Brenna emerged from the covers, "Yeah, I want to go shopping in New York. Want to come along?"

Rebecca always marveled at how good Brenna looked first thing in the morning.

"Right, as if I have a choice, seeing as I'm assigned to your security detail."

"Well, Miss Pissy, we can fix that. Collin, fire her."

Wide-eyed, Collin's head swung back and forth between them. "Huh?"

"Fire her, then I can hire her, and I won't have to listen to all this garbage because I'll be the one signing her paycheck," Brenna said brightly. "As if she ever turned down an opportunity to go shopping in her life. Rebecca, guess what? I'm rich."

Rebecca regarded her with a sorrowful expression then turned to Collin, "This is news? Is she really that oblivious?" She looked back at Brenna, "If you didn't know that before now, you're the only one. Shit. I thought you were the smart one."

~~~

In her mind, Brenna envisioned an orgy of shopping and partying in New York, the sort of thing she'd never done before. The first obstacle to her fantasy occurred when she sat down with Callie, Irina and Rebecca to plan out their trip.

Irina Moore was a twenty-one year-old succubus, a wilder, who had been rescued from a succubus hunting team in New York a few weeks earlier. Barely five feet tall, with blonde hair, a beautiful face and voluptuous body, she looked like a vision of a wanton angel. A prodigy, speaking eight languages, her sweet personality and innocent blue eyes beguiled everyone she met.

Although her mother was a telepath and a succubus, her father was a normal human. They had been hiding all of her life, though Irina wasn't sure exactly why. All she knew was that they feared being found by other telepaths.

"No, I'm not going to allow you to buy me a new wardrobe. I'm not some rich girl's remora. I have a job. I make enough money to pay for my own clothes." Rebecca crossed her arms, leaned back in her chair and shook her head.

"I feel the same way," Irina said. "If you want to loan me some money until I can pay you back, that's one thing, but as a gift? No."

13

Everyone's eyes widened as the room grew noticeably cooler. Brenna sat back in her chair, her enthusiasm from moments before replaced with a stony expression.

"Let me explain something to everyone. I don't have a wardrobe, I have clothes. Mostly clothes that don't fit and look like shit. I want to look nice for a change. There are only two women I know who are anywhere close to my own age. I'd like to go out occasionally, go clubbing. You know, go to nice places, not just a student bar. And I'm not going to go out looking like a million dollars with a couple of ragamuffins wearing clothes off the rack from Wal-Mart.

"You, Miss Protector, cannot wear jeans to a nice restaurant, they won't let you in, and I'll be without security and you'll get fired. And you," she said, turning to Irina, "do you really think your boss wants you showing up for an important dinner meeting wearing an Ohio State sweat shirt?"

Her friends both opened their mouths but Brenna cut them off, raising her voice, "I'm not finished!"

She held out her hands in a placating gesture. "I'm not talking about outfitting you for the rest of your lives. I'll pay for you to establish a basic wardrobe. One so that Seamus won't be ashamed to have you sit at the table with him for the Solstice Festival. After that, you make enough to enhance and maintain it. I want to do this. But if you won't let me, I'm going to pout, and sulk, and make everyone miserable, and believe me, I know how to do it."

Callie burst out laughing. "Damn, that's the worst threat I've heard in a long time."

Brenna winked at her. "I'll tell you what, I promise not to spend more than one week's income on the three of us, okay?"

Rebecca eyed her warily, "How much is that?"

"None of your business. You're my protector, not my financial advisor. Oh, come on, I've been unwell, don't you want to make me feel better?"

Both young women's faces relaxed and they began to nod.

"Oh, Brenna, that's beyond the pale," Callie exclaimed. "I knew you could be a manipulative bitch, but that's going too far."

The other two women looked at her in confusion.

"She's using Influence on you. Succubus Influence."

"It's in the interest of a good cause," Brenna said softly, looking down at her lap, her cheeks coloring.

"What?" Rebecca surged to her feet. "You're using your womanly wiles on me? Jesus, Brenna, I, I feel so used."

They all broke out in laughter.

In the end, she managed to convince them, and the trip was set for the week before Thanksgiving.

~~~

Brenna's shopping trip set off alarms throughout O'Donnell's security organization, starting with Collin. Listening to Brenna and Rebecca plan set his teeth on edge. He immediately went to Seamus, Brenna's grandfather and patriarch of the Clan, who blew sky high and sent for Callie.

"What the bloody hell does that girl think she's doing? Didn't getting kidnapped and almost killed by that monster teach her anything?" Seamus stormed around his office. "I know she didn't grow up in our world, but she needs to understand we have enemies."

Callie calmly let him blow off steam, watching him with a slight grin.

"Do you plan to bundle her in bubble wrap and store her away until there's no danger in the world?" Callie asked.

He stopped and turned to her. An alert triggered in the back of his mind, but he wasn't sure exactly to what he was being alerted. Callie was much too calm, much too amused.

15

Cautiously, he moved to the front of his desk and sat on the corner, watching her warily.

"You knew about this," he accused.

"Oh, yes, I'm the first one she mentioned it to. Despite what you might think, she doesn't take off in a vacuum and do things just to upset you and Collin. If I thought it was a bad idea, I'd have put a stop to it immediately. Father, you're being over-protective again. You have a charming, but unnecessary, tendency to do that with women."

"You think it's a good idea?" Seamus' eyes almost popped out of his head.

"Yes, I do. She's had a number of shocks over the past six months since we found her, and this will be cathartic." She held up her hand, forestalling his protest. "Do I think going to New York when there are still succubi hunters prowling around is a great idea? No. Do I think we can use it to our advantage strategically? Yes. Besides, she understands she'll be blanketed by security."

Seamus goggled at her, then whirled away and started pacing.

"Father, if you wanted to go hunting people, people who don't have an O'Donnell Gift on their side, what kind of team would you send?"

He wheeled about and studied her with narrowed eyes.

"Daughter, your devious mind is at work. Why do I feel as though I'm in London in 1966 again?"

Callie laughed with unfettered glee. "Does that still bother you?"

"The parallels are too striking to ignore."

Chuckling, Callie stood and walked to his sideboard. Pouring two drinks, she said, "Amazing you still remember that. And now that you mention it, it is somewhat similar." She handed him his drink. "Shall we explore our options?"

Shaking his head, he took a sip. "She's not her mother. Maureen had been trained in her Gifts since birth."

"No, she's more powerful than her mother, even as powerful as Maureen was. She's not much younger than Maureen was in 1966. Combine her with Rebecca, use Irina as bait, throw Collin, Kallen and Jeremy into the mix, and we have a formidable team. I'll be there along with Siobhan and Caroline. I really can't imagine anyone being able to stand against us. Hopefully we can resolve this problem."

"Callie, my dear, you have an evil mind." He took a deep breath. "Okay, let's explore our options. Please remember I'm an old man. Try to spare my poor, weak heart."

Callie laughed.

~~~

"What do you mean I'm being reassigned? I'm not going to be one of Brenna's Protectors anymore?" Rebecca had been called to Collin's office. Totally bewildered, she stared at him, trying to make sense of what he was telling her. It felt as though she'd been kicked in the stomach.

"Rebecca, a member of the family has asked to have you reassigned, and after careful consideration Kallen and I have agreed."

"Does Brenna know about this?"

"Brenna was the one who requested your reassignment."

Her face fell and she slumped in her chair.

"I can't pay you as much as she requested, but I can give you a fifty percent raise now, and if your performance warrants it, and Kallen agrees you've progressed far enough in your training, you'll get the other fifty percent in six months."

"What the hell are you talking about?"

Collin couldn't keep a straight face any longer. "You're being promoted to Team Leader over Brenna's security detail with thirty Protectors assigned to you. She said a low-level Protector shouldn't be telling her what to do all the time, and if you wanted to be in charge of everything, I should give you your wish and put you in charge. You'll need to go through Small Tactics School and Operations Planning, so figure out what her schedule is going to be and fit them in."

"I've been through Small Tactics."

"Not the Team Leader course."

"And I report directly to her?"

He nodded, smiling.

"That manipulative bitch!" Rebecca stormed out of the office.

~~~

Rebecca was ready to go back to waiting tables. She was sure she'd never worked so hard in her life. The logistics of two members of the family traveling were daunting. Kallen helped because Callie was going, and made sure Rebecca didn't miss any details, but mostly he watched.

Kallen O'Reilly was the most senior Protector and known as "Callie's Shadow." He and Callie grew up together and were lovers when they were young. He headed Callie's protection team and was single-mindedly focused on her wellbeing. He took the lead in mentoring and training Rebecca when she first joined the Protectors.

Brenna didn't want to stay at the New York compound, so they made reservations at a small luxury hotel in Midtown owned by O'Donnell Group. All the employees were Clan, and Caroline had reserved the top two floors for them. It was a favorite of telepaths, especially those visiting from Europe. Rebecca had to go through the background profiles of everyone who already had reservations for the time of their stay. Any new reservation requests were forwarded to her before the reservations were confirmed.

She also had to coordinate security with the New York office. They would supply additional manpower, boosting security at their hotel as well as at the hotel next door, which Siobhan told Brenna was a good succubus hunting ground.

One bright spot was that Collin allowed Rebecca free rein in picking her team. They were all much older than she, experienced, and she'd worked with them before. She picked ten women, and Brenna insisted all thirty Protectors be given a thousand dollars each to go into DC and buy new clothes. Considering the amount Rebecca had spent on outfits for a two-day operation the previous summer, it wasn't overly extravagant. She was surprised that Brenna was funding the entire expedition, but Callie had explained the arrangement that she'd made with the Clan.

"So she's really paying my salary? She wasn't just kidding?"

"She's paying for all of her security, now and in the future. She and Seamus had an interesting discussion on the subject. It all comes out in the wash. She's funneling all the rents that the Clan owes her into a fund to pay for her living expenses. It was the best compromise they could reach."

Callie was impressed at how creatively the young woman could curse.

Rather than deal with the logistics of busing everyone to an airport and flying to New York, Rebecca rented two buses and requisitioned two vans. Kallen added a stretch limo in the city to chauffeur their charges around. The New York office would supply any additional vehicles that might be needed.

After almost two weeks of preparations, she ushered the shoppers onto the bus. With several bottles of wine and a lavish picnic, they were on their way. After her first glass of wine, Rebecca fell asleep and didn't wake up until they reached Philadelphia.

~~~

It was a circus when they checked in. Kallen stood off to the side and laughed at Rebecca until she turned to him, frustrated half out of her mind, "Am I really in charge of this clusterfuck? I mean, really in charge?" He agreed she was, and she put him in charge of moving the luggage to their rooms. His smile died. "I am, or I'm not. Take the luggage, or take charge of this mess, your choice." He looked at forty people milling around the small lobby trying to check in and took charge of the luggage.

The four women had two connecting two-bedroom suites on the top floor. The rooms were sumptuously appointed in a style that would have made Seamus comfortable, with antique furniture, oil paintings on the walls and down comforters on the beds.

Siobhan O'Conner was originally from a small village in northwest Ireland and her voice still carried a soft Irish lilt. Now fifty-five, she looked to be in her early thirties and was the Clan's main intelligence operative in New York's financial and political circles. She showed up about an hour after they checked in to take them to dinner. Assuming they would be tired from their trip, she hadn't arranged any, as she called it, "entertainment" that evening.

Rebecca had been especially frazzled when she got to the suite she shared with Brenna. She pulled a Protector named Robbie into her room and closed the door. Shortly after Siobhan arrived, she emerged freshly showered, smiling and relaxed. Robbie trailed after her, also freshly showered and smiling. Brenna looked at her questioningly and Rebecca said, "I needed a little stress relief."

Siobhan took them to a famous old steakhouse in Midtown, a place of dark wood with tobacco stained single-use clay pipes hung on the wall, signed by celebrities such as Winston Churchill. Looking at the prices on the menu, Rebecca was reminded again about the cost of this trip. In addition to their party, Kallen and three other Protectors sat at a table nearby, and Brenna insisted that takeout dinners be sent to the six Protectors waiting outside.

Afterward they returned to their hotel and peered into the hotel bar. A quick scan showed a few occupants, but only Callie saw someone interesting. She greeted a man at the bar by name in French, and he invited her for a drink.

"You kids run along," Callie said. "I haven't seen Francois in years." The smile on her face told them she was staying.

The rest of them went to the hotel next door, much larger and more contemporary in decoration. On a Monday evening, it was full of business travelers. Siobhan coached the younger succubi as to their Glam and gave them some pointers on the judicious use of Influence and their pheromones as they took a table near the center of the room.

She raised an eyebrow and grinned as Rebecca projected Charisma, simulating the succubi's Glamour. "Nice. Callie's been teaching you?"

"Callie and Cindy," Rebecca said. "Cindy taught me techniques for simulating the succubus Talents."

Siobhan studied her, then said something that surprised the three young women. "You have the soul of a succubus. Are you a half?"

"I don't know. What's a half?"

"A carrier of the succubus gene."

"Yes."

Siobhan nodded but didn't say anything else. Rebecca looked at Brenna who shrugged.

Brenna knew from Rebecca that their Protectors hated having to deal with succubi on the hunt, but in a bar full of norms the available men were transparent. Tiny Irina scored almost immediately, using strong Influence to lure a tall, muscular man in his early forties and giving him a pheromone burst that glazed his eyes.

Watching them leave, Siobhan said, "Need to teach that girl some subtlety. You don't need to use that kind of blast in a place like this. Brenna, just dribble your

21

pheromones, let a small amount leak out, but don't blast the room unless you're looking for group sex."

Brenna flushed, "I've never done anything like that. I, I don't even know what I think about that."

Siobhan looked at Rebecca, "You've done some of that, haven't you?" Rebecca colored, but nodded. Siobhan cocked her head, obviously studying her with more than her eyes. "That's a very nice lust you're projecting, and, hmmm, strong pheromones for a non-succubus. My, my, Cindy did teach you nicely. You could fool someone that's never met one of us."

The waitress approached, telling them that various gentlemen had offered to buy them their next round of drinks. Soon they had company, and shortly thereafter all three retired upstairs. Rebecca's choice was a very tall black man who told them he had been a basketball player in college.

Brenna's partner was an enthusiastic lover, but without much stamina. She drained him and went back down to the bar with a nice Glow but feeling unsatisfied. Irina was sitting at the bar alone. The bartender came over to take her order, and in a chiding voice asked, "You ladies aren't charging for it, are you? Because if you are, I'll have to ask you to leave."

Gaily, Irina told him, "Oh, no, just on holiday and trying to have a good time."

Brenna entered his mind, and while steering his thoughts away from any suspicion of prostitution, told him, "We just graduated, and we're having a last fling before we get married." He laughed and gave them a conspiratorial wink.

After he served their drinks and went off to tend to other customers, Brenna commented, "Not that there's anything wrong with charging for it. I've been told most of the independent succubi make their livings as courtesans. It's considered an honorable profession in telepathic society, just another way of using their Gifts. Siobhan takes escort gigs sometimes." She looked around. "I'm sure that's a bit more high class than trolling in a hotel bar."

She showed Irina how to dribble her pheromones. They chatted for a while, deciding on their next targets. Another very tall man approached Irina. After a short conversation and an extra puff, he invited her to his room.

Like them big, do you? Brenna asked.

It gives me a nice full feeling <laugh>, although my real preference is a well put together guy around five six. I like kissing during sex.

As they left, Brenna's attention was drawn to the companion of the man Rebecca had taken upstairs. He was even taller and more muscular than his friend. Catching his eye, she smiled at him and exerted a bit of Influence. He came over to the bar and struck up a conversation. He was taller close up, at least six foot ten, and told her he was a rookie with the New York Knicks. He had played earlier that evening, then met his friend, a teammate from college. He had three days off until he played again.

"You must be very good, to play professionally," Brenna said.

"Honey, I'm *very* good," he said with a flirtatious laugh.

"I don't suppose you'd like to prove that, would you?" Brenna flirted back.

She implanted a suggestion in his mind, and he called the bartender over, asking if the hotel had any vacancies. The bartender made a call, and told him that he could pick up his room key at the front desk.

In the room, Brenna turned up her Glam and gave him a burst of pheromones. Turning, she lifted her hair over one shoulder, baring her zipper. He moved behind her and pulled it down, slipping his hands inside and peeling her dress down her arms. His hands slid around her and his huge hands cupped her breasts, squeezing them hard, just

23

short of pain. She gasped, throwing her head back against his chest. One of his hands moved down across her stomach, lower, inside her panties, cupping her and spreading her legs. One long finger pierced her and he lifted her almost off her feet. Pleasure flooded her, radiating from his hand throughout her body and setting off fireworks in her head. Her knees gave way and only his hands kept her upright.

When she finished shaking, she moved away from him and turning, finished undressing. Watching him, she eyed the largest male organ she had ever seen, even in a porno movie. Standing in front of him, her eyes were on the level of his nipples.

She reached her arms out and said, "Pick me up."

He cradled her bottom in his huge hands and lifted her without effort. She wrapped her arms around his neck and her legs around his waist. He bent his head to kiss her, their mouths meeting, savoring, exploring. The soft skin of his hard shaft rubbed against her slick folds. Writhing, she managed to sheath him in her to the hilt and they let out a simultaneous moan, "Ohhh. My. God."

He moved, stretching her and she felt her heat rising as his deep, strong thrusts sent her soaring over the edge, then before she came down, he lifted her again, driving her to an even higher peak. Her world narrowed to the feel of him inside her. Lowering her to the bed, he drove into her harder and faster, filling her as no one ever had. He plunged into her until he was close, but not wanting to lose him, she pushed him away and worked him to his climax with her hands and mouth. In return, he pleasured her with his mouth, deftly licking and sucking, driving her into a frenzy and twice bringing her to orgasm.

Very pleased, they exchanged cell phone numbers. They stroked each other, kissing and chatting, until he slipped his hand between her legs and kindled the coals of her desire into a raging bonfire.

24

Blasting him with pheromones, she aroused his attention again, mounting and sheathing him with a cry of joy. In her experience, men were much slower the second time and she rode him for over an hour, his mouth feasting on her breasts and her lips, his hands teasing her nipples, her clit, clenching her buttocks. Twice during that time, she received spears from her Protectors checking to see if she was all right, the first time from Jeremy, then later from Rebecca.

Oh, yeah, I'm doing just fine <smile>, she told her friend, and in a burst of exhibitionistic enthusiasm invited Rebecca into her mind.

My God, he's as big as a horse!

<smile> Yes he is.

Rebecca started to withdraw, but Brenna invited her to stay. She felt Rebecca's hesitation, but her curiosity won out. When he finally reached his climax, spilling into her, Brenna discovered that a man that big, an athlete in his prime, held a very large reservoir of life energy. It poured into her, escalating her orgasm to tremendous heights. She felt Rebecca jolt, sharing her orgasm and the Glow his energy created.

She cleaned up, dressed, and met Jeremy in the hall.

"That's quite a Glow," he grinned. "Have a good time?"

Suddenly self-conscious, Brenna blushed. On the elevator down, she asked him, "Do you think I'm a slut? Honestly, Jeremy, what do you think of what we're doing?"

"Only a man of low quality would use such a word. If a man can't appreciate a woman who is willing to share herself, her pleasure with him, then he's an idiot," Jeremy said.

"Brenna, I've known succubi all my life, and enjoyed spending time with both Siobhan and Cindy on occasion. It's who you are, and speaking for myself, I think you're

25

wonderful. You bring joy to people, and there's far too little of that in the world."

She digested that. "What do you think of Rebecca?"

He reached out and hit the stop button. With an intense look on his face, he said, "Rebecca is one of the finest women I've ever met. She's smart, brave, and loyal." He smiled, "And damned good looking, too. I don't know what she's told you about herself or what you've heard, but her problem isn't a problem to the people she works with."

He punched the button to start the elevator again. "Women such as you and Rebecca and Callie deserve to be put on pedestals. A woman who's willing to share her affection happily and freely is a treasure."

They were joined in the lobby by his team and Rebecca. Brenna shot a sharp glance at her friend, who appeared to be Glowing. When they reached their room, Rebecca gushed, "Jesus, that was awesome. I've never had an orgasm like that in my life."

"You had an orgasm?"

"Oh, hell yes. You kicked me over and the boyos I was with in the bar thought I was having an epileptic seizure." She shook her head in mock sorrow, "But I'm afraid you've ruined me. Sex will never be the same again."

"You're Glowing."

Rebecca's smile widened, "Am I? Well, thank you very much. I feel like I'm walking on air."

"Rebecca, you know you can talk to me about any kind of problems, don't you?"

Stiffening and looking away, Rebecca said, "I don't have any problems, except trying to coordinate everyone tomorrow. Well, good night."

~~~

When Siobhan came to take them to breakfast the next morning, she took one look at Rebecca, then turned to Brenna.

26

"You're taking on hitchhikers?" Siobhan shook her head, "Brenna, don't do that, you'll ruin her."

After breakfast, they piled into the limo and drove uptown to the design shop owned and run by Alice Callaghan for the past hundred years. Although Alice had 'died' twice, and the shop was now officially owned by her granddaughter, there was no doubt among the knowledgeable as to who was still in charge. She had sewn most of Brenna's mother's clothes.

As their appearance changed so slowly, telepaths had to change their identities several times during their long lives. Many changed careers, or in Seamus' case dropped out of the world entirely. At one hundred thirty years of age, Alice was an attractive, vivacious middle-aged woman whose brown hair was streaked with gray.

Things had changed in the custom clothing design industry in the hundred years since Alice first opened the shop, and she had not stayed behind. The first thing she had the three young women do was strip to the skin and stand on a platform where an electronic scan was made of their bodies. Feeding their measurements into a computer, Alice explained she could generate the patterns for any kind of clothing they might order.

She also scanned Callie, as her measurements were three years old. "You haven't been to see me in a while, Miss Callista. I was beginning to wonder if you'd found another dressmaker."

Siobhan was a regular customer, and that day was in for a final fitting for her Solstice gown, formfitting, strapless and fire engine red.

Alice read off their measurements. "Almost exactly your mother's measurements," she told Brenna. "About half an inch larger in the bust and half an inch wider in the hips."

"See? I'm a fat ass," Brenna told Callie.

There was a sharp smacking noise, and Brenna jumped, turning around to stare wide-eyed at Alice, holding the part of her anatomy that had been slapped.

"That's not fat, and that's not where you're bigger," Alice told her. "You're half an inch wider between the pelvic crests, and watch your language, young lady."

Irina stared wide-eyed, Rebecca was choking, trying not to laugh, and Callie and Siobhan were chuckling.

That could have been you, Miss Potty-mouth, Brenna told Rebecca through a directed mental thread.

Yeah, but it wasn't, and you can bet I'll be watching my language.

"Young lady," Alice told Irina, "you have been able to get away with not exercising because of your age and being a succubus, but unless you want that nice, soft figure to degenerate into cellulite and mush, you need to spend more time in the gym."

She praised Rebecca, "My dear, you have the most incredible body. It's obvious you take good care of yourself. If you ever want to model, I'm sure I can get you some work here in New York." Rebecca beamed. "I do hope, though, that you'll do something with that hair before you appear in public in one of my dresses. I would call it a crime, but that would be too flattering."

Brenna smirked at Rebecca.

Alice sat down with each of them and discussed colors, both their preferences and what she thought would look best on them. An assistant took each of the women aside and showed them computer-generated pictures of women with bodies similar to theirs, wearing different kinds of clothes, different colors, and asking them to rate the clothing on a scale of one to three. They also showed them different fabrics, asking if they liked how the fabric looked and how it felt, not just how it felt on their hands, but against their arms, legs, breasts and cheeks.

After two hours, the girls, clothed again, sat down with Alice. "All right, we have your measurements, your preferences. We know what we think looks good on you, and what you think looks good on you. So, what are we doing?"

Brenna leaned forward, "We each want six evening dresses, six cocktail dresses for nice occasions, six club dresses, at least two of those LBDs, foundation garments, and a line of upscale casual clothing for both indoors and out. We also each need a dozen business suits, half for warm and half for cold weather. Two of mine for each season should be pantsuits, but you'll have to ask them about their preferences. I think Rebecca probably wants more pants than skirts, but that's up to her. Blouses, of course, and accessories. I'd also appreciate recommendations of what to buy, and where, for things you don't carry."

Gasps came from the two young women sitting beside her. "And don't listen to them as far as cutting back. I'm paying, and I'm not going to argue with anyone about it. I've worn hand-me-downs and garbage my whole life, and I'm not going to be ashamed of how I look anymore."

"Do you know what that's going to cost?" Alice studied her.

"Yes, ma'am, I do. Alice, we all just graduated from college. We're starting out in our professional lives, our social lives, and all we have is stuff that keeps us from being arrested, clothes off the rack from the cheapest stores. You know how hard I am to fit, and I can't imagine Irina's much easier, all those curves and tiny as an elf. And Rebecca, well, she'd look good in a gunny sack, but I don't want to be seen with her in one."

Alice answered her with peals of laughter.

"Well, Brenna O'Donnell, you definitely know your mind as well as Maureen did. I'll take your money. For

29

foundation garments, will you take what I think is appropriate, style and quantity?"

"Yes, ma'am."

"Two of you are succubi. Do you want these clothes to reflect that, or be more conservative?"

"For me, about two-thirds succubi wear, one-third more conservative," she looked at Rebecca, "Conservative or …?"

"Brenna? You said you weren't going to do this," Rebecca pleaded.

"I said I'd spend one week's income. That's what I promised."

"Jesus, how much do you make?"

"I told you, none of your business. Now, do you want to dress sexy or not?"

Callie sent Brenna a thread, *Before or after taxes?*

I don't think I got that specific.

Callie chuckled.

The rest of the week, in between stops at Alice's shop to make decisions on fabrics, colors, and styles, they went shopping for shoes, boots, purses, coats, makeup, and other things. Brenna also spent an afternoon with Alice learning more about her O'Neill shielding Gift which they shared.

They took Rebecca to a fancy hair salon and had her hair done to Alice's specifications. Tossing her head and letting her hair settle back into place, her smile lit up the room. The others agreed Rebecca had never looked better.

But the highlight of the week for everyone was Brenna taking her mother's jewelry to the appraiser's. Prior to leaving on the trip resulting in their deaths, Brenna's parents left an ornately-carved box with her. They told her that if anything ever happened to them, to sell the jewelry to pay for her college education. Through several foster homes, she had hidden the box, and had qualified for scholarships and grants to pay for college. Surprised to discover Brenna still had it, Callie insisted the jewelry be appraised for insurance purposes, but even she was stunned at the final number.

Her friends watched in awe as the appraiser pulled incredible piece after incredible piece from the box.

"Twenty-seven point five million dollars?" Brenna's eyes were big as saucers.

"Twenty-seven million, five hundred seventeen thousand dollars, yes," the old man replied. "It's a rather remarkable collection, with some very unique pieces."

The signature piece, a sapphire, diamond and platinum necklace and earrings had appraised at ten and a half million dollars, "I have never seen a matched set of sapphires this large that are this perfect." A ruby and gold necklace was valued at two and a half million, "A truly incredible piece."

He estimated a collar necklace with five rows of diamonds she had loaned Rebecca for her first dinner with the family at seven hundred fifty thousand, the matching bracelet one hundred fifty thousand, and the earrings at fifty thousand.

"I was wearing a million dollars' worth of diamonds?" Rebecca breathed.

The pearls were judged to be of the highest quality. More than two dozen pieces were valued at six figures.

"You hid this in the back of your closet under the laundry hamper?" Rebecca asked.

Numb and clutching the box to her chest, Brenna stumbled out of his shop into the limo. "I need a drink."

~~~

Chapter 3

*We are all ready to be savage in
some cause. The difference between
a good man and a bad one is the
choice of the cause. - William
James*

Taking advantage of the opportunity Brenna's
shopping trip afforded them, Collin and his security forces
scheduled an operation to take out the succubi hunting
teams in New York.

Six weeks before, Irina Moore had come to New York
to interview for a job as an interpreter at the UN. A man
she met there gave her an invitation to a charity event.
When she attended it, a team of succubi hunters tried to
intercept her.

Their plans had been derailed by Siobhan O'Conner
and Brenna's redheaded alter ego, Samantha. They spirited
her out of the trap. When Caroline O'Connell, the Senior
Vice President of O'Donnell Group in New York, went to
Irina's hotel to retrieve her luggage, the hunters ambushed
them. Subsequently, a deadly succubi-hunting team in DC
had been dealt with, but the leaders in New York were still
operating.

Jayson O'Rourke, O'Donnell's Director of Operations,
had promised Irina he would ensure she got another shot at
the position she'd applied for at the UN. Having now taken
a job with the Clan, she was no longer interested in the UN
job, but the groundwork had been laid for her to resume the
interview process if she chose. With Irina's help, they
reactivated her application and scheduled interviews.

During her previous trip, she completed her initial
interviews and had a second day of interviews scheduled.
Of the people she interviewed with the first time, only one
wanted to meet with her again. It was the man who gave

32

her the invitation to the charity event. Irina told the O'Donnell strike team that he originally wasn't on her interview list, but was added after her first three interviews.

"Are you comfortable with this?" Callie asked Irina, carefully watching her face. The young succubus looked as though she should still be in high school.

"Well, I won't say I'm not scared, but I want to do it," Irina said, twisting a long strand of blonde hair around her finger.

Shaking her head, Callie pressed, "You've told me you're not a brave person. You know what happened when we used Brenna as bait for these people."

"Yeah, I know," Irina's voice softened and she dropped her gaze. She stared at her lap for a full minute, then lifted her cornflower blue eyes. "All my life, my Mom has been afraid, hiding. She and Dad don't have much of a life. I guess I made a decision that I don't want to live that way when I approached Siobhan and Samantha."

Her eyes focused and the blue seemed to grow darker. "Callie, I'm always going to be small. Rebecca calls me a mini-succubus. She doesn't say it to be mean, but I get tired of people treating me like a child. I want what she has, what Brenna has. People's respect." Her expression grew intense. "The only way people are going to respect me is if I earn it. I know there are a lot of different ways to do that, but doing something even though I'm scared is one way to earn respect from myself. And that's where I have to start."

With Irina's help, Rebecca built and implanted a construct in the young succubus' mind. She explained it to Irina as being a stage set, intended to fool another telepath. Constructs were often used to create false identities. In this case, it recreated the Irina that existed prior to her meeting the Clan. The construct didn't contain her knowledge of the Clan and reinstated her leaky shields. The real Irina still existed as a watcher underneath. Only she or someone with the Lindstrom Gift could see the construct or collapse it.

33

With Brenna hitchhiking in her mind underneath the construct, Irina met with the UN official for her interview.

"I hope you're feeling better," Konrad Rosenberg smiled at the diminutive girl sitting nervously in his office.

"Oh, yes sir," Irina smiled nervously, "I think it must have been some sort of food poisoning. I felt fine when I met with you, but that evening I became deathly ill. I'm fine now."

"It's too bad you didn't have the opportunity to attend the party I gave you the invitation for," he said.

"Oh, no, I went," Irina assured him. "I don't know if it was what I ate before I went, but I got sick while I was there."

"Well, I'm glad you're feeling better." What followed was a perfunctory repeat of their earlier interview. At the end, he made sure to find out where she was staying while in New York.

The hotel name she gave was a setup. That night, when Irina returned to the sham hotel, over a hundred Protectors were waiting, inside and out.

Irina rode the elevator to the third floor. When she emerged, room keycard in hand, a man was waiting. Irina nodded at him and turned to go down the hall. A hand closed around her upper arm.

"Hey," she said as he tried to pull her to him, "what the hell?"

Another man stepped out of the alcove where the ice machine was located. As he approached, she saw a syringe in his hand. She kicked the man holding her in the shin and wrenched her arm away. Backing down the hall away from them, she started draining their energy.

Doors opened on both sides of the hallway on both sides of the elevator. O'Donnell Protectors poured out of the rooms and captured the men inside an air shield.

Hauled into Irina's hotel room, Brenna smashed their shields and turned their minds over to Collin and his Protectors. Rebecca collapsed Irina's construct.

"We did it," Irina squealed, bouncing up and down and laughing in exultation. "That was the most amazing thing I've ever done."

She hugged Rebecca. "You were right. It was like watching a performance. I was so nervous, but the Irina in the construct was cool as a cucumber. I never would have been able to pull it off." She beamed as various people congratulated her on playing her part so well.

Protectors appropriated the hunters' clothing, and Caroline, almost a hundred years older than Irina but short and blonde, took Irina's place.

Taking their captives' car, Jeremy and Kallen drove to the rendezvous site at a brownstone on the upper west side and hauled Caroline to the front door. Kallen knocked. When a man answered the door, Kallen hit him in the face and bulled his way inside.

All three were extremely powerful telepaths with the Gifts for Air Shielding and Neural Disruption. Covered in air shields, they charged into the house, Jeremy taking the stairs two at a time while Kallen and Caroline split up and fought their way through the ground floor. Five more Protectors followed them in.

Caroline confronted two men and a woman in the living room. One discharged a bolt of electrical energy at her, but her air shield deflected it. She returned a stream of disruptive neural energy. Her assailant jerked, convulsed, and fell to the floor twitching as his nerves discharged randomly and commands from his brain ceased to make proper connections.

"Give it up or I'll do the same to you," she said to the other two people. The man pulled a gun, but was too slow. A silenced pistol spat over Caroline's shoulder as the Protector following her was faster.

One man tried to flee out the back door, but the team waiting there captured him and thanked him for opening the door.

On the third floor, a woman fired a gun at the Protectors coming up the stairs. The bullet bounced off Jeremy's air shield, and when he charged into her, she slipped and tumbled over the railing, hitting the bannister below, and bouncing down to the first floor.

Within five minutes, they subdued and captured the men and women in the house.

They rounded up seventeen telepaths. The woman who fell from the third floor was dead of a broken back, and the man Caroline burned out was euthanized. Four others, including one with a bullet in his shoulder, were hurt and taken to the healers at the New York compound.

Interrogations ensued immediately. Some of them had knowledge of CBW personnel at the UN and other operations in New York. Protectors were dispatched to apprehend three more operatives associated with the succubi hunters. The captives were transported to the Clan's compound to have their minds thoroughly ransacked. Once the O'Donnell Clan was through with them, their Gifts would be burned out and their minds would be stripped of their memories.

~~~

The next day, the most important operation commenced.

The Center for a Better World, CBW, was the most powerful European rival to the O'Donnell Clan. Based in Berlin, it presented itself as a philanthropic organization. In reality, it served as a front for a consortium of German, Austrian, Italian and Eastern European Clans.

Philosophically, the consortium was the polar opposite of O'Donnell. Their basic unifying belief was that telepaths were a superior race whose rightful place in the world was to rule, and normal humans should serve them. During

36

World War II, those Clans backed the Nazis and Fascists. During the Silent War of the late 1940s and 1950s, they fought to control Europe. O'Donnell and its allies were victorious, forestalling those plans.

CBW had a small U.S. headquarters in Washington, DC, that Seamus tolerated, and a larger contingent in New York operating out of the UN. Most of the foreign Clans had some presence in DC and at the UN. The UN actually served the same function for the Clans as it did for national governments, giving them a neutral ground to meet and communicate.

The operations against succubi in New York were not within the boundaries Seamus was willing to tolerate. Reports of succubi and other young telepathic women disappearing had become more numerous, and at least two succubi had been killed.

Several teams entered UN headquarters using various guises. Some entered wearing UN security uniforms, some as tourists, others as credentialed national representatives or UN employees. Collin and a team of four computer experts took control of the security center, disabling cameras throughout the building and crashing the servers.

Brenna, Rebecca and three Protectors, all dressed in conservative business suits, went to Rosenberg's office, blurring their presence in the minds of everyone they passed.

When they entered his office, his secretary jumped to her feet, lashing out with a bolt of mental energy. The attack was deflected as Brenna had her team covered by her O'Neill mental shields. Rebecca walked up to the secretary and punched her in the nose. The secretary fell back in her chair, blood gushing over her blouse. Battering through her shields, Rebecca captured her mind.

"Did that feel good?" Brenna grinned.

"That was for Irina. She told me his secretary was creepy," Rebecca said, rubbing her knuckles.

Opening the door to the inner office, Brenna said, "Good morning, Herr Rosenberg." She smashed his shields and took control of his mind. The Protectors plundered his thoughts, discovering the entire structure of CBW operations and personnel at the UN and throughout New York City.

Rosenberg reported to three different people. A member of Siegfried von Ebersberg's Clan, his superior in that regard was another important official of the UN. Rosenberg also reported to CBW intelligence in Berlin and to Lord John Gordon in London. It was Gordon who was running the succubi hunters, though most of the personnel were supplied by von Ebersberg. Young succubi such as Irina and Brenna were delivered to von Ebersberg. Older ones such as Cindy had been delivered to Manfred Gless before his death.

He knew that those delivered to Gless, the monster Brenna had run into near DC, were destined for murder. The fates of those sent to von Ebersberg weren't as clear to him, though he did know his Clan dealt in prostitution.

One piece of information that came as a surprise was that they were also hunting women who only carried the succubus genes. The Kashani Gift, usually called the Succubus Gift, was the result of a sex-linked gene complex. Brenna inherited it from both parents, while Rebecca had inherited it from only one of her parents. Brenna was a succubus and Rebecca wasn't. Von Ebersberg was collecting both, the younger the better.

When they finished, eyes blazing with rage, Rebecca placed her finger against Rosenberg's head and sent a stream of Neural Disruption energy into his brain. His body stiffened then slumped.

Shocked, Brenna asked, "Did you kill him?"

"No, I burned out his Gifts. He's head blind."

Leaving Rosenberg's office, they went searching for his superior in von Ebersberg's Clan.

How's our time? Rebecca sent to Collin. *We know who the kingpin is. Do we want to take him out of here?*

No, too risky. We can give you another fifteen minutes, but that's it.

We won't have time to do a thorough interrogation.

Collin was silent and Rebecca waited for instructions. In the meantime, Collin opened a secure elevator for them. They rode it to another floor.

I wish we could capture his mind, the way Brenna did Gless, Collin finally answered Rebecca.

We're not letting the bastard into Brenna's mind, Rebecca responded.

No, I'm not suggesting that, just wishing. The tone of his mental thread carried the same revulsion Rebecca felt, remembering how dangerously close Brenna had come to being killed.

Arriving at Johan Karlson's office, Rebecca took the lead. All of the strike team members, including Brenna, wore bulletproof vests under their clothes, but she wasn't taking any risks with Brenna's safety. CBW operatives had proven quite willing to use conventional weapons.

"We have an appointment with Mr. Karlson," Rebecca said, battering through his secretary's shields. Brenna shattered the shields of the other three telepaths in the office and the Protectors blurred everything from the minds of the two norms present.

Pushing through the door to Karlson's private office, they were met with bolts of electrical energy and spears of neural disruption. Karlson was a powerful telepath and he didn't intend to let them capture him. Brenna's shields blocked the neural disruption while Rebecca's air shield deflected the electrical energy. The lights went out. Karlson's office had windows across one wall and they could see in his office, but the outer office was plunged into darkness. One of the Protectors kindled a small ball of fire on his palm to provide light.

Brenna smashed Karlson's shields and took control of his mind. He screamed, sinking into his chair, holding his head in his hands.

I have notification of a power failure in your area, Collin sent.

Karlson used electrokinesis, Rebecca told him.

The women rifled through his mind.

There's an intelligence gold mine here, Rebecca told Brenna. *Isn't there some way to take his mind with us?*

I don't know. Brenna enfolded his soul with her mind and attempted to pull it out of him. It didn't budge.

Rebecca reached into him, grabbed his soul and pulled it into her mind. Karlson shuddered and his body slumped.

"Shit," Brenna said, turning frantically to Rebecca, "he's dead. Put it back."

Rebecca pushed Karlson's soul back into him. Brenna stimulated his heart and he took a shuddering breath.

The women looked at each other, relief in both their faces.

Karlson had a heart attack. Can we get him out of here in an ambulance? Brenna sent a spear to Collin.

Hell yeah, that works. I'll have people there in a few minutes.

A doctor and two EMTs soon appeared. Within half an hour, Karlson was loaded into an ambulance driven by an O'Donnell Protector. With Karlson safely sedated in the O'Donnell infirmary, a team went to work mining his knowledge. The succubi hunting in New York and Washington was over.

Twelve more CBW operatives were rounded up and the rival Clans' communication network was compromised. Not only had they disrupted the succubus hunting operations, but CBW's U.S. operations as a whole.

~~~

Alice had told Brenna and her friends that she could have some clothes ready for them the end of the week. The

40

rest would be shipped to West Virginia where her sister Elise could make any final adjustments that might be necessary. Wanting to see the best first, Brenna asked her to make the Solstice dresses so they could try them on before their trip ended. On Thursday morning, they went to a fitting, discovering Alice also had a second dress ready for each of them. They would have new dresses for Thanksgiving.

Callie felt as proud and happy as a new mother watching the wonder on the girls' faces as they looked at themselves in the mirror. She remembered how she felt the first time she put on one of Alice's creations, seeing the tall, awkward girl she had always thought of herself turned into a beautiful swan. It changed her self-perception and her life. For the first time, she had seen the beauty her father had always praised.

Before they left the shop, Brenna and Alice went off alone, and when she came back Callie asked, "So, did you keep your promise?"

"Of course, before taxes."

After the fitting, Brenna insisted they go to Tiffany's. All of the female protectors were with them that day, and as everyone wandered around the store, Callie began to wonder if that was an accident. Brenna wandered about, talking to everyone, looking at the pieces people showed her, and in the end bought a rather plain jade choker necklace that fanned across her upper chest, pointing to her ample bosom, a nice watch, and a ring for Collin.

Callie watched her speaking at some length to a manager when she went to pay.

"Forgive me for being suspicious, but is there a reason we came here?" she asked Brenna. "And how much was that receipt you just signed?"

"Why, Callie, how could you possibly suspect me of manipulating something for my own selfish purposes?" Brenna asked, her eyes artificially wide.

41

"Perhaps because I know you."

Brenna smiled and looked around at her party gazing into the cases, some purchasing things. "I'm just doing a little Christmas shopping."

Callie remembered Brenna standing with each of the women, looking at jewelry they pointed out, most then reluctantly turning away because they couldn't afford it. She remembered her own longing look at an exquisite choker of yellow diamonds, and talking herself out of the hundred fifty thousand dollar price tag.

"You didn't."

"Of course not," Brenna scoffed, "you're a hundred-millionaire yourself. If you really wanted that necklace, you'd have bought it. I only really went overboard for one person and a little overboard for another."

Callie didn't bother to ask whom. "She'll yell at you."

"No she won't," Brenna told her with a chuckle. "She'll be speechless."

"So what are you giving me?"

Brenna chuckled, "Nice try. You'll know when you pull the end of the bow."

"You didn't see anything you really wanted?"

"Get real. I've got over a hundred pieces in that box, and I haven't worn a fraction of it yet. I need more jewelry like I need another hole in the head."

The group was getting ready to go, gathering near the entrance, when Callie made a mad decision. She crossed to the showcase where the yellow diamonds were displayed, and motioned the saleswoman over. "I'll take that," she said, pointing. Turning, she met Brenna's smiling eyes.

That evening, Siobhan took them to her favorite club. There was a live band, and the crowd was a little older than in some of the places she'd taken them earlier in the week. With a small bribe to the door screener, she arranged for the Protectors to be able to rotate in and out of the club freely. Since telepaths were able to clear their systems of alcohol at will, Kallen had acquiesced with allowing them to party freely.

Everyone was having a good time, dancing and flirting. Callie danced with the same man several times and then disappeared. Worried after a while, Rebecca checked the restrooms. *Brenna, have you seen Callie? I can't find her.*

She was dancing with that blonde guy, but I don't see him either.

I'm going to check outside.

Okay, I'll come with you.

They went outside, the late fall evening rather chilly, but didn't see Callie or the man. Increasingly worried, they walked around the building. In the alley, they saw a man standing in front of a woman who was backed against the wall. She had her arms around his neck and one leg around his waist, high heel and panties hanging from the end of her foot. What they were doing wasn't in question.

"My God, that's Callie!" Rebecca was scandalized.

A voice behind them made them jump, "And I'm sure she'd appreciate some privacy. I know my men would appreciate you going back inside so they can go with you and get warm," Kallen said in a droll voice.

"You love her, doesn't that bother you?" Rebecca asked.

"Yes, I love her enough to want her to be happy. I don't make her happy, not that way. Aren't you the wrong one to be talking about someone having sex in an alley?"

Rebecca's face flamed so bright Brenna could see it in the dark.

"Go back inside, she's safe, and she's doing what she enjoys doing," Kallen said.

Chastised, they went.

When they sat down at their table, Siobhan asked, "You do know what the primary purpose of panties is, don't you?"

43

"Uh, what?" Brenna asked.

"To keep your ankles warm, silly. Don't worry about Callie. Kallen takes care of her."

Sunday morning, after a riotous evening out on the town ending in a bacchanalia in their hotel, they loaded up the buses. Dropping by Alice's shop, they picked up the clothes that were ready, and headed for West Virginia.

"Ok," Brenna turned to Irina, "what's the final score?"

Pulling out her smartphone, Irina punched a few buttons, "Rebecca fifteen, Brenna twelve, Irina nine."

"Whoo hoo! I won!" Rebecca raised her arms in the air and did a little dance in her seat.

"What are you talking about?" Callie had a very perplexed look on her face.

"Modeling offers," Irina explained.

"How many runway offers?" Brenna asked.

"Rebecca twelve, Brenna and I, none."

"It's the legs," Brenna pronounced.

"Yep, the legs," Irina agreed.

"How many lingerie or nude?" Rebecca asked.

"Brenna nine, Irina six, Rebecca none."

"The boobs," Rebecca said. "And who knows if those were really legitimate offers or if they just wanted to see them."

Brenna stuck her tongue out at Rebecca.

"What were the others?" Callie asked.

"Mostly modeling makeup," Irina said. "Brenna had one for shampoo, and Rebecca had one offer to do dish soap commercials. He thought she had pretty hands."

~~~

Chapter 4

The more you love, the more you
can love--and the more intensely
you love. Nor is there any limit on
how many you can love. If a person
had time enough, he could love all
of the majority who are decent and
just. - Robert A. Heinlein

When they arrived back at the estate, Brenna sent a spear thought, *Collin, where are you?*

In your room.

Our room. I'll be up in a few minutes.

She walked into her room and began taking off her clothes while emitting bursts of pheromones, saturating the air. "Strip, Doyle, I have something for you."

Grinning, he did as he was told, and watched as she walked nude toward him.

"I'm yours, your play toy. Do with me what you wish." She smiled, "It's my penance for leaving you alone. Want to play?"

Merging their minds, he fondled, licked, and played with her body, pleasured her, and had her pleasure him. As the night progressed, they changed positions several times, being careful to control his climax. By midnight, both were thoroughly frustrated, exhausted and unsatisfied.

~~~

Cindy Nelson, recuperating from her abduction and torture at the hands of a succubus-hating telepath, had been moved from DC to the estate while Brenna was in New York.

Brenna talked to Cindy about the problem, but came away without any answers. Cindy mirrored her frustration, saying that was the major reason she and Seamus didn't live together and she spent so much time in Washington.

"Brenna, it's just too hard when you're together all the time. You want him, he wants you, and you can't consummate the act. You have to watch what you're doing all the time, and you can't just enjoy each other."

Brenna mentioned a book Rebecca had found in the Clan library, *The Succubus Gift*, but Cindy didn't read sixteenth century Gaelic. "You should ask Siobhan. She'll be coming for Thanksgiving."

That night, Brenna's frustration reached a peak. She made the mistake of giving Collin too large a pheromone dose, and both of them failed to monitor his excitement level. Brenna wanted him so badly, wanted to lose herself in their lovemaking, and she did. She was in the middle of an orgasm when she reached farther into him, deeper in his mind than she had ever gone, and touched his soul. His reaction was immediate, reaching out for her, and their souls merged.

Their souls became one, resonating with the same energy. Her orgasm grew, her pleasure soaring, and she took him along with her. It was impossible for either of them to separate from the other. The world went away, and only BrennaCollin, CollinBrenna existed. In that maelstrom of wonder, pleasure and sensation, of becoming one person, he climaxed, triggering her again in the middle of the orgasm she was already riding. His energy flowed into her, the Glow starting to grow.

No! No, damn it! Not yet! Not now! The most wonderful feeling either of them had ever had, their love merging them into one person, and she was ruining it, ending it when it had so much farther to soar.

Frantically, she began trying to push his energy away, feed it back to him, anything to keep from draining him. She felt him begin to slump and fade away from her. Reaching into that place in her mind where his energy flowed into her, where the Glow originated, she tried to block it. She touched something in that place, and suddenly the energy flow changed. It still flowed into her, changed into the glowing energy that fed a succubus' need, but then it flowed back out of her into him and he held it.

He stopped fading and strengthened, the bond between them held, their souls stayed together as one, and watching his face she saw his eyes clear and take on a quality like her Glow. Pulling his face back from her, he rose to his knees, lifting her off the bed into his arms. She wrapped her legs around him and felt him drive into her with new power. Their lips met and their souls merged completely. They stopped being two separate people, instead becoming one soul bonded in love. She knew they truly belonged together. They would always be together.

Neither knew how long that merge lasted. Lying next to each other, she opened her eyes, and a moment later he opened his.

"What did you do? My God, that was incredible, and I'm still awake."

"I, I'm not sure. Are you okay? Do you … I mean, are you …"

"I feel better than I ever have in my life. I'm a little tired, but I'm not drained. What happened?"

"I didn't want you to go. I, I think we merged our souls. Is that possible?"

"Yes, but if they don't resonate, if they're on different frequencies, they push back apart."

"They didn't push apart."

He smiled, "No they didn't. Brenna, the term 'soul mate' originated with telepaths. It's said a person may have more than one soul mate in their life, but only death can separate you."

She smiled, a bit shakily, "So now I have to kill you if I want to get rid of you?"

"Afraid so."

"Oh good," she snuggled even closer to him, nestling her head against his chest, "that would be so much more satisfying than just giving you a ring back or something."

He laughed. "Seriously, what did you do? Will it work again? Do we have to merge our souls for it to work?"

"I don't know. I just touched a place in my mind, the place where your energy is turned into my Glow, and it was like throwing a light switch. The energy flowed into me, through me and back into you."

After a while, they made love again. Without the pent-up sexual frustration, it was slow, gentle, languid, and extremely satisfying. She pleasured him with her muscles, and he teased her with slow, deep strokes that gave her a sense of warmth and well-being. They merged their souls, reveling in the joy of finding someone that not just fit but completed their beings. His climax began to build and she encouraged him, their merged minds building each other's pleasure. When he finally spilled in her, she flipped the switch as her orgasm triggered. They took each other soaring again, lost in each other, lost in their pleasure. His energy flowed into her, changed, and flowed back into him.

She fell asleep with her head resting on his shoulder, feeling his hand stroking her hair. She had never felt happier or more satisfied in her life.

~~~

Collin awoke in the morning to some very pleasurable sensations. Something warm, soft, and heavy was bouncing on his hips, and a part of him in that same region was very warm, wet and happy. Opening his eyes, he saw Brenna staring down at him.

"Do you know what I'm doing?" she asked in a very cheery voice.

"Uh, well, I could take a guess," he replied sleepily.

"I'm having morning sex. Isn't that wonderful?" Her cheerfulness grated on his nerves.

"Sure, I guess so."

"Smug boy. It's probably old hat to you, but I've never had morning sex, not with the same guy I had evening sex with."

"Oh." He suddenly realized why she was so happy.

"Collin, I was thinking, I don't think we have to do a soul merge for it to work. I think I know how to do it anytime. But," she leaned forward and kissed him, "if I'm wrong, you'll still wake up in time to carve the turkey."

She began moving faster, her muscles rippling over him, driving him deep within her.

"Well, you're going to find out pretty quickly if you keep that up."

Their minds merged and she felt his passion build. He spilled inside her. As his climax triggered her orgasm, she tripped the switch in her mind. Grinding down on him, body upright, she arched her back and thrust her beautiful breasts forward, a beatific look on her face. He watched in awe as she shook in the throes of her pleasure. Her internal muscles rippled over him, pleasuring him far beyond anything he'd ever known. He realized he'd never seen her in this state, her Glow building and her entire being becoming radiant. The familiar drain of his energy started, but then it flowed back into him, changed and glowing.

When her orgasm had spent its force, she fell forward, her hands on either side of his head and her hair falling like a black shower around them.

"Do you always come that hard?" he asked.

"Only when a man comes inside me," she panted. "It's completely different than an orgasm you give me other ways. I might come several times before you do, but the last one is mind shattering."

She clenched him tight, her muscles working. With a burst of pheromones, massaging him with her muscles, he felt himself growing harder again.

"You're going to kill me," he gasped.

49

The predatory smile on her face was almost frightening. "Maybe, but you'll die happy."

He couldn't argue with that, and when she began to move again, he discovered he didn't care. He made it into the office two hours late with a huge smile on his face.

~~~

Cindy had told Brenna she was spending two hours each morning with Elsie Cavanaugh, the Clan's senior healer, and two hours each afternoon with Dorothy, Elsie's daughter. The healers used their Gift to speed her healing. Elsie was two hundred five years old and incredibly cantankerous. Brenna had been studying with her for three months.

Bursting into Cindy's room, she found Elsie deep in a healing trance. "Cindy, guess what? Oh, sorry."

Elsie opened her eyes and fixed her with a glare. "My, my, it's the succubus. Finished gallivanting off to New York? Well, it's good you're back. I can use you. I don't have the energy I need to do this properly, and I see you're glowing. Sit down and let me have some of that extra energy."

"Uh, I can help, but I don't really have any extra right now." She sat down, merged her mind with Elsie's, and began helping her strengthen Cindy's bones.

Elsie gave her a look of disgust. "Bah, you don't. Why not?"

"That's what I came to tell Cindy, I found a way to have sex without draining the man."

Cindy's eyes shot wide open and she tried to sit up. Elsie pushed her back down.

"That doesn't do me any good. What we're doing is very draining. If we had more energy we could help her heal faster. That's one of the reasons succubi make the best healers. Your mother was one of the strongest healers I've ever seen. Go out and drain a few men and she could really make a difference on an injury like this." She shook her

50

head. "I'm only a half. I take a man and all it does is balance me."

"Half of what Elsie?" Brenna asked, puzzled. Cindy went very still on the bed at Elsie's words.

"Half a succubus, what do you think I'm talking about? Pay attention, girl. Well, nothing to be done for it this morning, but I want you in here tomorrow, ten o'clock sharp, and I want you to have a full Glow on. The more the better. Every day, you hear me? We need to get her up out of this bed, and the only way we're going to do it is to accelerate healing those bones."

She got up and tottered to the door.

"Elsie, what do you mean that taking a man restores your balance? What balance?" Cindy asked.

"I told you, I'm a half. My energy balances get all out of whack, since I can't store energy the way you can. I take a man and restore the balance, but I can't keep in balance. My dam was the same way. Had a sister, she was a succubus. You're lucky, you two. It's hell being a half." With that, she shuffled out the door.

Brenna turned to Cindy, seeing a wide-eyed startlement on her face that matched her own feelings. "Rebecca," they said in unison.

"I wonder if all the carriers have the same problem," Brenna mused. "Collin, for instance. You don't suppose …"

"… that's why he can't keep it in his pants?" Cindy finished. "Oh, my God, that would explain so much. Both my parents were carriers."

"When we were in New York, Siobhan asked Rebecca if she was a half. I'd never heard the term before," Brenna said.

A thought, a memory, flitted through Brenna's mind. She sat down and chased it. When did she learn … then she had it. Genetic diseases, a course she took at the medical school.

"Cindy, Callie has it all wrong. The succubus gene isn't a sex-linked recessive, it's a sex-linked dominant." Brenna said.

Cindy looked puzzled.

"Hang on a second, let me get Callie up here. She's the expert. I've just had a few courses in genetics."

Callie, unless the business is on fire, can you come up to Cindy's room. We just learned something very startling from Elsie. Brenna sent on a spear thread.

On my way.

When she arrived, Brenna told her what Elsie had said, and Cindy told her about her parents and the conversation she'd once had with Rebecca.

"When we ran that operation where Rebecca played a succubus, I was trying to gage her lust levels, you know, trying to figure out if she could really project enough to simulate what we do with our pheromones. She told me that she has to have sex once or twice a day. Has to. Otherwise, she said her mind starts to fog and she gets so distracted she can't think of anything else. She said all the Protectors know, and they were kind enough to help her out when she needed it."

Cindy shook her head. "Can you imagine? A beautiful young woman like that saying men are kind enough to have sex with her when she needs it? It blew my mind. But it also made me flash to my parents. Both of them would go nuts if they were celibate for more than a day."

"Maureen once told me her parents were that way. I'd forgotten until just now. But they're both carriers, too," Callie said.

"Too much information, Callie," Brenna said, shaking her head. She didn't even want to think of her grandparents having sex. "What I don't understand, is why didn't you recognize this before?"

Pursing her mouth and shaking her head, Callie said, "The genes have been lost in this country. Think about it.

52

All the succubi in Clan O'Donnell were born in Ireland. We obviously have some carriers here, but no succubi have been born in the U.S. O'Byrne and O'Neill have at least a dozen each, and there are a lot outside the Clans in Ireland and Britain. The genes are also rare in Europe, where the Inquisition was strongest."

Callie took a deep breath and looked away, her eyes unfocused. "I should call your grandmother O'Byrne. We're probably reinventing the wheel."

"Callie, when I took a genetic diseases class, they made a clear distinction between recessives and dominants," Brenna said. "For a recessive-caused condition, you have to have both genes for the condition to manifest, right?" Callie nodded. "But some conditions are caused by dominants. And if you get both sides of a dominant pair, the condition is much more severe."

She saw the light come on for Callie. "What you're saying is the succubus gene is a dominant. The people with one gene manifest the Gifts associated with the gene complex. But if you have two copies of the gene, the manifestation is far more severe, in other words, you get a succubus."

"Exactly. Elsie said that her energies get unbalanced, and since she can't store the energy like we can, having sex only corrects the imbalance, but she can't keep it in balance. Our ability to manipulate energies, shifting them where we will, keeps us from getting out of balance in the first place. It explains why Rebecca and Collin become increasingly agitated and distracted the longer they spend between sexual activity."

Brenna thought for a moment, then said, "That would also explain why we have much stronger energy Gifts. My ability to drain and project energy is much stronger than Rebecca's and I know hers is stronger than Dorothy's.

"Okay, I buy it as a working hypothesis, but what good, other than as an interesting fact, does it do for us?"

Cindy answered, "It might do a lot for the people who have the condition, psychologically, if nothing else. Callie, I don't think you realize how much of an impact it makes on these people. They can't control their behavior, behavior that's considered sinful, outrageous, even disgusting by society at large. They hide, they're ashamed, they think they have some kind of moral failing.

"In our society, succubi are treated mostly with respect. But the poor women who only have half the Gift are treated with derision and disgust. Siobhan and I might joke about being genetic sluts, but we know how much we gain from our condition. Poor Rebecca really is a genetic slut, and she gets nothing out of it except shame. She feels she has to hide what she does."

Callie stood, "I wonder how many we have? I need to check my database."

"Hold it," Cindy commanded. "I'm sympathetic to Rebecca, but Brenna came in saying something that is life-altering for me. What was that about sex without the Drain? Controlling that's the ultimate dream of every succubus. If I could do that, I'd be able to have a real relationship with Seamus." The look in her eyes was that of a hungry tiger.

Callie sat back down.

"Well, Collin and I had sex last night," Brenna's eyes took on a far-away, dreamy look, "and we merged our souls, it was so beautiful."

Callie jerked as if she'd been slapped, staring at Brenna.

"That's nice. Get to the good part," Cindy said.

"Then we had sex again, and a third time. This morning we did it three times again."

"When you say sex …?"

"Sex. He came inside me, the energy drain started, and then his energies flowed back to him."

"You drained him, and then fed him back his energy? I've tried that, it doesn't work."

"No, not like that. You know the place where their energy goes and is transformed into the Glow? There's a switch there you can flip. The energy flows through you and then back into him. I'm not pushing it, it's automatic, and he's able to hold it."

"Show me."

Brenna opened her mind and attempted to show Cindy the switch, but it wasn't there. "Cindy, I'm not making this up. Ask Collin. He even glows a bit. He says the energy coming back into him is changed."

Cindy was quiet for a couple of minutes, obviously listening to something mentally. "Well, he's telling me the same story you are, so either this is the cruelest joke you could dream up, or you stumbled onto, well, something." She sneered, "Or you're both delusional, something I'm not going to entirely discount." The sneer faded into a sad expression.

~~~

Callie checked her database and talked to Elsie, then called Caylin O'Byrne in Ireland. Afterward, she met with Brenna again. The gaps in their knowledge compared to what Callie was told by the older women were astounding. Brenna went to see Collin.

"Honey, I need you to tell me about your woman problem, and be honest with me." She walked around his desk, took his face in both hands and kissed him soundly enough to curl his toes. "Collin, I'm not trying to trap you. I've been in your mind enough that if I wanted to poke around and make your sexual habits an issue, I'd have done so already. But I need to know about your love life, in a general way, and about your mother."

"My mother?"

Brenna nodded, sitting back on his desk. "And if you're willing to be honest with me, I'll screw your ears off before I leave. Deal?"

He grinned, "You really don't play fair, do you?" He took a deep breath, "Ok, ever since puberty, I'm horny all the time. I don't mean in the way most boys are horny, but in an obsessive way. I think about it all the time, and it's only gotten worse as I get older. If I don't get it at least once a day, preferably more than once, I get so distracted, so antsy, that I have to go looking for it. And if it's long enough between times, then I don't care who I screw, which can cause problems if it's someone I don't like and don't want to see again. Enough?"

"Do you ever feel as though you're energized afterward?"

"Always. It's like drinking a pot of espresso. My mind is clear and focused."

"Do your partners feel tired?"

His brow furrowed in thought. "Now that you mention it, yes. Most women anyway."

"But not succubi, or Rosie or Rebecca."

"Yeah, how'd you know?"

She nodded, "And your mother?"

He took another deep breath, "My mother is the same way only she has a couple of regulars, men she's been seeing for decades. She seems to need it about once a day. That and my father's drinking were the two issues I remember growing up. She would call him a drunk, and he'd call her a slut."

He grew very quiet then looked at her, "May I inquire as to the reason for these questions?"

"We think you're an incubus, that the uncontrollable urges you experience are genetic in origin. We're trying to make sense of something Elsie told me today. She's a carrier for the succubus gene, as are you, Rebecca, and your mom. Cindy's parents are, too. So was my dad. All of a sudden, a lot of things started to come together. Cindy was the one who really identified the issue, but as soon as she voiced her suspicions I could see it, too."

56

"I'm an incubus?" he said, a smile slowly growing on his face. He started laughing.

"Your succubus girlfriend isn't complaining," Brenna said. "I'm rather in favor of having an insatiable lover." She started unbuttoning his pants.

~~~

Brenna went to see Rebecca next. "We need to talk. I need you to tell me about this deep, dark, secret you seem afraid to discuss with me, but every Protector in the valley knows about."

She explained what they had discovered. When she finished, Rebecca was silent for a long time then turned her face to Brenna, eyes full of pain. "Are you trying to tell me that all the pain I've endured, all the ridicule, the shame, the pregnancy scares, are because I have a damn gene that makes me act this way? You get two of them, and everyone thinks you're wonderful, but I only get one and my life is a train wreck? God damn it! Some son of a bitch can't keep it in his pants, knocks my mother up, and I pay the price my whole damn life?

"Go away, Brenna. I've been alone my whole life. Just go away. You don't want to be around someone like me."

Brenna felt the pain roll off her friend like an ill wind. "I'm not going away. You're the one who set the rules. Remember? I'm here, and I'll always be here."

"Damn you, damn you to hell." Rebecca stepped toward Brenna with her fist raised. Brenna simply stood with her hands by her side, pity in her eyes.

"I told you to get out. Leave me the hell alone."
Brenna didn't move.

"Oh God, oh Jesus, why me? Why don't you leave? Please leave. Please?" Brenna still didn't move.

Rebecca broke, sobbing. Brenna enfolded her in a hug, feeling Rebecca's tears soak her shoulder. She cried until she didn't have any more tears to shed, misery in every line of her face. "So, now I know what the problem is, what the hell do I do about it?"

"The same thing you told me to do when I discovered I'm a succubus. You can't change it, you can't deny it, all you can do is decide how you want to face it. It's not your fault. Everyone who knows you well respects you. Are you listening?"

Rebecca stared at her, incomprehension plain in her face. "You don't care? You're not ashamed of me? How can you respect me?"

Tears rolled down Brenna's cheeks. "Good God, Rebecca, I'm a succubus. I'm a fucking genetic whore. Built for pleasure. A natural predator. We're made for each other. The whore and the slut. God help anyone who messes with you, because I'll make them sorry there isn't a hell they can escape to."

~~~

After a discussion with Collin, Brenna went out to fulfill Elsie's expectations. He gave her a list of Protectors scheduled to be off duty. Rebecca went through the list and made recommendations. She went to their barracks on a mission to add a little cheer to a few Protectors' day.

Brenna met with Elsie and Cindy the next morning and Elsie used the energy she had collected. It was obvious how much Cindy benefited from the healing session and Elsie directed her to be prepared for a similar session each day.

When Siobhan came in for Thanksgiving and found out what Elsie had directed Brenna to do, she volunteered to bear some of the burden. "After all, it's not like I'm going to be celibate while I'm here. If I can contribute, then of course I'm willing to help."

Cindy lost no time in telling Siobhan about Brenna's fantastic assertion. Rebecca brought her the old book from the library, and Brenna once again tried to explain what she'd done, how she had found the switch and how it worked, but Siobhan just shook her head. There wasn't anything to show. Brenna had already established that the switch was only there when a man's energy triggered her Glow.

The next day, Siobhan told Cindy and Brenna, "I've been reading that book, *The Succubus Gift*, and it's very informative, very thorough and accurate. I tend to agree with your mother's notes. I think it was written by a nun who was a succubus and possibly a healer. I found a couple of passages that suggest a succubus doesn't have to drain her lover. There's reference to a technique that can be used to circumvent it, but there's no details. The author is so condemnatory. She says succubi only use the technique with a man they love, then goes on to say that since succubi are incapable of love, it's rarely if ever used and therefore she's not going to waste any time describing it. The fucking bitch!"

~~~

Thanksgiving was traditionally a family occasion. Some non-family members of the Clan were usually included, such as Siobhan, personal friends, and some top-level executives that were very close. Brenna, who had been without family for so long, was stunned that the table was set for sixty people. It was the first occasion that she and her friends had to wear their new dresses from Alice's shop, and she knew the other two young women felt as wonderful as she did.

Seamus' younger children Jill and William, Callie's half-sister and half-brother, had flown in, as had Brenna's other grandparents.

William Wallace was forty-five and regional manager of the Clan office in South Africa. She soon discovered his primary interests were sailing and fishing, and he was very keen to talk about them.

Jill McConaghy, forty years old, was Seamus' youngest child. Slender and pretty with shining brown hair and sparkling blue eyes, Jill was lively and vivacious, quick

59

to laugh and an interesting conversationalist. She served as regional manager of their Hong Kong office, overseeing all of their Asian interests. Brenna knew she and Callie were very fond of each other and soon understood why.

On the other hand, her distant cousin Rodric, sitting on one side of her, was a boor and a letch. He made numerous references to her being a succubus. She smiled, answering some of his comments politely and ignoring the rest. During one such exchange, she received a spear thread from her grandmother, *Don't you think it would be easier to just agree to meet him after dinner and kill him? I'm sure it would take days before anyone realized he wasn't breathing, the difference between that and his normal demeanor being so slight.*

Brenna choked on her food, causing concern in the men sitting beside her. When she finally got herself under control, she shot a look at her grandmother, who smiled sweetly back at her.

Her grandparents expressed their desire for her to visit them and she managed to catch Callie's attention.

"I'd love to come, but there are security difficulties in my traveling with the troubles we've been having lately."

"Caylin," Callie intervened, "If you're amenable to a late spring visit, I think we can work out the security and logistics. I know Brenna wants to go, and is very curious to see where her mother grew up." On a spear thread, she told Brenna, *You really don't want to visit Ireland until late spring. It's a cold, miserable place in the winter.*

Brenna glanced out the window, where it had started snowing. *Completely unlike warm, sunny West Virginia?*

You'll notice your grandparents are here for a three month visit.

Yeah, but they're going to Florida in January.

After dinner both William and Jill asked her if they could meet with her the next day. She chatted with Jill for some time, fascinated by her tales of Asia. "I'm dying to meet your friends," Jill told her. "Callie seems especially taken with that wilder Protector you've adopted and the new succubus is darling. Would you mind introducing me?"

Brenna's cousin Jared stepped forward. "I'd appreciate an introduction to her also. Darling isn't exactly the word I'd use, but I suppose 'hot' would be uncouth, wouldn't it?"

She led them to where Rebecca was talking with the tall, redheaded older man she was sitting beside at dinner and Irina was attempting to be polite to Rodric. She introduced everyone. Irina and Jared made an instant connection. The man Rebecca was with turned out to be Kallen's older half-brother Sean, head of her grandparents' security team. He and Rebecca were discussing their possible trip to Ireland.

Gazing around the room, half listening to Rebecca wheedle an introduction to Sean's tall, redheaded son and Jill and Irina chatting in Russian, Brenna suddenly realized she felt at home here. She drifted off from the group and sidled up to Collin, putting her arm through his and leaning against him.

When she and Collin got back to their room, she was surprised to find Irina standing outside her door. With a glance at Collin, Irina pulled Brenna aside, "Can you show me that trick? You know, the one that keeps you from draining a guy?"

"I've tried to show Cindy and Siobhan, and haven't had any success."

"I know, you told me. What I mean is can you *show* me? You know, let me see how you do it."

Brenna shot a glance at Collin, "You mean, *show you*, like let you watch me do it?"

Irina colored slightly and nodded her head. "Yeah, that's what I mean."

Brenna thought for a moment, looking at Irina's pleading eyes. *Collin, would you mind having this voyeur watch us make love? She wants to see how I do the energy feedback trick, and I've had zero luck trying to explain it to any of them.*

He looked startled, then thoughtful. *Hell, I'm not bashful. It's up to you.*

She told Irina she would send her a thread, and looking happy Irina retreated to her room on the second floor. Brenna chuckled at Irina's impatience. It seemed the young succubus had arranged to visit Jared later and didn't want to keep him waiting too long.

~~~

Collin began with the lightest of touches, his fingers stroking her face, her neck, her hair. A delicate shudder rippled through her body, and heat began to grow between her legs. Lifting her hair away from her neck, he reached behind and unhooked the clasp of her halter top, pulling the straps apart and releasing them. They fell, leaving her uncovered to the waist.

His hands brushed lightly over her breasts, down over her stomach, then slid the dress down over her hips and thighs. Stroking her inner thighs, he brought his hands back up, lightly touching her shaved mons with his fingertips.

"God, I love your hands," she purred.

Smiling, his lips moved to her neck while his hands cupped the curves of her breasts. She slid her hands under his shirt, loving the feel of his warm skin and taut muscles. Tipping her head back, she reveled in the sensations he aroused as he tasted her. His kisses increased their intensity. When he sucked her nipple into his mouth she moaned, pushing against him.

Managing to pull his shirt off, her hands moved to his pants. The pants fell to the floor and he pulled her down to the bed, continuing to kiss her breasts. She ran her fingers through his hair while his mouth sucked and teased.

She gasped as his fingers slipped between her folds, stroking her with feather light touches. He groaned, penetrating her with his fingers, tickling the spot she loved, hearing her whimper, his fingers pleasuring her with a constant rhythm, matching his hot kisses to her breasts and neck.

Reaching for his erection, she touched the tip and he shuddered. Thick, long, and hard, he was ready to fill her aching need. Spreading her legs further apart, she gave him a burst of pheromones, causing his nostrils to flare. With a smile, he removed his fingers, bringing them to her mouth where she sucked her essence off.

Desire enveloped them, pushing them to find the pleasure their bodies sought. He positioned himself at her entrance, and pushed into her in one long thrust.

Brenna purred with approval, feeling him stretch and fill her. Locking her eyes with his, loving the determination written on his face, she returned his eagerness and desire with her own. Lost in the moment, she almost forgot to send a spear to Irina.

"Harder. I want it harder," she panted.

He increased his speed and force, rising to his knees and putting his hands under her thighs, pulling her up and toward him, driving deeper into her. She cried out, urging him on. Her cries escalated to small whimpering screams and he thrust into her harder and harder, her hips rising to meet him. She could feel his energy grow as the big moment neared, then he spasmed and so did she, his energy pouring into her, taking her over the edge and feeding her orgasm. She writhed underneath him, basking in the Glow, their bodies joined, sharing their orgasm. Through the fog, she flipped the switch, returning his energy back into him. Through their link, she heard Irina gasp as she saw and understood the process.

Irina had stayed in the background, but both were aware of her presence. It was very different to have someone else in their minds, experiencing all that they created together.

Collin exhaled, laying back on the bed. Brenna felt Irina's exultation.

Thank you both so much <smile>, Irina sent, *Collin, you have no idea how much this means to me,* and then she was gone from their minds.

"Collin, honey, I hope we didn't completely exhaust your exhibitionistic urges, because I have a feeling we're going to be asked to perform again." She cuddled up to him. "You did a very good thing tonight. I don't think you can totally appreciate what this means to us. It makes a real relationship possible, something I was told I'd never have." She twisted so she could kiss him. "I love you, Collin Doyle." Her hand traveled down his torso. "Want to practice making babies again?"

~~~

Brenna's meeting with William demanded all the focusing skills she'd developed from sitting through six years of boring classes. Although he asked her a few pertinent questions, he was happiest when talking about his boats. He came away from the meeting seeming pleased that she shared his interests.

Getting together with Jill was an entirely different kettle of fish. Seamus' youngest was no fool and she was extremely interested in Brenna's plans for her inheritance and especially what she planned to do with O'Donnell Development. She was also interested in Brenna's research into the brain and listened raptly to her theories about the Telepathic Gifts.

~~~

Brenna and Jill went riding for a couple of hours, cold though it was. Rory, the stable master and her grandfather's oldest friend, met them when they came back into the stables. "Brenna," he said very seriously, "I haven't seen my grandson since that friend of yours' disappeared with him last night."

"Rory, the last I heard she had him chained to the bed and was turning him into a sex slave. Why, do you really want him back?"

He roared with laughter. "Brenna, Miss Jill, it's good to see the two of you together. Does an old man's heart good to see the best of the new generation getting on with each other."

"Which old man would that be?" Jill asked, looking around as though she might spot him. "Rory, I keep telling you, hanging around with old people will make you feel old. Spend more time with Helen."

He chuckled, "Damn, if I don't miss having you around."

His demeanor suddenly turned serious. "You girls going to take over this place and run it?" He reached out and put his hands on their shoulders. "Don't you let anyone say you can't. Listen to Callie. Seamus will back you. Just bulldoze over all of them, you hear? You're the two best things happened to this Clan since Seamus was born. He knows it, and Callie knows it."

He stepped back, looking sheepish, and mumbled, "Sorry, forgot my place. Hope you enjoyed your ride." Turning, he walked away, his face blushing red. Brenna turned to Jill, seeing a mirror of her own astonishment in her face.

"What was that about?"

Jill shook her head, then comprehension dawned on her face. "He's a precog you know. He saw something. Damn, I wish I knew what he saw."

~~~

Chapter 5

*Behind every great woman is a guy
looking at her ass. - Author
Unknown*

Jill drove down to DC on Monday and flew out on Tuesday, promising to be back in two weeks. Brenna and Rebecca rode with her into the city to spend the next few days Christmas shopping.

"Brenna, you already bought me a boatload of clothes. You're not going to get me something for Christmas too, are you?"

"Oh, maybe an accessory or two, maybe a new flogger," Brenna said, smiling.

Rebecca chuckled. "Just don't go overboard, okay? I don't know if I've said thank you enough, but thank you again. You don't have to buy my love."

"Perish the thought, I know you're cheap," Brenna laughed. "But let me have my pleasures, okay? Believe me, I got more pleasure out of seeing you in that new evening dress than you got from wearing it."

~~~

It was a warm sunny day in Washington, unseasonable for late November. Sean enjoyed just walking around. He had been over to the National Mall, although he hadn't gone inside any of the museums. There would be plenty of time to do that later, perhaps on a day when the weather wasn't so nice.

Walking north from the Capitol, he planned to stop into a pub he remembered for lunch. It was too early to begin working on his assignment -- that would take place after dark. For now, he could enjoy the day and the pleasant sight of the two young women walking in front of him.

Dressed in tight blue jeans, they definitely were among the nicer attractions he'd seen that day. The taller one moved like a dancer, slender and oh so enticing, her high-heeled boots clicking on the pavement. The shorter, wider one had a nice arse, but he was sure the loose peasant blouse hid a chubby figure and the tight jeans probably contained more fat than he preferred. No fat on the other one, though, of that he was sure. He smiled to himself. A typical pair, tall and slender would be pretty, and her chunky friend with the long braid would be happy to take any attention that might spill over.

They were going in the same direction he was, and it didn't occur to him that after three blocks they might think he was following them.

Suddenly they stopped, whirling about. They were younger than he had imagined, and the tall one was even prettier. She took several steps toward him, and the shorter one moved away from her, off to his left.

"Why are you following us?" the tall brunette asked, a definite menace in her tone.

For the first time, he attempted to read her mind and was shocked when he hit an unyielding shield.

"I wasn't following you. We just happen to be going the same direction," he replied, unsure of himself.

She smiled with all the friendliness of a hunting lioness, "A telepath following two telepaths by accident? I think that's stretching coincidence a little far, don't you?"

He threw power to his shields and tried to trigger an air shield about himself. His Gift failed, and he felt a moment of panic. He glanced at the other woman, and decided panic wasn't such a bad idea. Fear churned his stomach as he realized his attention had been on the wrong woman. The short one was a succubus.

He attempted to step backward and discovered he was covered in an air shield projected by one of the women. None of his Gifts responded when he tried to trigger them. One of them was an O'Neill, and had covered him in a mental shield so tight he was helpless. Unearthly beautiful,

67

the shorter woman smiled, the look in her eyes freezing him and making the other woman suddenly look benign.

"Drop your shields," the succubus told him, her voice a soft, melodic purr that caused an immediate and inappropriate response south of his belt. "I won't ask you a second time."

A soft tap against his first level shield was followed by a blow that staggered him. Wide eyed, his head filled with pain, he complied.

All of them, she said in his mind. *Either you give me all nine levels, or I take them, it's up to you how much pain you want to bear.*

Sure he was going to die, and equally sure he was powerless to stop her, he dropped his shields and allowed her to look at his soul. She captured him, holding his soul with her mind. The women turned and walked off down the street. He followed on a mental leash.

"Damn, he was telling the truth," the short succubus told her friend. "He was just going the same place we are to lunch." She laughed, "He thinks you have a nice ass."

"Me?" the taller woman said in surprise.

"Yeah, he thinks I'm fat."

"So what are we going to do with him?" The tall woman's voice held a note of confusion.

"Let him buy us lunch. Then we'll take him back to the house and let the boyos rummage through his mind. After that, I guess we'll burn him out, drain his memories and send him on his way. Kind of a pity. He really isn't a bad guy, just a little shady. But he's hunting prey for Siegfried, so I don't have a lot of sympathy for him."

Sean started to sweat. The off-hand way she discussed his future was more than unsettling. He was terrified.

Entering the pub, the tall woman asked for a table and they were seated away from the other diners.

"Sean McDermott, I'm Brenna and this is my friend Rebecca. Order whatever you like, since you're paying,"

68

Brenna laughed. "*We* certainly won't spare your credit card."

He discovered that although she was in control, he could speak and order for himself, including a pint of Guinness. The women also ordered lunch and beer as well as three shots of Midleton's. They definitely weren't sparing his wallet.

When their drinks arrived, Brenna hoisted her whiskey and toasted him with a grin, "To new friends with deep pockets."

Tossing back their drinks, he felt the whiskey slide over his tongue and burn its way to his stomach. It brought a bit of soothing numbness. They ate their lunches and then his captors had him pay the bill, with an extremely generous tip.

Rebecca called for a van. McDermott was taken into custody by Protectors and transported to the DC compound where he was locked in a basement cell. Brenna called Collin and explained what had happened. Kallen was dispatched to DC to interrogate the captive and decide what to do with him.

~~~

Kallen entered McDermott's cell and watched the blood drain from their captive's face.

"You really stepped in it this time, Sean," Kallen drawled. "What were you thinking? White slavery? I always thought you had more sense, not to mention a higher sense of morality."

"White slavery? What the hell are you talking about? Kallen, I don't know what those women told you, but I don't know anything about that. Hell, she's got my mind, look for yourself." McDermott was sweating. He had met Kallen O'Reilly a couple of times and was fully aware of the O'Donnell assassin's reputation.

The women had never told him their last names or whom they were working with. All he knew was he'd run into the strongest telepaths he'd ever met. That they were two beautiful young women who looked to be barely out of high school was a trap he'd never imagined.

"Just exactly what did you think von Ebersberg hired you for?" Kallen gave him a sardonic grin.

"He's looking to recruit young women, especially succubi. I'm supposed to find them, make initial contact to determine if they might be amenable to working in Europe, and notify him. From there he'll interview them and perhaps make them a job offer. That's all."

Kallen cocked his head, silently listening to someone, and then laughed, "Rebecca says if you think he's paying your rates for that, you're too stupid to breed. The good news, Sean, is they're backing off the idea of burning out your Gifts. The bad news is they think you should be neutered."

McDermott swayed in his chair and Kallen thought he might faint.

"Or, there's a third option."

His eyes glassy, McDermott gasped for air. "God, Kallen, who are those women?"

"Boyo, you ran into two of the most dangerous women on the planet. That's Seamus O'Donnell's granddaughter and her shadow."

McDermott's eyes rolled up in his head and he slid out of his chair to the floor.

Brenna, Kallen sent, *I think you have yourself a lap dog. Whatever you want him to do, he's yours.*

Rebecca, also listening through his mind, responded, *I think we can implant a construct with a compulsion and send him back to Europe to gather intelligence on Siegfried's network.*

We'll pay him, of course, Brenna added, *but we don't trust him as a free agent. If he screws up and betrays us, the compulsion will kill him. If not, then he'll be all right.*

Kallen walked over and picked up the water pitcher sitting on a small table. He poured its contents over McDermott's head.

Brenna, come on in, Kallen sent.

Brenna and Rebecca walked into the room. Sputtering and blinking water out of his eyes, McDermott first saw Rebecca.

Then Brenna entered, her hair out of the braid and falling like a black wave across her shoulders. She wore a low-cut blue wrap dress that accented her wasp waist and curves, matching heels and a single strand of pearls. She was one of the most beautiful women he'd ever seen, even if the smile of amusement on her face was at his expense. He couldn't remember why he had thought she was fat.

"Good evening, Sean," she said in a sultry voice. "As Kallen said, we have an offer for you, assuming you don't mind working for a chubby chick."

"Uh, no, uh, I mean I'm listening, I mean I don't think you're fat …," he stammered.

Her smile broadened and she laughed, "You just think I have a big ass. Well, so do I. It's rather refreshing to receive an honest opinion.

"Ok, here's your choice: you're going to work for O'Donnell. We'll pay you a monthly salary and your expenses will come out of it. If at some point you think expenses are too high, present us with an expense report and receipts and we'll review the situation."

Kallen lounged against the wall. "You can help yourself by supplying all the information you can on what you're doing here and anything else you know about Siegfried's operations," he said. "We can get it from your mind, but I'd like to see you actively help us."

McDermott was nodding at all of this.

Rebecca stepped forward and leaned down to look into his eyes. "We're going to embed a construct on your ninth level with a compulsion. If you ever betray us, or attempt to

71

disable the construct, the compulsion will burn out your brain. You don't have any black on your soul, a little bit of brown, but no black. You've never raped a woman or coerced her into sex. Don't. That will also trigger the compulsion. Any questions?"

Her tight smile held no humor. He still wasn't sure which of the women was scarier.

"Do I have any choice?"

"What I've outlined is the only choice I'm prepared to offer," Brenna said. "Of course, you can let Rebecca have her way with you and go free."

His eyes widened. Glancing at Rebecca, he found it hard to breath. "You wouldn't really castrate me?"

"Oh, no," Rebecca grinned. "I'd never do *that*. Burn out the nerves to a man's groin, yes, but I'd never castrate someone. That's so crude, don't you think?"

Kallen leaned over and in a soft voice said, "She's not joking. You'll find they're both rather devoid of a sense of humor about certain things."

"Wha … what do you want me to do?" McDermott said, obviously shaken.

"It seems some of our European brethren are capturing succubi. We've shut down some of their operations, but your presence indicates there's more work to do," Brenna said. "You're going to help us."

Brenna's face hardened, "Siegfried wasn't going to offer jobs to the women you identified, or if he did, the jobs would be bogus. We think he enslaves them and either pimps them or sells them."

McDermott took a deep breath, then shook his head. "All I did was look at your arse, and I'm going to pay for that the rest of my life?"

"No," Brenna leaned close to him, "you agreed to take money from a slaver to identify targets for him. You didn't ask any questions you didn't want to know the answers to, and thought that would protect your soul. Don't give me

72

any of that 'poor me' crap. Do you want to see what you were doing?" She projected an image of Cindy Nelson, near death after being captured by Siegfried's goons. It was accompanied by Brenna's emotions when she first saw her friend's battered body.

She backed up quickly and managed to save her shoes. McDermott was violently sick.

"Be glad you ran into me first," Brenna said. "If you'd been successful at all in your assignment for von Ebersberg, I wouldn't have spared you. Get your head on straight, Sean. Your world is black and white now, and I'm the white. If I tell you the sky is pink with purple polka dots, that's your reality. You're going to spend the rest of your life doing what I tell you. I suggest you learn to like it, it'll be a lot easier."

Brenna turned and walked out of the room.

Rebecca stepped up beside him and spoke in a conversational tone. "She's being merciful. You're lucky she didn't turn you over to me."

They implanted the construct in his mind then put him back on the street.

~~~

With the entire Clan on alert, Brenna found herself being far more aware of what went on around her. The day after she and Rebecca captured Sean McDermott, they were having lunch in a restaurant in downtown DC near the White House.

"Rebecca, see that young girl over there? She's a telepath and so's the guy with her," Brenna pointed out a couple just sitting down. The girl looked to be in high school, but with a fully mature woman's body. That description might have been made about Irina. At twenty-three, Brenna looked a bit older and Rebecca, at twenty-four, looked old enough to attend college.

Rebecca casually scanned the two, then froze with her fork halfway to her mouth.

"She's wearing a construct," she said. "Why would a young telepath wear a construct?"

Brenna slipped into the girl's mind.

"Damn," she exclaimed, "I've been trying to figure out how they did it. It's the construct."

"You've lost me," Rebecca said.

"How Siegfried controls a succubus. They're implanting a construct."

"She's a succubus?" Rebecca looked skeptical. The girl was pretty, but definitely not in the same class as the succubi she knew.

"No, she isn't. She's a carrier."

It took a moment for that to register, but when it did, a grim expression set on Rebecca's face.

"Are you saying," she started.

"Yeah, that guy's her pimp. He's whoring her for big bucks. They're taking a lunch break between appointments."

"Shit. The perfect whore, someone who can't say no," Rebecca looked sick.

The man suddenly sat up and started looking around. When his eyes scanned over Brenna and Rebecca, he stopped and gazed at them intently. He turned back to the girl across the table from him and said something. They both stood and walked toward the exit.

Brenna started out of her seat, but Rebecca put a hand on her arm.

"Pay the bill. I'll have Carly tail them," Rebecca said. On a spear thread, she contacted the leader of Brenna's protection team.

Carly, there's a man and a young girl coming out of the restaurant. Tail them. I don't care if they see you, but don't let them out of your sight. They're telepaths. Brenna and I will be out in a minute.

Brenna hurriedly paid the bill and they went out to the sidewalk. A Protectors' van filled with the items they had bought shopping that day pulled up to the curb.

"Why would someone pay extra for a telepath?" Brenna asked as they settled in the van.

Rebecca shrugged. "Who knows what they're training them to do. With a construct, you can make someone totally compliant. Whatever the customer wants, she'll do. I guess she could also enhance the experience, make the guy think he's having the climax of his life."

"Shit, she wouldn't even have to screw him. Implant a memory, steal his wallet, and he'd still be happy as a clam," the Protector sitting in the front seat said.

Shaking her head, Brenna said, "I don't have anything against prostitution, but I don't think she's doing it willingly."

"It's not prostitution," Rebecca said, her lips a thin line, "it's serial rape."

Carly told them on a thread that the man and girl were picked up by a car driven by another man. They followed the car for several miles, then pulled up behind it when the trio pulled into a driveway in a suburban area just inside the beltway.

Protectors poured out of the three vans Carly had involved in the chase. The driver of the car pulled a gun and immediately screamed and fell writhing on the ground holding his head. The other man attempted to fight using mental weapons, but also fell. Rebecca ran into the yard and grabbed the girl, pulling her back to the van.

The door to the house burst inward off its hinges and two Protectors dived through the opening. A gunshot sounded inside, then all was quiet.

We've got them all, Carly reported. *These two plus two inside.*

A few minutes later, she called Brenna inside. Rebecca stayed in the van with the girl.

"Brenna, there are five other girls in here," Carly told her when she walked into the house. "I don't think they're running a brothel, but what we're finding definitely looks like an escort service. None of the girls look old enough to drink."

That was an understatement. The girl outside looked younger than Irina, who was twenty-one, and she was older than those inside. A couple looked like they should be playing with dolls instead of men.

Scanning their minds, Brenna found all were implanted with constructs.

"Hi, my name is Brenna. We're not going to hurt you. Can you tell me your names?" she asked the girls sitting in an upstairs bedroom. They watched her silently with wide eyes.

"We've blurred the minds of the people in the house next door and across the street," Carly said. "It's the middle of the day and most people aren't home, but someone might have reported that gunshot. Can we take everyone and get the hell out of here?"

Brenna nodded. "Your show, Carly. Thanks." She took the hands of the two youngest girls and led them from the house.

The Protectors took the computer and all the files they could find and followed them.

~~~

Seamus teleported from West Virginia to San Francisco, then to DC, bringing Lydia McCarthy. Lydia was the Clan's best construct artist and Rebecca's teacher. Siobhan, who also had the Lindstrom Gift and had worn more than fifty constructs as an O'Donnell operative, flew in from New York. Siobhan sometimes worked as an escort and was very familiar with the escort and courtesan culture in Europe and New York.

They also brought in Dr. Moira O'Reilly, a Clan psychiatrist specializing in telepaths and especially wilders' and children's problems. Moira was a very strong telepath with twelve Gifts, but not the Lindstrom Gift.

Cindy and Brenna's attacker the previous month had worn a construct when Brenna first met him. Obviously, someone with the Lindstrom Gift was working with both the succubus hunters and the prostitution ring. Collin hoped Lydia and Siobhan might gain some clues as to who it was.

Before collapsing the constructs in the girls' minds, they studied them in detail and read the memories the girls had collected. What they found sickened Brenna.

The girls ranged from thirteen to nineteen. All had been kidnapped, all had been sold over and over to a wide variety of wealthy customers. None were succubi, but three were S-gene carriers. Two were from O'Donnell Clan families, one missing for over a year, the other missing for two years. The nineteen year old that Brenna and Rebecca first spotted had been living a life of forced prostitution for three years.

In addition to being sold for sex, two of the girls showed scars from physical abuse consistent with being used by sexual sadists. Their memories confirmed it.

Lydia took Moira through the girls' minds, then gave her a briefing describing the constructs and what she thought still might exist of their original personalities.

"The constructs are ninth level, implanted at the level of their souls and expanded out through all the layers of their minds. Very intricate. The person who built these was very good at their craft. However, they're also cookie cutter. All of them are identical with the exception of their names. That means the original builder may be thousands of miles away, or even dead. Anyone with the Lindstrom Gift could set them up in someone's mind."

"It would make sense to sell girls with the constructs already in place," Siobhan commented. "Capture the girls, implant the constructs, turn around and sell them for a big profit. You'd save on the training expenses and don't even have to damage the merchandise. That sounds like the kind of business von Ebersberg would like."

"I think we should collapse one of the constructs, probably on the youngest girl, and see what we have," Moira said with a resigned expression. "We'll have to notify her parents at some point."

Lydia collapsed the construct and Moira immediately entered the girl's mind and laid a Comfort on her. Watching the psychiatrist closely, Brenna saw the blood drain from her face. Shaking, Moira fumbled for a chair and dropped into it.

Concerned, Brenna knelt down in front of her.

"Moira? What is it?"

Taking a deep breath, Moira shook her head. It took her a full minute before she whispered, "There's nothing there. She's like a baby. They took everything away from her before they planted the construct."

~~~

Chapter 6

We say that slavery has vanished from European civilization, but this is not true. Slavery still exists, but now it applies only to women and its name is prostitution. - Victor Hugo, Les Misérables

Collin and his Protectors battered down the shields of the men who had held the girls. In-depth interrogation over three days revealed they were a small ring. They had paid between a hundred thousand and two hundred fifty thousand each for the girls, constructs already implanted. In the past year, they'd cleared over three million dollars.

The ring procured the girls from a contact in New York. Twice in the past three years they'd sold new girls they had abducted to that contact. The broker told them those girls would have a construct implanted, then sold either to the west coast or overseas.

The only truly useful information the Protectors obtained was the identity of that contact, their client list, and the knowledge of two other rings.

"Call Charles Farrell," Seamus said. Farrell was the top-ranking telepath inside the FBI. "We could be chasing this type of thing forever. Time to turn it over to people who make their living doing police work."

"I can't believe the amount of money they're spending to buy these girls," Collin said. "And the price for succubi is off the charts. Those guys were quoted twenty million for a succubus with a construct."

Seamus sighed. "The profits are huge. The last estimate I saw pegged human trafficking as a thirty-two billion dollar industry. That's thirty-two billion a year."

"What makes a succubus so valuable? I'm still trying to get my mind around it," Brenna shook her head.

Rebecca spoke up, "Think about it. A woman sex slave can earn a pimp two hundred fifty thousand dollars a year. A succubus can be sold for a hundred thousand a night."

Seamus nodded, "And Siegfried von Ebersberg has a long history of trafficking women, specializing in exotics. He started after World War I, and prohibition and the depression in this country became a bonanza for him."

"We also have intelligence that the Chinese are working on selective breeding programs," Collin added. "Succubi genes and eggs might find a ready market. The Germans may be doing the same thing. Twenty million may seem high until you start counting the ways you can market the goods. It's not just sex."

"The disruptions in Russia and Eastern Europe in the nineties provided a new source of beautiful women," Seamus continued. "It revitalized Siegfried's business. I wonder if he really knew what he was getting when he took Gless on.

"Brenna, I know you don't want to hear this, but I'm going to increase security on all the succubi again."

"So much for running away and joining the circus, huh?"

Collin chuckled, "You won't even make it past the driveway."

~~~

As the FBI broke up several prostitution rings, they recovered a number of telepathic girls. One disturbing thing they found were five young S-gene carriers who were college students when kidnapped.

Rebecca spotted a common factor. All had gone to their student health centers seeking counseling for their sex addiction. All had been referred to an outside counselor who specialized in such cases. Three were Clan, the others wilders.

Charles Farrell met with Moira, Rebecca and Brenna at the Washington compound. Brenna and Rebecca had never

80

met him, though they knew of him from his work in attempting to find Cindy when she had been kidnapped.

"When I was in college, I did the same thing," Rebecca said. "It didn't help, of course, but the problems of having this condition are so severe, it causes you to want to fix it. It can be all consuming, and once you get out of your parents' home, you feel as though you have the freedom to seek counseling."

"I'm glad you spotted this trend," Farrell said. "I went back and did a database search, and identified twelve more women who were referred to him that are missing. Ten of those are known Clan."

"I think that's amazing so many telepathic girls have gone missing in this area," Brenna said.

Farrell ran his hand through his hair and shifted in his seat. "It's not just in this area, or from a single school, that's why it was difficult to spot. This guy has built a practice by approaching colleges throughout the Atlantic region. These seventeen girls went to twelve different schools in five different states."

"I'm going to have Collin do a search on missing Clan members," Brenna said. "Some of the girls we've found are too young for college. I wonder if any parents fell for this guy's pitch."

It was decided to mount an operation with Rebecca and Irina as bait.

Dr. Jonathan Detweiler had a PhD in psychology from a prestigious German university. He'd moved to the States seven years ago and aggressively built a practice as a sex therapist by contacting student health centers and offering his services as a consultant. He currently listed forty-three colleges and universities as clients, and also worked with several large city school districts. He had published a number of highly regarded papers in psychological journals and many psychologists sent him referrals.

"I've met him a couple of times," Moira said. "When you requested this meeting, I made a few calls and two of the therapists I talked to refer patients to him. He's very well-known and respected."

The original plan was to create constructs for both Rebecca and Irina, but Rebecca brought up a potential problem. "We know a construct artist is working with these people. Suppose it's him? If it is, he'll detect the construct and it will blow the deal. Let me go in and just give him me. If he is a Lindstrom, I'll collapse Irina's construct before she goes to see him. We'll just have to be good actresses."

Lydia implanted a construct in Irina, relying heavily on Rebecca's own experience to create the personality and memories. As she built the construct, Lydia, normally exuberant and happy, became increasingly withdrawn. Brenna could see something was bothering her.

Callie's contacts inside universities, along with the FBI's influence, created identities and enrollments for them at West Virginia University.

Telepaths mature late compared to normal humans, and with their long lives look far younger than their chronological ages. At twenty-four, Rebecca was older than any of the women who had gone missing, but she still got carded at most bars. Irina could easily pass as a college freshman.

The evening after Lydia finished the construct, Brenna found her sitting on the broad front porch. She sat staring out into the twilight, arms wrapped around herself, rocking slowly in her chair.

"Are you okay?" Brenna asked.

Lydia turned a tear-streaked face toward her. "I've built hundreds, maybe thousands, of constructs. That was the hardest thing I've ever done in my life. My God, Rebecca's been through so much pain."

Brenna put her arm around the older woman and hugged her. "Yes, I know. I've been through some of it with her. But now that she knows what causes it, she's dealing with it and starting to heal. Moira is working with her, and we're trying to identify girls with the condition at an early age. My grandmother has been consulting with them on a program she uses in Ireland, and Rebecca is helping Moira develop coping strategies for them. That's helping her a lot."

~~~

One of the selling points for Dr. Detweiler's services was his willingness to travel to his patients. For student health clinics, this was a Godsend. It would be almost impossible for students to travel long distances for therapy.

Rebecca and Irina went to the counseling center on separate days, made appointments to meet with a psychologist, and received referrals to Dr. Detweiler. When they contacted him, he made arrangements to come to Morgantown the following week. While they waited, the two women treated the time on campus as a vacation, cutting a swath through the willing young men they met.

As soon as Rebecca walked into the room at the health center to meet Detweiler, she was thankful she hadn't worn a construct. She had no way to know if he had the Lindstrom Gift, but he was a powerful telepath. During their meeting, he gently and cautiously probed her shields.

It didn't take much acting for Rebecca to reenact the first interview she had with a counselor in San Francisco five years before. As a strong empath, Rebecca left feeling that Detweiler had bought her performance without reservation.

She met Irina at the student center coffee shop and collapsed her construct, then coached her as to how to approach her interview. Irina wouldn't present as a sex addict the same way an S-gene carrier would, but rather as someone whose sex addiction stemmed from trying to

83

figure out why her relationships with men turned out so badly.

Irina's mother was a succubus, and she had known about the effect she had on men from an early age. But conversations with Brenna had given her a good idea of the confusion her friend had gone through when she became sexually active.

"I don't understand it," Irina told the doctor with tears misting her eyes. "I don't think I'm bad looking, but … but … we make love and then they don't even call for two weeks. I don't want to be a one-night stand. I want someone to love me. I keep hoping the next guy will be different."

Detweiler's methods became very clear. He made appointments to meet with them in Morgantown in two weeks, but he suggested he was willing to provide extra free counseling if they could drive to his office in Philadelphia on the weekend.

"I couldn't believe how excited he got when I walked in," Irina said after her meeting with Detweiler. "He said he could help me with my self-image problem." She laughed, "I thought that's what high heels were for."

"If he's ever seen a succubus, it would be impossible to ignore what you are," Rebecca said. "He's probably counting his money already."

Irina's brow furrowed. "Most succubi aren't short."

"I wasn't talking about your height. Irina, you may be the only woman in the world who's prettier than Brenna. It's pretty obvious you're not really human."

The diminutive blonde gasped and stopped walking, staring at Rebecca. "Nobody's prettier than Brenna."

"That's what I would have said before I met you. Besides, you smell like a succubus. Come on, let's get on the road. We need to figure out what to do next. I think we've set the hook."

"I took a shower this morning," Irina muttered as they approached Rebecca's car.

Rebecca smiled at her. "I know that. What kind of perfume are you wearing?"

Irina shook her head. "I don't wear perfume. Everything I've ever tried stinks when I put it on."

Rebecca chuckled. "None of you wears perfume. You smell like flowers naturally."

~~~

Back at the manor, they met with Collin and some of his lieutenants. Moira and Brenna also sat in on the meeting.

"What are our objectives here?" Collin asked the group. "From my viewpoint, we want to capture him, set him up as a mole and follow him to the broker in New York."

Brenna chuckled, "I'm not volunteering as bait, but wondering if you need me for backup."

"We definitely need backup," Kallen said. "The op we ran with Brenna proves even the most powerful telepath can be taken down with the right drugs. Considering your range, you can link with Rebecca from a block away and never be in danger."

Rebecca called Detweiler and made an appointment to meet him on Saturday. She showed up dressed in a form-fitting dress rather than the jeans she'd worn on campus. After half an hour describing the problems she was experiencing, he turned the conversation in a different direction.

"So you're from San Francisco?"

"Yes. I wanted to get away from there, that's why I came east to school."

"Are you close to your parents?"

"No, I don't have much contact with them. I have a scholarship, so they aren't paying anything."

"Do you have friends waiting for you today?"

85

"No. I didn't even tell anyone where I was going. I'm not very proud of why I'm here."

Detweiler leaned back in his chair, folding his hands across his stomach.

"And you're twenty-one?"

"Yes," Rebecca said.

"I'd like to try to hypnotize you. I've had very good results with it in similar cases."

Alarm bells went off in Rebecca's mind, and in Brenna's, sitting in a coffee shop at the end of the block.

I think we need to get ready to move, Brenna sent to Jeremy.

Detweiler took Rebecca into another room, had her lie on a thin bed-like couch, and dimmed the lights. She reached out to the electricity in the walls and drew it into her, ready to discharge if he touched her. He started into a droning speech, telling her she was growing drowsy. She closed her eyes. Rather than listen to him, she described what was happening across her mental link to Brenna.

After about five minutes, Detweiler touched her neck. Rebecca reacted immediately, discharging electricity into him and assaulting his shields.

Show time, boys and girls! Brenna broadcast to the team waiting outside Detweiler's office. She fed energy to Rebecca through their link.

Detweiler fell backward, missing his chair and falling to the floor. Rebecca covered him in an air shield to prevent him using any mental or physical weapons against her. She didn't know what Gifts he might have, but it would stop weapons such as Pyro or Electrokinesis.

He gained his feet and attempted to charge her, but ran into the air shield. She battered against his shields, but he put up stiff resistance. Fearing he might have a Gift that wasn't blocked by the air shield, she bolted toward the door, only to find it locked.

Brenna, I can't get out of here.

86

We're on our way, her friend answered.

If he has the Rivera Gift, I'm toast.

Drain him.

Rebecca reached out with her mind and started drawing his life energy into herself. With the energy Brenna had been feeding her, her reserves were full and she wasn't able to store it, so she fed it to Brenna through their link. The succubus soaked it up like a sponge.

Detweiler struck at her with a projection of pure mental force. She absorbed it and sent it on to Brenna. He tried again, but the projection was much weaker this time.

Rebecca heard banging in the outer office. Not on the door to this room. She struck at his mental shields again and the outer shield covering his fore mind fell. He reeled, clutching his head. Sending another assault on his next level shield, it fell as well. The third level held out longer.

The banging now was on the door to this room.

Get out of the way, we're going to blow the door, Jeremy sent her. She dived to the floor behind the couch.

Go for it, Rebecca told him. The door blew off the hinges, flying into the room and bouncing off the air shield surrounding Detweiler.

He screamed, fell to the floor, and lay still. Brenna and the Protectors walked into the room.

"I have his mind. You can drop the air shield," Brenna said, reaching down to grasp Rebecca's hand and help her to her feet.

"Took you guys long enough. He's tough. I thought I'd never get through his shields," Rebecca said, sitting on the couch. Her hands were shaking and she clasped them together.

"He has the Kilpatrick Gift, double shielding. He also has Electro and Pyrokinesis. That air shield might have saved your life," Brenna said. "He doesn't have the Rivera, though. No neural disruption."

Jeremy hauled Detweiler to his feet. "He's fully mature, and if he has the Kilpatrick Gift, that's why you couldn't get through his shields."

"She got through three," Brenna said.

Stopping in mid stride, Jeremy's head snapped around to look at Rebecca. "Jesus, you're going to be hell on wheels when you grow up."

Rebecca tried to give him a smile, but failed. "He scared the shit out of me."

One of the Protectors held up a syringe. "With good reason. He didn't stick you, did he?"

"No. I freaked out as soon as he touched me." Rebecca started shaking again. "I remember Brenna getting drugged, and if someone could capture her with drugs, I didn't have any doubts what it would do to me."

Brenna sat down beside her and hugged her close.

Coming out of the building, they discovered the Protectors stationed outside had captured two men who evidently were responding to a mental call for help from Detweiler. They loaded all their prisoners into a van and headed for Baltimore.

As they drove off, a woman emerged from the building and watched them drive off. She reached for her cell phone and made a call.

~~~

Collin planned an operation to capture the broker in New York. Detweiler had been thoroughly interrogated. His contact for selling young women was the same contact from whom the first prostitution ring they had broken was buying young women.

The broker was John Brockington, an Englishman tied to Lord Gordon, and listed his profession as a consultant. He was also known to Johan Karlson, the man Rebecca and Brenna captured at the UN.

Collin ordered surveillance on him after the UN raid, but Brockington had flown to England the next day. He'd come back two weeks later, but the day they captured Detweiler, he flew to England again and did not return.

~~~

Brenna always covered Rebecca with her O'Neill shields when they were out in public together. Rebecca had very strong shields due to her Kilpatrick Gift, but Brenna still worried.

"Lydia, some of these girls had constructs for years. Is there any permanent damage from that?" Brenna asked.

"No, not that I know of," Lydia shook her head. "This Gift has been known for centuries. You can do harm with a construct, implant commands, but the construct itself is benign."

"Those girls had ninth level constructs implanted at the ninth level. Is that how they always work?"

Lydia smiled at Rebecca, who took that as a cue to answer Brenna's question.

"You can implant a construct at any level. We could put a nine level construct in your first level," Rebecca said.

Brenna cocked her head, looking thoughtful. "So we could build a nine level construct of your mind and implant it in your first level?"

"Yeah, but what would be the purpose?" Rebecca looked puzzled, and so did Lydia.

"Protection. I'm trying to figure out how to build a trap for someone who doesn't have the O'Neill Gift."

Lydia's eyes widened. "That's brilliant. Yes, I think I see what you're getting at."

"But how do you simulate a soul?" Rebecca asked.

A slow grin spread across Lydia's face. "By constructing a thought package that looks like a soul. I'll bet I could do it. Most people have never seen another telepath's soul."

It took a week to create the construct and implant it. When they were finished, they showed Rebecca's mind to

Irina and Collin, neither of whom had the Lindstrom Gift. They didn't detect the construct.

~~~

"I'm not pleased to see you here," the Lord said, glaring at the man who stood before him in his study. It was a pleasant room, dark paneling lined the walls and a fire burned in the fireplace. The Lord didn't offer his visitor a chair.

"I didn't feel as though I had any choice," John Brockington said, shifting uncomfortably from one foot to the other. "Detweiler has been captured as have von Ebersberg's men at the United Nations." He took a deep breath, "If Miranda hadn't seen them at Detweiler's office and warned me, I might have been taken, too. The FBI has rounded up several of our customers, and it appears to be but a matter of time before they break the others. O'Donnell seems to be quite determined to stop our business venture in the States."

Lord Gordon thought about this news, taking a sip of his cognac and regarding the construct artist who had run his operations in the U.S. As upset as he was with Brockington, the man was correct. If he'd been taken, O'Donnell would have the full story on Gordon's operations, not just in the U.S. but also in Ireland, England and the Continent.

"Well," he said after a long period of silence, "until I can figure out exactly what damage has been done, you can work with our clients in Ireland. Did Miranda come with you?"

"Yes, I didn't see any reason to leave her there. Detweiler knew her too well."

Gordon nodded. "Take her with you to Ireland," he said, and then dismissed Brockington.

~~~

Chapter 7

All witchcraft comes from carnal
lust, which in women is insatiable. -
Malleus Maleficarum, Heinrich
Kramer, Inquisitor of the Catholic
Church, 1486

The guests started flowing in through the Washington-area airports the week before Solstice. The main manor house had one hundred bedrooms and the two guest wings each had sixty more. Each bedroom was equipped with its own bath, making the O'Donnell manor house one of the most expansive private homes in the world.

Brenna had always been impressed by the large, well-appointed kitchen, but for the holiday season they opened up another area that in itself was twice the size of the everyday kitchen. Another thirty people were brought on in the kitchen alone, and the number of Protectors on the estate tripled, half being used to expand the serving staff.

The night Jill arrived with her boyfriend Tom, an impromptu party convened in Brenna's suite. Two dozen young people spent the evening drinking, talking, flirting, and generally having a good time. Those who had been to previous Solstice celebrations at the estate filled in the newcomers.

Winter Solstice, or Alban Arthan in the old Gaelic tradition, was celebrated by decorating the house with greens, especially mistletoe and holly, but also evergreen branches throughout the house as a promise that nature will be green again in springtime when life returns to the land. Traditionally, it was a festival of rebirth. In Newgrange, Ireland, a Neolithic passage tomb and temple structure is said to be over two thousand years old. The sun shining through a window the morning after Solstice symbolizes the insertion of a ray of light by the Sun God into the womb of Mother Earth. It was believed this would bring new life to the world come spring.

As celebrated in the O'Donnell household, the Solstice Ball, occurring on The Longest Night, is a formal ball in the nineteenth century tradition. The women dress in formal evening gowns, the men in white tie and tails. Protectors serve, circulating with drinks and food and a sumptuous buffet is set in the grand ballroom. The symbolism of the Sun God impregnating Mother Earth is a major feature of the ball.

A section of rooms on the second floor is left empty for anyone's usage. Although the ball itself is the height of decorum, any woman can approach any man and invite him to escort her up the grand staircase in view of the whole room to the upstairs bedrooms. This is often accompanied by applause and cheers from the onlookers.

A featured attraction at these events had always been Cindy and Siobhan, obvious symbols of sexuality and fertility, the priestesses on earth of the Goddess. With the arrival of Callie's old friend Antonia Federicci, there would be an unprecedented five succubi at the ball.

Succubi are viewed as the superstars of the night, their trips up the stairs cheered by all, their beauty, glamour, and freely-given favors a symbol to release inhibitions and a benediction on the actions of the other women. Historically, the number of children born nine months after the ball exceeded the number born throughout the rest of the year. Although not everyone in the valley could attend, Seamus funded several satellite events in the village.

~~~

"Brenna, come in," Callie said. "I want you to meet Antonia Federicci, one of my oldest friends and a friend of your mother's. Antonia and I have known each other since the late forties, when I was footloose and fancy free, traveling around Europe after I graduated from college. It's a rare treat for me to have her visit."

Antonia was an eighty-five year old Italian succubus. In the period after World War II when the Clans fought for dominance, her Clan had been a loser, decimated by an alliance of fascists. She maintained her Clan ties, but now was a wealthy international lawyer and independent courtesan.

They sat and talked for some time, and in the course of their conversation Antonia asked about her adventure in hunting Cindy's kidnappers. During that time, Callie had contacted Antonia and found out that several succubi in Europe had also been attacked and two of them killed. Brenna recounted her ordeal.

When she came to the part about channeling a lightning bolt, Antonia chuckled, "I'll bet that hurt."

"Really hurt. I don't think the human body was meant to have that kind of power run through it. I think I'm really lucky it didn't fry me."

Callie and Antonia exchanged looks.

"Brenna," Antonia began, "there are some adepts who can channel the lightning. They're sometimes called Storm Queens and Kings, and the most powerful of them are succubi. The problem is not what you did, but how young you were when you did it."

Brenna gaped at her in surprise.

"Antonia was known as a Storm Queen during the war," Callie told her. "It's one of the reasons I wanted you to meet her. Other than you, she has more Gifts than any succubus on record, fifteen like your mother, including the O'Neill Gift."

"I'm sure you're tired of hearing cautions concerning the use of your Talents," Antonia said with a smile, "but Callie tells me that you are a, what did she call it, oh, yes, a neuroscientist. You study the brain and the nervous system, is that right? Well, what happens in the brain during the process of maturing from adolescence to adulthood?"

"Additional layers of myelin are laid down and, oooh, I understand," Brenna said with her eyes wide. "Myelin is the insulator for our nerves. I don't have enough insulation yet."

"Exactly, and if you study our brains, you'll find the myelin sheathing far thicker than in a norm, and thicker yet in those with certain Gifts. I know people tend to say that only succubi are physically different from norms, but that's not true. There are many differences, subtle differences. If you had attempted to hold the power from the lightning you might have burned yourself out, but when you get older you'll be able to."

Antonia reached out and touched her arm, "Brenna, I would be glad to help you understand your Gifts. There is much more to succubi than most people give us credit for. But I'm also hoping to learn from you. Callie has been telling me that you've discovered a way to keep from draining your lovers."

"Collin has agreed to help me show you, all of you, if you're up for a sex show this evening," Brenna said, her face growing very warm.

Antonia's smile was answer enough. "Tell me where and when. Should I bring popcorn?" Brenna's blush deepened, and Antonia leaned forward, laying her hand on the girl's face, "Oh, I'm sorry, I didn't mean to make light of it. You're young and shy, and I deeply appreciate you doing this for me, for us."

That evening after dinner, Brenna wheeled Cindy into her and Collin's room to join Antonia and Siobhan, sitting with a bottle of wine at the table. Collin lit a few candles, and turned out the lights. Undressing, she joined him on her bed and they began to stroke each other, becoming aroused and less conscious of their audience. He lay back on the bed and she straddled him, her hair creating a tent about them, shutting everyone out. "This is better, huh?" she whispered. He pulled her close and kissed her.

94

"Yes," he whispered back, "I can pretend they're not even here."

She mounted him, and as they established a rhythm she opened her mind to the other succubi. She helped him come quickly, using her muscles to pleasure him in just the right places, and as he built to his climax she felt the anticipation build in the women around the table.

She took him over, his energy flowing into her and triggering her, she flipped the switch that hadn't been there even a moment before. His energy flowed into her, changing and carrying her Glow back into him. His fingers dug into her hips, holding her firm against him with just her muscles milking him. His hips bucked and he spilled into her. Her arms buckled and she fell onto his chest, lying there panting and feeling her Glow.

When she recovered, she sat up, throwing her hair over her shoulder, and turned to the women watching them. All three were crying, tears silently running down their cheeks. Siobhan pushed out of her chair, striding to the bed and gathering both of them in her arms, kissing both their faces, her tears warring with her smile. "Thank you, oh God, thank you so much." She let go of them and put her face in her hands and sobbed.

"It was there, it's been there all along, and I never noticed it, never thought to look," Antonia whispered softly. Cindy leaned forward, her arms wrapped around her middle, her forehead resting on her knees.

Brenna jumped up and ran to her, putting her arms around her shoulders. "Are you all right? Cindy, are you okay?"

Cindy raised her head and opened her arms, wrapping them about Brenna's waist. "Oh, honey, I'm so all right," her tear streaked face held a beatific expression. "My God, Brenna, I can finally say yes to him, I don't have to feel guilty for loving him." She smiled, "You should be wearing a bow. This is the best Christmas present of my life."

Wearing a robe, Brenna wheeled Cindy back to her room, watching the other two succubi walk down the hall to the stairs. She was startled when she heard Cindy send a spear thread to Seamus, and then realized that Cindy had purposely included her. *Darling, can you please come to my room? Brenna gave us our Christmas present early and I'd like to share it with you.* She turned her face to Brenna, "Do you think you could help me dress a little bit?"

Brenna found a baby doll teddy in one of Cindy's drawers and helped her put it on. Turning down the covers, she helped her get into bed, propping her up on the pillows. She went to the bathroom and got a washcloth, cleaned the tear streaks from her face and helped her to put on some lipgloss and blush and powder. She looked beautiful, even with her hair only half an inch long.

Brenna answered the knock on the door, stood on her tip toes to give Seamus a kiss, then went to her own room leaving him standing in Cindy's doorway staring at the woman sitting in the bed.

The next morning at breakfast Seamus walked in with Cindy in his arms. Her chair materialized by his, and he lowered her into it. Both had a Glow. "Excuse me, I have an announcement to make. I have asked this beautiful young lady to be my wife, and she's said yes."

Brenna gasped.

"There's a caveat. She wants a long engagement and won't set the date." He shrugged, his smile growing larger.

The room erupted with congratulations. Brenna received almost simultaneous spear threads from them, *Thank you* from Cindy, *Bless you, Brenna O'Donnell* from Seamus.

~~~

At mid-morning, Brenna was called to the front door. A pile of boxes and garment bags sat in the foyer. She sent spears to Irina, Rebecca and Callie, *Clothes are here!*

Sorting through what had arrived, Brenna found the evening gown she'd ordered for Cindy. *Seamus, can you bring your blushing bride to Elise's rooms? Her solstice dress has arrived and needs a fitting.* She carried Cindy's things to Elise, who smiled and told her she would make it her first priority.

Carrying her own things to her room took two trips with an assist from Collin. He shook his head at everything stacked on the bed, table and sideboard. "I wondered how long it would take for you to fill these closets. You're even quicker than I thought."

There was a knock on the door, and turning, she found Alice standing there. "I haven't been to one of these bacchanals in years, but I just couldn't stay away this year, especially when Antonia came by the shop right after Thanksgiving and ordered two new dresses."

Collin excused himself and Alice came in and began helping Brenna unwrap and put away the clothes, smiling as she tried on various garments, exclaiming in pleasure at each one.

Alice encouraged her to try them on and was gratified at her reaction to a simple pair of black slacks. "Oh, my, God. Alice, you're a magician!" She squatted down, feeling only a slight tightening over her bottom, straightened, and turned looking at herself in the mirror, spinning and trying to see herself from different angles.

"Brenna, there's a triple mirror in the closet."

"There is?" She went to the closet and looked around confused. Alice came in behind her and pulled out a folding panel, revealing three floor length mirrors.

"Gertrude and I were friends," Alice said. Gertrude was Brenna's grandmother, Seamus' wife, and Brenna had inherited her bedroom.

When Brenna got to the boxes with the foundation garments, she found that many of the boxes held sets with bra, panty and garter belt, and some also included matching hose. Then she opened a box and just stared. "What is this?"

Alice smiled, "That's for your solstice dress, that's what goes underneath."

"But, what is it?"

Alice burst out laughing. "It's a corset, haven't you ever worn, or at least seen one?"

"Maybe in Playboy."

Alice had her strip and put it on. Sapphire blue with lace over satin, it was rather stiff and she had a bit of a problem cinching it around her waist. It provided stiff shelves for her breasts to rest on, but didn't cover the nipples. It flared over her hips and had garter straps hanging from the bottom. There were matching lace-topped hose but no panties. "Alice, there aren't any panties here."

"And what would you need panties for on The Longest Night? You'd just lose them. Here, put on the hose and let's see how that dress fits. I only have tomorrow if it needs any adjustments."

"The corset is kind of tight."

"Yes, dear, I know. I told the girls that you'd be able to fit into a twenty-two inch waist, and I was right."

Brenna rolled her eyes, then rolled the hose up her legs and hooked them to the garter straps. "These are the softest stockings I've ever felt."

"Silk is so much nicer than nylon, don't you think?"

She put on the dress, a sapphire colored chiffon and lace one-shoulder evening gown. The sparkling bodice of beaded lace had a diamond shaped keyhole cutout and the center pleated A-line skirt was slit on the side to mid-thigh. Alice zipped her up, then handed her a pair of matching four-inch spikes. Looking at herself in the mirror, she was stunned. Alice walked around her, pulling at the fabric here and there. "Yes, I think it will do. Does it feel all right?"

Just then, she received a spear from Rebecca, *Is Alice with you?*

Yes, Brenna answered, *we're in my room.*

Good, Irina and I will be right up, Rebecca sent.

Shortly there was a knock on her door and Rebecca entered with Irina wearing a bathrobe. "My God, Brenna, that is stunning!"

"Alice, I think this is a little tight." Irina pulled the robe apart, revealing an emerald green corset similar to Brenna's. Her waist appeared incredibly tiny.

"Oh, no, I don't think so. It's only twenty inches. One of my girls wanted to try for Scarlett O'Hara's sixteen, but I decided that might be a little too much."

"I can't breathe. I know I won't be able to eat anything," Irina protested.

"Dear, you'll be so nervous that you won't be able to eat anyway. You can live on the fruits of love for one night."

The three young women stared wide-eyed at her.

"What about the panties?" Rebecca asked. "This outfit and another one are missing the panties."

Brenna chuckled. "I was told that panties are superfluous, and I'd probably lose them anyway."

Irina's eyes almost popped out of her head.

Rebecca eyed Alice critically. "And what are you wearing tomorrow night?"

Alice smiled, "Something my girls designed for me, but I assure you, the outfit doesn't have any panties either."

~~~

Siobhan called a meeting of all the succubi in Cindy's room right after breakfast and had invited Rebecca and Jill as well. When they all gathered, she produced three bottles of red wine, a basketful of glasses and two huge boxes of chocolates. "Breakfast of champions," she proclaimed.

"Ladies, this is an historic occasion. Never has the O'Donnell Solstice Ball hosted five succubi -- I checked. In 1928, there were four, but one of them was over a hundred fifty. I thought we should get together and decide what kind of show we're going to put on."

Rebecca spoke up, "Some wag has already dubbed it 'The Dance of the Succubi' and it's spread. There are pools going all over the place and some of the betting is outrageous."

Puzzled, Brenna asked, "Betting on what?"

"Damn near everything, who will go up the stairs the most times, who will be the first one up the stairs, whether Cindy will take anyone at all, whether Brenna will participate, you name it, someone is betting on it."

Siobhan chuckled, "How are the odds running for most times upstairs?"

"You're the leader at one-to-one odds. I tried to bet on Rosie Thompson, but they wouldn't take my bet. I think Collin tried to bet on her, too." She blushed, "They also refused the bets of the seven Protectors who tried to bet on me. Succubi only."

Looking thoughtful, Cindy asked, "What are the odds I won't take someone?"

Rebecca smiled, "Need someone to place a bet for you?"

With a sly smile, Cindy nodded.

"No problem, I'll have Rosie place it. No one would suspect her. I think I'll take a little of that action myself," Rebecca laughed.

"Who is Rosie Thompson?" Siobhan asked.

"The most notorious woman in the valley," Rebecca answered, looking straight at Cindy, "a succubus-gene carrier. She's a little older than Collin and Jared and they're all old friends. She's a legend among the locals. A really nice lady, really sweet, I like her a lot."

"Okay, back to business. If this is going to be the succubi show, we should give them a show, don't you think?"

"Why did you invite me to this meeting?" Jill asked. "I'm not a succubus."

"Because you're a genius organizer," Siobhan answered with a smile, "with a wicked and naughty mind. We aren't prejudiced, just predatory. Besides, I know you like wine and chocolate."

Siobhan popped a truffle and washed it down with a sip of wine. "Now, for those of you who haven't attended before, there are some basic rules, which will be explained to all new guests at dinner this evening. This is the most civilized and discreet orgy you'll ever attend. No sexual activity in the main ballroom, not even necking. All activity takes place upstairs, or if you're really hot to trot, I suppose you could use one of the closets on the main floor.

"Men do not ask, period. Any man seen or reported to be propositioning women will be escorted out by the Protectors. Brenna's grandmother's rules, I understand, and they've held up for a hundred years. Women approach the men and ask, 'Sir, would you do me the honor of conducting me to a more comfortable place?'"

"You're kidding," Irina said, laughing, "a formulaic proposition?"

"Yep, and if they accept they will offer you their arm. If they decline they will make some kind of lame excuse, but that doesn't happen too often and is definitely frowned upon. On the other hand, it is considered bad taste to go too far outside your age range. Collin might have a couple of old ladies ask him, but it's not likely. It would also be considered poor form for Antonia or me to prey on an eighteen year old. We're supposed to leave them for you girls. The men may ask you to dance, indeed are expected to, but you can ask the men as well."

"Any questions?"

"Uh, yeah," Brenna looked uncertain, "How many men am I supposed to ask? I mean, do I have a quota or

101

something? I heard Jill say she took five men upstairs last year."

Jill laughed, "I've slowed down as I've gotten older, but it really depends on you, one or a dozen. How many last year, Siobhan?"

"Twelve, but I have a date this year so who knows, I might go slow."

"Jesus, twelve men in one night? When do you breathe?" Irina asked in awe.

"You sort of get in a rhythm, you know? I mean, you're not going upstairs to spend hours gazing into each other's eyes. That's why you leave the one you really want until last. But who knows how it will go this year. It's always been bang and drain, but with Saint Brenna's gift, I think things will be a bit different."

"Saint Brenna?" Jill looked around. "What gift? What am I missing here?"

Cindy smiled at her. "Your father and I made love this morning. Didn't you notice my Glow at breakfast?"

"Well, yeah, but ..." she trailed off, the implications of Cindy's statement starting to sink in. She turned wide-eyed to Brenna, "What did you do?"

Irina giggled, "She found the answer to the most important question in the world."

By lunch they had a plan, simple but flashy, with the aim of assuring the ball would achieve the proper atmosphere from the beginning. Something that wasn't in their plan was Seamus pulling Brenna into his study and informing her that he wished her to perform the benediction at the beginning of the ball. He gave her a phrase to memorize and told her to announce it to the gathering upon his entrance.

~~~

Chapter 8

The major effect of the succubus' presence is a lowering of inhibitions with regard to sex and lust. Slowly, the populace begins to shrug off its ingrained social mores. Males and females begin to desire her. The decreasing of inhibitions extends to all people; people feel less and less social pressure to restrict themselves in their romantic pursuits. The people become less and less concerned with others, and more and more intent on fulfilling their own desires. - Bishop Jerome du Bois, 1544

In addition to the main dining room, there were two smaller dining rooms in the main house and two in each of the guest wings. A light dinner was served in all locations at six o'clock, giving everyone a chance to eat and then take care of any last minute preparations before the ball began at eight. Officially, it ended with sunrise, but few people were ever still awake by then. Brenna had plans to greet the sunrise with Collin in their room, but to start the evening they made love before they showered and dressed. Other than escorting her into the ball, he would be on his own for the evening.

Brenna wore her mother's sapphire necklace set, her hair brushed all to one side. Seen in profile from her left, it appeared she had short hair, or it was all up. From the other side it looked as if a black waterfall was cascading from her head down over her shoulder and arm. The final touch was her makeup, sapphire-blue eye shadow with matching blue lipstick and fingernail polish.

Jill's room was next to hers, across from Cindy's. Brenna stopped in to see if Cindy needed any help and came out into the hall just as Jill emerged. They walked down to dinner together. Jill wore a tight yellow sheath in a Chinese style, hugging her minimal curves but making her look taller. "I may have to slip into the kitchen and borrow a knife," she confided, "I think this thing is too tight to dance in. I should have had them make the slit higher."

"I just hope I don't make a complete fool of myself. I only learned ballroom dancing this fall," Brenna replied. "Collin's been teaching me, but if the guy doesn't know what he's doing it will be a disaster. If you need any comic relief, just find me on the dance floor."

A twenty-four piece orchestra would play from eight until one with a break at ten, and since the sixties, a rock-and-roll band would take over and play from two until four. Most of the older people would be ready to retire by then and the younger people would take over the dance floor.

Collin escorted her into the ballroom at eight just as the orchestra started playing. It was already crowded, a swirling maelstrom of color from the women's gowns mixed with the black of the men's suits.

By tradition, everyone waited for Seamus before the festivities started. He was supposed to take the dance floor first and for the past twelve years had escorted Cindy onto the dance floor to begin the festivities. The other four succubi stood together near the entrance with their escorts while they waited. It seemed as though everyone was watching them, but Brenna hoped they were just watching the entrance for Seamus.

She eyed the broad, curving, open staircase that swept up one side of the room leading to the second floor bedrooms, wondering if it was there just for the purpose it served at this ball. The people who normally occupied those rooms had cleared out for the night, making arrangements to stay elsewhere. Irina's room was one of them. *Irina, where are you sleeping tonight?*

Jared has graciously offered me a place <smile>. It's rough being a homeless refugee.

Seamus wheeled Cindy into the room, setting her chair at the edge of the area around the dance floor. He bent down to speak with her then straightened.

The other succubi stepped forward onto the floor, three of them circling until they each reached a cardinal point, Cindy holding the south. Brenna glided to the center of the floor. The orchestra faltered, then quieted. Siobhan, at the north point turned and sent a spear thought to the conductor. After a moment, they started a new piece of music, the traditional waltz to kick off the evening.

Boosting her Glam to the maximum, the Goddess-like projection that succubi serving as Her priestesses traditionally used, Brenna raised her arms in the air, and threw her head back.

"On this, the Longest Night, we call on our Mother to bless us, to embody the women of the Clan with Her will and Her desire, that they may take into their bodies our offering to Her and pray She shall let the sun rise on the morrow."

She released a burst of pheromones into the air, knowing the other succubi, Cindy included, had done the same. Out of the corner of her eye, she saw Cindy standing with her arms raised in front of her chair, Seamus steadying her with one hand on her shoulder.

Brenna dropped her arms and waited while Collin walked out to her, took her in his arms and swept her into the waltz. The other succubi's dates would be doing the same thing. Seamus held Cindy, swaying to the music at the edge of the floor. Randolph led Callie onto the floor and then other couples began to filter out. As they whirled around the room, Brenna and the other succubi continued to saturate the air with their pheromones.

105

When the dance was over, she moderated her Glam back to medium. Collin bowed deeply to her, kissed her hand, and said with a smile, "Most beautiful lady, I hope you enjoy yourself. I shall see you in our room, and believe me, I'm looking forward to it." He led her toward the front of the room near the bar and the orchestra and took his leave.

She snagged a glass of champagne off the tray of a circulating Protector and he winked at her. She winked back. Men asked her to dance and she managed not to disgrace herself. It was the most magical night of her life, something out of the movies.

Then Noel Campbell, head of their San Francisco office, stepped in front of her and asked in his Scottish accent for a dance. She had noticed Noel when he first arrived at the estate but hadn't had a chance to talk with him. Tall and dark haired, incredibly handsome, Noel looked as though he had just stepped from the pages of a men's fashion magazine. He was a wonderful dancer and she almost felt graceful as he twirled her around the floor in his arms. When the dance ended, she looked up at him and repeated the ritual formula. He looked startled, then pleased and offered her his arm.

When they took the first step onto the staircase, a gasp went up from the throng and then applause as they climbed.

"I had hoped to spend a little more time at the party this evening but it would be rather stupid of me to refuse the most beautiful woman in the room, wouldn't it?" Noel smiled at her.

She gave him a coy, sideways look and smiled. "I have a special surprise for you. I think you'll enjoy it."

"Oh, no doubt I will."

They went to Irina's room, passing several others. Brenna felt a bit more comfortable using it than a stranger's. Entering the room, she filled it with her pheromones and kicked her Glam to high. Taking her in his arms, he kissed her deeply. She fumbled with his pants, managing to unfasten them and take his erection in her hand. He pushed her back against the wall, raising her skirt, and plunged his hand between her legs.

He took her standing with her back against the wall, his hands gripping her hips and she opened her mind to him. They shared their pleasure gazing into each other's eyes as he drove her to her crest again and again. She met him thrust for thrust, desperate and greedy. Then she felt him reach his climax, his energy spilling into her along with his seed. She flipped the switch and saw his eyes widen. Using his energy and his pleasure to enhance her orgasm, she fed the pleasure he was giving her back into him.

When they came back to themselves, he stared down at her. "How?"

She smiled, "We discovered an ancient trick. Do you like it?"

He pulled her to him and kissed her deeply.

"Come visit me in San Francisco. I'd love to show you the city," he told her as he escorted her back to the ballroom.

"I was kind of hoping I might get a chance to spend some time with you again before you leave," she answered. "I'd like to get to know you better."

"I thought, I mean, aren't you …"

"With Collin? Yes, but he won't mind us spending an afternoon together."

When they appeared at the top of the stairs, Brenna sending a burst of pheromones into the room as a signal she'd returned, a murmur started below. As they descended, everything came to a halt. She was obviously Glowing, and he even had a bit of a Glow, but he was upright, awake and smiling. No one knew what to make of it.

Siobhan met her at the bottom on the arm of a man with a startled look on his face. "I was waiting until you came down. I wanted to see the expressions on people's faces. It was priceless, they're all wondering if you're some kind of succubus prude or virgin or something."

"I guarantee not a virgin," Noel answered.

Siobhan laughed and continued up the stairs on the arm of a very confused gentleman.

With the first succubus' journey up the stairs, the dam was breached and a steady stream of people was soon traveling the staircase in both directions. The dancing became more energetic, the laughter a little louder, the smiles larger. She received a spear from Cindy and turned to Noel as she took her leave from him. "Noel, I realize this is a small breach of protocol, but the circumstances are special. When you've recovered a bit, Cindy would like you to drop by and say hello." The look on her face told him all he needed to know.

"I'll do that," he smiled. "I've always been a great admirer of hers. Thank you, Brenna, and I look forward to seeing you again."

She ate a couple of canapés and drank a glass of champagne, watching the people and enjoying the music. She watched Rebecca and Irina go up the stairs and then Antonia on the arm of a tall, distinguished looking man with white hair. She danced with a couple of men, asking the second one to escort her upstairs.

She returned in time to see Noel approach Seamus and Cindy. They chatted for a bit and then Cindy put her hand on his arm and said something to him. He bent down, scooped her up in his arms, and carried her up the stairs. Smiling, Seamus watched them go.

Rebecca appeared at her side, nudging her and directing her attention to Jill. "You're getting outdone. That's her third already." They watched her take a man's arm and head toward the staircase.

"Are you enjoying yourself?" Brenna asked her.

"Oh, hell yes, I love it. Oh, my God, will you look at that?"

Brenna turned, and saw Seamus escorting a woman upstairs. She blinked, trying to make sense of what she was seeing. Turning, she searched the room for Callie. She found her on Collin's arm, heading for the stairs. Her world started spinning and she reached out for Rebecca, who steadied her.

"I think we're undergoing culture shock," Rebecca murmured. "Either that or someone spiked the champagne with hallucinogens. Oh, there's someone I wanted to try. I'll see you later." Brenna watched her cross the room and sidle up to William. That convinced her hallucinogens were the answer.

She decided to stop worrying about other people, and approached a handsome young man she didn't recognize to ask him to dance. While they were dancing, she noticed Irina watching them and realized she had asked him just before Irina had. When the music stopped, she thanked him and drifted to the buffet, seeing Irina approach him and take his arm. Irina shot Brenna a grateful look.

Thinking of Noel, she decided that she should probably not show favoritism. She approached Nigel Richardson, director of the London office, and asked him to escort her upstairs. Later, she found Todd Harwood of the Dallas office and took him upstairs also.

Before she knew it, the rock band was setting up, the crowd had thinned, her feet hurt, and she had the most marvelous Glow going. The last two men she had taken had both asked her to drain them, saying they wanted a true succubus experience. She obliged them, notifying the Protectors so they could be moved into their own rooms.

She had last seen Rebecca going upstairs with a man on each arm. Earlier, Siobhan had taken Seamus up and Cindy had taken Collin. Antonia had taken Callie's

109

husband Randolph, Brenna's grandfather Fergus, and Kallen's half-brother Seamus. Her grandmother Caylin had taken at least two men upstairs that she'd seen.

One man who, in spite of his good looks, had been avoided was Kallen. She'd heard he enjoyed very rough sex and Rebecca had warned her to stay away from him. On a whim, she approached him. "Kallen, if I ask you up, will you be gentle with me?"

He looked at her oddly. "No, but I won't hurt you. I'm not a gentle man, Brenna."

She considered, "Kallen, would you do me the honor of conducting me to a more comfortable place?"

"It would be my honor, Brenna." He offered her his arm and they went upstairs. He took her to his room on the third floor.

Inside, she gave him a pheromone burst and started taking her dress off. He stripped in a hurry, then grabbed her and pushed her forcefully into the wall. Putting his hands under her bottom, he picked her up and pushed her ankles up onto his shoulders. He was huge, almost as large as the basketball player in New York, and he plunged into her without any foreplay at all, hammering her. The angle of the position allowed him to drive as deeply as she could take, and she took it all. It was rough, hard and fast, and his stamina was incredible.

She just hung on, mindlessly surrendering all control. Her body shattered, sending rockets from her groin to her brain in an endless stream. Waves of scalding heat roared through her blood. In the distance, she heard a woman's voice whimpering, saying over and over, "More, yes, more, God, more."

He pulled her away from the wall and carried her to the bed, dropping her on her shoulders and driving her into the mattress. Lost in a continual orgasm for over thirty minutes, scorching heat filling the space between her legs, she felt like a bomb had gone off in her mind when he finally spilled into her, and forgetting entirely about the switch, she drained him. He rolled off her and smiled. "Thank you Brenna, you're such a sweet, lovely lady. I hope you enjoyed your first ball. Good night." He closed his eyes and slept.

She lay there beside him and waited for the earthquake to end. It took her some time to put herself together and make it back downstairs. Collin sent her a thread saying he had to check security after the ball ended at four, and he would see her in their room around sunrise. Irina was dancing to the rock band with Jared, and Jill was dancing with Tom. Rebecca wasn't there. Seamus and Cindy had retired, as had her grandparents, Callie, Antonia, and most of the older people.

After Kallen, she didn't have any desire for another man. She soon wandered upstairs, going to her room and making a cup of hot chocolate. Watching the moon travel across the sky out her window, she let the images of the evening play across her mind without really thinking about them.

Dawn was breaking when Collin came in. He stripped and took a shower, then came to bed. They made slow, gentle love, and fell asleep in each other's arms.

~~~

Chapter 9

*The people I'm furious with are the
women's liberationists. They keep
getting up on soapboxes and
proclaiming women are brighter
than men. That's true, but it should
be kept quiet or it ruins the whole
racket. - Anita Loos*

The Christmas tree was erected on Solstice day, a giant twenty-foot spruce tree. Although she wasn't involved in decorating it, Brenna was told that traditionally everyone hung at least one ornament, often something with a personal meaning. She'd wracked her brain trying to think of something. Rebecca, who had been there the previous year, hung a silver ball with the year the family found her written in glitter. Finally, Brenna took the teddy bear she had carried through multiple foster families, wrapped a bit of ribbon under his arms, and tied him to a branch.

She spent all her free time between Solstice and Christmas wrapping presents. She did a lot of her shopping online and had some anxious moments waiting for some presents to arrive. By paying expediting charges, she had even managed to get Noel's present there on time.

Many of the guests from Solstice had left over the next couple of days, traveling to spend the holiday with their own families, but Callie told her the number of people staying for Christmas was higher than normal.

Whatever their stated reasons, Callie suspected Brenna was the reason for the large turnout at Solstice and the number of people staying over for Christmas. Everyone wanted to meet Seamus' prodigal granddaughter and was curious about her, especially after the Gless incident. A twenty-three year old PhD, a succubus who looked exactly like her mother, a telepath of unexplored power, she was an enigma that everyone wanted to meet.

Brenna was unaware of the intense scrutiny being leveled at her. Completely oblivious of the Clan's internal organization and politics, she didn't know the entire power structure of the Clan and its allies had gathered at the estate for the sole purpose of figuring out how she fit into the Clan, what her future role would be, and what the relationship of each of them would be with her. She just knew she had a lot of relatives, the Clan had a lot of people who were important and wanted to talk with her, and she had a lot of presents to wrap.

~~~

On Christmas Eve, Seamus wandered into the ballroom and found Callie standing near the tree, its lights providing the only light in the room. He walked up and put his arm around her and she leaned against him, marveling at how being close to him still made her feel safe, as though everything was right with the world.

"It seems there are more presents than I remember from previous years," Seamus said after looking the tree over.

"That's because Brenna hasn't been here in previous years."

"But, I mean, aren't there a lot of presents?"

"Dad, see that pile over there on the right side? All those are *from* Brenna."

"Good God, who did she buy presents for?"

"Everyone."

"What do you mean, 'everyone'?"

"Everyone. The family, her friends, her lovers, the kitchen and household staffs, the Protectors, the stable hands … everyone. That doesn't include the seventy-two that she shipped off to New York, Baltimore and Washington. She bought a present for Tom Moody, the cop that was first on the scene in Spencerville. She said he was kind to her."

"How many?"

"Two hundred twenty-five here, I think. I've been trying to keep count since the pile started growing the beginning of the week. God knows where she's been stashing all this stuff. I did find out from Mrs. McCarthy that she acquired keys for a couple of empty bedrooms on the third floor, but what she did when we filled those rooms for Solstice I don't know."

"Well, you and I always get presents for the staff, so it's nice she thought of them."

"Dad, you and I give them gift certificates, bonuses, bottles of wine, things like that. Every one of those is individualized. Every one will mean something to the person who receives it. Every one has a meaning to her. I asked about some of them. She can tell you about the person and why they want or need the particular present. You know Karen Parker?

"Cute little brunette who works in the kitchen?"

"Yes, she's getting married this spring. There's a set of high-quality cookware for her kitchen. There's a down comforter for Jeremy. She told me she got cold in his room. There's an envelope for Mrs. Doyle, two tickets and a week's reservation at a resort in the Bahamas for February. Jewelry for Rebecca and Irina, a knife for Kallen's collection, half a dozen things for Collin, from the practical to a lovely ring, a pair of silver spurs for Rory … I've found something for everyone except me."

"No present for you?"

"She said *someone* told her I'm a present-peeker, so mine isn't there. I wonder who might have told her that?"

He chuckled, "If the shoe fits, Callie."

"I haven't done that since I was a kid."

"Okay, so that explains a lot of that pile of loot, what about the rest?"

114

"At last count, there's one hundred twenty-seven presents *for* Brenna. And who knows how many aren't under that tree. You're aware of what Rory and his boyos got her, aren't you?"

"Yes, Rory told me. It seems she's made an impression on people."

"She does that. She's made an impression on me. I've known her six months and I love her as much as I do Jared or Jill. She's as special, and infuriating, as you are."

"Funny, I could say the same thing. I haven't thought of your childhood, adolescence, and scorched-earth after-college years so much in a long, long time. I suppose we should be grateful she's fallen in love with Collin. I hate to think of how wild she might be if she didn't have a reason to come home at night."

"I'm not sure if he's really a calming influence so much as an anchor. The influence she's having on him though is nothing short of amazing. I think the boy's growing up."

~~~

Guests were warned Christmas at the manor house provided a minimum of service. Most of the household and kitchen staffs spent the day with their own families and only volunteers and single Protectors were in the building. A buffet was set out for breakfast and dinner would be served. Otherwise, residents and guests were on their own and the staff on duty would sit with the family for dinner.

Waiting for the official eight o'clock start to the festivities on Christmas morning, Callie wandered around the ballroom sipping her coffee with a camera around her neck. Callie's passion was photography, and she'd documented the family for decades. She immediately noticed a bundle of five boxes that hadn't been there the night before, with a tag reading 'Aunt Callie'. When the present rush scramble ensued, she headed for it first, her curiosity almost boiling over.

Sitting amidst the torn paper, she gazed in wonder at Canon's latest top of the line professional camera, with the three lenses she didn't already own and a fourth to replace the one she had dropped and dinged at the Grand Canyon seven years before. Callie immediately set the camera around her neck aside, put her new one together and started snapping pictures. She had to be reminded she still had other presents to unwrap.

Rebecca sat and stared at the diamond collar necklace, three strands, with matching earrings. Irina's blue eyes filled her face, her mouth worked, but nothing came out. She pulled the three-string pearl choker and earrings out and put them on. Callie thought the picture of her in pajamas and bathrobe with that jewelry on was one of the best she took that morning.

Brenna's presents were an eclectic mix. The girls in the kitchen gave her a hand-lettered coupon book, redeemable for the dessert of her choice every month. The household staff gave her an electric teapot for her room and a collection of teas. The Protectors pitched in on a calf-length, suede sheepskin coat. An envelope contained a note from Rory and the boyos at the stable saying to come see them to get her present.

Callie gave her a pair of handmade riding boots, and her gift from Seamus was a saddle. Collin's gifts included a gold necklace with matching earrings worked in the shape of a graphic from the Kama Sutra. The set definitely couldn't be worn to church. Rebecca and Irina embarrassed her with an outfit that made her blush when she unwrapped it in front of Seamus. The black corset, garter belt, panties, knee-high stiletto boots, leather handcuffs and flogger were beautiful, but …

Alice's present almost stopped her heart, a thigh-length mink coat, thick and dark and the softest thing she had ever felt. When she tried to protest it was too much, Alice

116

laughed. "Don't say I can't afford it, not after I had the most profitable December ever."

Wearing a new pair of sheepskin boots from Jill, the suede sheepskin coat the Protectors had given her and a knit wool hat from Jeremy, she walked down to the stables. The presents for Rory and his boyos and her new saddle floated along behind her on a telekinetic leash.

When she got to the stable, she passed out the presents. The horses, the stables, and the down-to-earth men and women who worked there were one of the major joys of her life. But she wasn't prepared for their present to her.

"We didn't bring your present up to the house because you would have just had to bring her back down here, and it's rather cold this morning," Rory started. Brenna gaped at him as one of the men led a black mare out of a stall. "A man over in Maryland had her for sale. Said she was a little too spirited for his daughter, but I figured you could discuss things with her and work out an accommodation."

"Oh my God. She's beautiful. What's her name?" Grins, leers and lifted eyebrows met her query, but no answers. Brenna looked from face to face, then a suspicion began to creep into her mind. "Oh no, you didn't. Succubus? Jesus, you guys are incorrigible."

"Coming from you," one drawled, "that's a compliment."

Rory grinned. "The man I got her from says she has a fancy for the boys. I'm hoping you'll let me breed a couple of foals from her."

She spent the next two hours getting to know her new friend, brushing her and feeding her carrots, then trudged back up the hill to the manor house for Christmas dinner.

~~~

Late in the afternoon, she wandered into Callie's parlor. Her aunt was deep in conversation with Jill and Noel.

As she entered the room, she heard Noel saying, "It seems a bit quick to make such an important decision, but I tend to agree with you. I don't think waiting will change the way any of us feels."

Becoming aware of her, the conversation stopped and they turned to look at her.

"I'm sorry, am I interrupting something?"

Callie patted the couch next to her, "Of course not, come join us and have some tea."

Brenna could tell Callie wasn't being completely honest, and the three looked uncomfortable, trying to find a different topic to discuss.

Callie poured her a cup of tea, and Jill restarted the conversation.

"Brenna, I know you've had a lot going on, and had a lot hit you in a very short time, but have you thought about what you want to do, what your future will be? Become an international jet-set party girl?"

Brenna laughed. "You mean become a professional succubus? I think that would get pretty boring. The sums Siobhan and Antonia say I could earn are pretty astounding, but I don't think that's how I want to spend my life, and I don't really need the money."

She took a sip of her tea. "I've been thinking a lot about the research I was trying to do at Hopkins. I really do love it. Now I have a population of true telepaths for research subjects, so I think I could really make some progress, really learn something. The problem we've discovered with the succubus carriers, maybe there's something we can do for them. We don't have to be slaves to genetics, we can try and figure out ways to either modify or enhance what genetics has handed us."

"You're thinking about going back to Johns Hopkins?" Callie asked.

"Oh, no, that would never work. I could never publish the work I want to do with telepaths. No, what I'm thinking

118

about is establishing a lab here. I haven't had a chance to thoroughly research it yet, exactly what the costs would be, but such a facility could be used for a lot of other things, such as Elsie's and Dorothy's clinic. It's just starting to take shape in my mind and I'd need to discuss it with you and Seamus, but I think it would benefit everyone."

"What kind of facilities would you need?" Noel asked.

"Well, a CAT scan and PET scan, a cyclotron, there are some mobile ones on the market now, a diagnostic lab that would expand Callie's and Elsie's lab facilities, things like that. It would need an additional power supply over what we have now, some of those machines draw a lot of electricity. If I can get Seamus to share that cost with me, we could build a modern facility that would enhance the valley's power grid."

"Where do you intend to get that kind of money?" Jill asked.

Brenna looked at Callie, "You said that gold just sits there, not generating any income." Callie nodded. "I can sell a portion of that, enough for construction and equipment and salaries for a few years. Finding the right people is more of a concern than money. I can't run a cyclotron so I'll need engineers and nuclear scientists. If I can find telepaths that can run it for me, who will take a salary and live out here in return for freedom to do their own research, then I can make it work."

Noel looked at Callie, then at Jill. "You're right, she's even more impressive with her clothes on, and that's saying a lot."

Brenna blushed.

They questioned her extensively for the next half hour. She discussed her interests in the Clan's future, their operations in Washington, and her desire to travel.

Feeling an undercurrent to this discussion, she folded her arms under her breasts, sat back in her chair and looked back and forth between them. "Now, suppose you three

119

conspirators tell me what you were discussing when I came in, and what this conversation is all about."

Their collective demeanor was that of a group of naughty children caught doing something they shouldn't have.

Finally Callie spoke, "We were discussing something you don't want to hear about, something that's going to set you off and send you into Seamus' office. Brenna, I'm going to ask you not to do that. The only way I'll be honest with you is if you promise to keep our conversation confidential, within this group. It's Clan politics, things you don't know about or understand at this point, and we don't need you doing any damage just because you get your nose out of joint."

Brenna surveyed them, seeing the same gravity on all their faces. "Maybe you shouldn't tell me. I don't think I want to get caught up in all that anyway. I'm perfectly happy just being a kid and letting Seamus and Callie make all the big decisions."

The obvious discomfort and squirming at that statement made her reconsider. Watching them, her own discomfort started to grow.

"Okay, tell me. I promise not to go whining to Seamus, and I won't shoot my mouth off in front of anyone else. But a warning, the man that's in my body every night is also in my mind. I can hide things from Collin if I want to, but I'd rather not build that kind of wall between us." She speared Jill with her eyes, "And if you think I have *any* secrets from Rebecca, get those thoughts out of your head right now."

She looked at Callie, "As for Irina, she doesn't know or care about this type of thing, and I don't know if she ever will. Her needs and desires are something completely different."

"You know she's in love with you," Jill said.

"I'm hoping it's just a young girl's infatuation, but if not I'll deal with it. At least she's not gay. A lesbian succubus is an impossibility, and though she may be bi, so far my relationship with Collin has her standing back. But that's my personal life and has nothing to do with anything you're concerned with."

Callie spent some time considering how to answer Brenna's questions.

"You know I'm not happy with my role as heir. It's not something I ever wanted, but I assumed it when Jack died because there wasn't another viable candidate."

Brenna sat up straight on the edge of her chair. "Whoa. Don't even go there. Jesus, Callie, I'm still a kid. Who in their right minds would consider naming me as heir when I've only been part of the Clan for a few months?"

She looked at their faces, and realized that's exactly what they were considering.

"Wait a minute. What do you have to do with Seamus naming an heir? Isn't that up to him?"

"Not really," Noel answered. "He has a veto, but the Council does also. The Clan isn't a democracy but it's not a dictatorship. Seamus holds his position not only by birth and personal strength and wealth, but because the Clan Council backs him. We have the power to depose him, or his heir, although that would never happen. But in the future, say if Seamus wanted to name William or Jared as heir, the Council would never go along with it."

Jill took up the explanation, "Seamus led the Clan here in the 1890s, and has done an incredible job building a single clan into a worldwide power. The Clan is far more than the O'Donnell Clan now. He did it by a combination of personal power and charisma, shrewd business decisions and investments, and a ruthless devotion to protecting his own when necessary. His vision has attracted a lot of talented and dedicated people over the past century plus."

"Brenna, Seamus is getting older," Callie said. "He has another four or five decades at most. The Clan needs a leader, another visionary to lead us into the twenty-second

121

century. That's not just talk. All of us will probably see it. Seamus foresaw the explosion of technology, of American power, of the development of a new kind of civilization a hundred years ago and it's served us well."

"The next hundred years will see change accelerate." Jill stood and paced. "Where do we fit in? What will our role be? I can't see it. I mean, I think I can see part of it, but I'm a tactical thinker. We need someone who sees big pictures, a strategic thinker who isn't afraid to take risks.

"Callie and I talked before I came for Thanksgiving. She told me she wanted to step down, and that was no surprise. But I thought naming you was crazy, and for just the reasons you cited. But you sold me. The first time we sat down to talk, I went and told her she was right. Do you know what you said that convinced me I wanted to follow you for the rest of my life?"

Stunned, Brenna shook her head.

"When I asked you about that operation you mounted against Gless. I asked if you ever considered that it might not be smart, that you could have sat back and let the Protectors hunt him down and you'd have been safe. Do you remember your answer?"

"I said it might not have been smart, but it was the right thing to do."

Jill nodded. "The person I want leading this Clan is someone whose soul is the true heir to what Seamus has in his soul. I want to follow someone who does what's right, and I'll follow her into hell with a popgun."

Brenna felt numb. Noel and Callie were nodding in agreement. "So what does that mean, what are you talking about doing? Hell, I don't know if I'd do the Samantha thing again. Looking back on it, it was incredibly stupid and got people killed."

Callie poured herself some more tea. "Are you aware your grandparents aren't part of our Clan? Fergus is Lord O'Byrne, and the O'Byrne Clan is allied with us, but not part of us. When your parents were married, the understanding between Fergus and Seamus was the heir to both Clans would come from Jack and Maureen's children. You're already the O'Byrne heir, although I'm not sure Fergus has discussed it with you."

Feeling more and more like she'd fallen down the proverbial rabbit hole, Brenna shook her head. She hadn't felt this disoriented since the night she'd walked into the Clan house in Baltimore for the first time.

"Unless I step down, Seamus can't propose a new heir," Callie said. "The annual Council meeting is scheduled for London in late April. I'm planning on proposing you to replace me. That will put the opposition off balance and they'll have to react on their feet. The reason for not talking to Seamus is, as long as he's officially unaware of this, he doesn't have to put it on the agenda."

Callie leaned forward, her eyes pleading, "Brenna, Dad and I have talked about this, in a discreet, roundabout fashion. We can't talk about it directly, but he knows you're the future of this Clan. The three of us wouldn't even be discussing it if we thought he disagreed."

Abruptly, Brenna stood, "I need to think about it. This is too much, too quick. And you were going to spring this on me in April? Out of the blue? Jesus, Callie, you should know better. Shit. You don't want it, what the hell makes you think I do? You're not even asking me what I want."

Callie's face was bright red and she couldn't meet Brenna's eyes.

"You thought you'd just cram this down my throat, didn't you? You don't want me 'storming in to Seamus'," Brenna gave a disgusted snort. "You knew what my reaction would be. This was your plan? It makes my plan for capturing Gless look good. Right now I wouldn't put the three of you in charge of planning a slumber party."

She fixed Jill and Noel with her eyes. "I don't like surprises. I react rather badly to them, as a matter of fact. Not always smart, but you're the ones who think I'm so damn smart. You think you want to follow me? Be careful what you ask for. You may find I'm not as laid back and benevolent as Seamus is."

Brenna's face was flushed, her voice harsh. "Jesus, Callie, get a fucking clue. No surprises. No. Goddamned. Surprises. Got it?"

Walking to the door, she turned. "Jill, *I'm* the manipulator, not the manipulated. I'm nobody's puppet. I've tried to tell people around here that I'm not all sweetness and light but no one seems to listen. I kill people who piss me off, for God's sake! I'm not happy with this at all."

She turned and stomped out of the room. The table with the tea on it rose a foot off the floor, then dropped with a bang, rattling everything on it and spilling their tea.

Jill licked her lips. "You did say she had a temper."

"She wasn't that angry," Noel said in a shaking voice. "She didn't rise to the killing edge."

Callie looked at Brenna's retreating back. "She wasn't kidding, you know. The sweetness, the generosity, the caring for people isn't an act. But she does have a temper, and she is a manipulator. If she thinks she's right, God help you if you get in her way. She won't lie to you, but she'll twist you every which way until you agree with her. And Jill, take the warning. Don't ever try to get between her and Rebecca.

Brenna went looking for Rebecca and found her in her room putting on makeup for a date with Kallen's nephew. "I need to talk with you. Can you postpone your date for a little bit?"

"Sure, you want to talk here?"

"No, let's take a walk."

When they were a couple hundred yards from the house, far enough that Brenna wasn't worried about eavesdroppers, she told Rebecca, "There's a group that wants to name me heir."

"Uh-huh. I didn't know anyone was opposed to it."

"What?" Brenna stopped in her tracks and stared at Rebecca. "You knew?"

Puzzled, Rebecca told her, "I thought everyone knew. You said 'group'. I didn't know you meant a specific set of people. Hell, almost everyone expects that you'll be named heir at some point. The staff all considers it to have happened already. We give you even more security than we do Callie. I know Karen and Caroline consider the designation a formality. I don't understand what the problem is."

"I don't want to be the heir, I'm perfectly happy letting Callie do it."

"But Callie isn't happy and you're far more qualified. People respect Callie, but people love you. They'll follow you the way they do Seamus. Hell, the way you're talking, it almost sounds like this is some kind of surprise."

"It is a surprise. How come everyone seems to be discussing this and I don't know anything about it?"

"God, you blow my mind sometimes. You pay enough attention to get everyone their heart's desire for Christmas, but you have no idea how people see you, what people think about you. Callie's been dropping hints that she wants out ever since you showed up, and she hasn't been subtle about it. The only mystery is whether she's going to announce she's stepping down before the Council meeting in London or wait until the meeting."

"You know they're going to do it at the meeting?"

"Of course. They have to have the whole Council ratify it. Have you paid any attention to the Clan organization and structure stuff Collin and I have been trying to tell you?"

When they got back to the manor, Brenna knocked on Jill's door. With an air of resignation, she told her aunt, "Rebecca says you're overthinking things. I guess the only person who didn't know what you're planning to do is me. She was surprised you think anyone will oppose it. Other than me, of course."

~~~

She entered her room and had no sooner closed the door than someone knocked. She opened it to find Irina and Siobhan standing there. "Brenna, Siobhan thinks she and I are cousins."

Siobhan entered behind her. "More than think. How many succubi named Mairead O'Conner do you think died in the King David bombing in 1946?"

"One maybe?" Brenna said, taken aback. She had no idea what the King David bombing was.

"Exactly. Her grandmother and my aunt died that day and I'm telling her it's the same person."

~~~

Antonia sat in Seamus' study and accepted a glass of wine. "Seamus, Federicci has always been grateful for O'Donnell's support. If not for you, we probably would have been completely destroyed in 1958, and my brother and I remember."

A sad look crossed her face. "But we're not much of a force anymore, and although I'll always be loyal to them, I've operated independently for the past fifty years. Being here, meeting your family, has me rethinking that. Specifically, meeting Brenna has me rethinking that."

She took a sip of her wine and sat the glass on his desk. "I'm here to offer you my services, as a lawyer, a succubus, and specifically as a trainer for your granddaughter. She's a special talent but also a special person. I think I have something to offer, and I'd like to be part of what you've built here."

He regarded her and took a sip of his whiskey. "As you said, your family loyalty has to be first in your consideration. If it wasn't, I'd question your values. So you can't really join the O'Donnell Clan. But if you'd consider working for me on contract, say one year to start with ten two-year renewable options, at a million a year, would that be acceptable? Duties as assigned, of course. I wouldn't ask you to fight for us, but if you ever volunteered, I wouldn't turn you down. I remember that black day in Tuscany in 1957."

She smiled. "That would be entirely acceptable. Thank you."

He clinked his glass against hers. "Draw up the papers, madam lawyer."

~~~

Chapter 10

I love to see a young girl go out
and grab the world by the lapels.
Life's a bitch. You've got to go out
and kick ass. – Maya Angelou

New Year's Eve was informal at the manor since the
true Clan New Year took place at Samhain. There were
parties, of course, but no big formal affair.

Collin had grown up in the valley, as had many of
Brenna's friends. Invitations to parties all over the manor
complex as well as in the village were sitting on her
dresser.

They went around to the parties in the village first. It
was snowing heavily, and the village looked like a picture
postcard. Brenna hadn't met many of Collin's friends, but
she had a wonderful time and met several people she
thought might become friends.

They moved next to the bash at the Protector's
barracks, which was in full swing when they arrived. It was
starting to degenerate from wild to debaucherous, and when
they left, Rebecca tagged along.

The party in the ballroom at the manor had a band, and
they planned on toasting the New Year there, then moving
to Brenna's room for final drinks. They danced a bit, then
Collin was called away. Shortly thereafter, Jeremy and
Robbie also left.

"What's going on?" Brenna asked Rebecca.

"Some kind of communications glitch I think. They're
having problems contacting all the posts on the perimeter.
It happens sometimes with the weather."

Irina had danced several times with two off-duty
Protectors, and coming back to their table after one dance
pulled Brenna aside.

"Would it bother you if I took off for a bit to drain a guy?"

"Oh, no. Go catch a Glow and we'll see you at the room."

Smiling, Irina went back to one of the men and they left through the kitchen door.

"Her taste in men is rather questionable sometimes," Rebecca commented sourly. "That guy is a jerk."

A man asked Brenna to dance. Before she made it back to the table, another intercepted her, and she went back out to the dance floor.

Rebecca saw the second man Irina was dancing with go out the kitchen door. She didn't like either of them. They had given her a hard time when she first joined, and had been extremely rude when she declined to sleep with them. Kallen had beaten one of them for calling her a whore. Seeing both of them going off with Irina bothered her, so she got up to follow and make sure her friend was okay.

She walked into the kitchen and found the men, but no Irina.

"I was looking for my friend. Did she leave?"

"Yeah, we fucked her and she left," the one named Seth said with a sneer.

That set off major alarm bells for Rebecca. Irina had gone seeking a Glow, and both of these guys were still standing. "Did she go out the back? It's snowing." She started toward the outside door.

Seth moved into her path. She felt Pete at her back.

"She said she was going home," Seth said.

Rebecca started to tell him to get the hell out of her way, but stopped when he pulled a pistol and pointed it at her. The two of them assaulted her shields, and with the guns pointed at her, she let Seth gain control of what he thought was her mind.

129

She sent a silent prayer to the Goddess for Brenna's idea. She'd been wearing the special construct that simulated nine levels for weeks and didn't even think about it anymore. He controlled the construct, but not her lower eight levels.

"She doesn't need you. Where's the other one? The old man's granddaughter?"

"She's with her boyfriend."

"Don't lie to me, Collin left. He has a communications problem."

Rebecca wasn't sure if the two would be able to hear her if she tried to send a mental message. With a pistol at her back and another in her face, she wasn't going to push these guys and get shot.

"I don't know where she is. She said she was leaving, that's why I came to find Irina."

"Well, she's gone. Now we need to figure out what to do with you," Pete said from behind her.

"One thing we're going to do is have her service us," Seth leered at her. "Take off your clothes."

He moved to lean up against the counter. Playing along, Rebecca reached back and unzipped her dress, shrugging it off her shoulders and letting it fall to the floor. She was wearing a bra, garter belt, panties and heels.

"Very sexy. You said once you wouldn't fuck me if I was the last man on earth. As far as you're concerned, I'm going to be. Come here, bitch."

"Seth, we don't have time for this, man," Pete complained. "We've got a tight window. We need to grab the black-haired bitch and get out of here. Mason and Stevens are waiting."

She moved toward Seth, stopping in front of him. He unzipped his pants and pulled out his penis. In doing so, his hand moved and the gun was no longer pointed at her stomach.

"Suck my dick, bitch."

She reached out and took his erection in her left hand. Leaning forward, she stumbled, her head bumping his shoulder and causing him to wave his arm to keep his balance. The pistol was no longer pointed at her at all.

"Clumsy bitch!"

Reaching past him, she pulled a butcher knife out of the rack behind him and swung it down with all her strength. He screamed, but her backstroke across his throat ended it. She whirled low, throwing an air shield around Pete. His gun was loud in the confined space. He screamed, clutching at his knee. The bullet had ricocheted off her shield. She battered down his mental shields, seized his mind and put him to sleep.

The rock band in the ballroom had prevented anyone hearing the shot. She crept to the door and through the window saw two more Protectors standing with their backs to the door. She didn't recognize either of them. The information she had gleaned from Pete's mind gave her their plan. These men had never been O'Donnell. Pete and Seth had been bought off and a snatch team was inside the manor.

Kicking off her shoes, she pushed the door open, holding out her left hand. "Hey, guys, see what I have."

The two men looked at her outstretched hand. The man on her left reeled back from her, his eyes wide and a sick look on his pale face. She shoved the knife into the kidney of the man on the right then stepped toward the other man. Her knee slammed into his groin and when he bent over, she hammered her knee into his face. He went down, blood spurting from his face, and she plunged the knife into his back.

And then she was running, shouting at the top of her lungs and broadcasting as strongly as she could mentally, *Security breach, hostiles in the compound, security breach at the manor, hostiles in the compound.*

131

Racing out a door at the back of the house, she spotted two men and a large splash of red moving away from her. Irina was wearing a red dress. She sped up, catching them easily. They whirled to face her. One man was carrying Irina with a pistol held to her head. The other man moved to her right to flank her.

"Hey! You're not going anywhere. Let her go. It's over," Rebecca called.

"If you want her dead, take one more step. We're leaving, and we're taking the little whore with us," the man holding Irina said.

Rebecca held out her hand. "Seth was cocky like you. Now he's not cocky at all."

The man on her right gasped, then retched. His gun wavered and she hit him with an energy bolt of Neural Disruption. He convulsed and fell.

"It's getting mighty lonely. If you're waiting for your friends inside, they aren't coming. They had a bitch problem," Rebecca said with a tight grin.

"You can have her back dead, or you can let me leave. Your choice," he said, his voice shaking.

"Oh, I think there are more choices than that," Brenna said as she walked up.

How can I take him without getting Irina hurt? Brenna sent to Rebecca.

Don't hit him with anything. If he convulses and pulls the trigger, she's dead.

"Yeah, there're more choices. You can come over here and leave with us."

"Okay, just don't hurt her." Brenna started walking toward him. Rebecca watched in horror, but when Brenna got close to him, she sent, *Catch!*

The gun disappeared from his hand and materialized in front of Rebecca. She dropped the knife and grabbed the gun before it fell. The man screamed, grabbing his head and falling to the ground, dropping Irina. She got up,

132

looked at him, and kicked him in the groin with her pointed-toe shoe. It evidently felt good, because after a pause she kicked him again.

"Very well done, ladies," Collin said. Rebecca whirled to see him walking toward her, a dozen armed Protectors fanning out around them. He took off his coat. "Are you going to keep that as a souvenir?" nodding to her left hand. She was still holding Seth's severed penis.

"Eww, no." She dropped it. "Yuck."

He took the gun and wrapped his coat around her shoulders. Suddenly she realized she was cold. Her feet felt like blocks of ice.

"Brenna, do you have his mind?" Collin asked.

"Yes, who wants him?"

"Give him to me." Brenna allowed Collin to enter the man's mind and transferred control to him.

"Are you hurt? Irina?" Collin asked.

"Bastard tore my dress." Irina kicked her kidnapper in the ribs.

"A couple of you loan the ladies your coats and help them back to the house," Collin said to the Protectors. "Their footwear isn't really appropriate for this weather." Collin picked Rebecca up in his arms, carrying her like a bride, and started back to the house. *Brenna, have the staff fill your tub with water. Not too hot, ninety-eight degrees, not hotter. Have them use a thermometer.*

Shock and cold hit Rebecca hard.

"Two gold stars Rebecca, you did well," his voice was calm, soothing. "It would be three gold stars, but you're out of uniform." She wanted to laugh, but her teeth were chattering so hard that her jaw hurt. She marveled at his strength, how solid he felt. She wasn't a small woman, but he never faltered, never stumbled, walking through foot-deep snow.

He carried her up three flights of stairs into the room he shared with Brenna. Mary, one of the household staff,

133

was in the bathroom and water was running into the huge marble tub.

"Turn on the shower please," Collin directed. "Warm, room temperature, not as warm as the bath." The woman leaped to comply. When she had tested the water and stepped away, he carried Rebecca to the shower. "Can you stand?" She shrugged.

He set her on her feet and Mary reached out to steady her. He stripped his coat from her and pulled her into the shower. He was still fully clothed. He positioned her under the pouring water, leaning her against the wall. He took off his jacket and threw it out on the floor, then started undressing her. Covered in blood, Rebecca was too numb to protest as he reached around her back to unhook her bra, then pulled off her other undergarments. He washed her, gentle but firm, and shampooed her hair. He heard someone pounding down the hall and into the room.

Callie charged into the bathroom and stared at them. The water running down the drain was red.

"My God. Rebecca, are you all right?" the anguish in her voice was enough to break Collin's heart.

"She isn't hurt, none of this is hers." He had her clean enough now to make that statement. When he'd first seen her outside, he'd called for the healers. Two of them were waiting next to the tub.

When the water ran clean, he picked her up and carried her to the bath, sliding her into the water.

"Shit. That's hot," Rebecca exclaimed.

"It's body temperature, Rebecca, you're just cold. You'll warm up." Collin stroked her hair. "None of the blood was yours. Are you hurt anywhere?"

She shook her head. He looked up and saw Brenna and Irina standing in the doorway.

"I'm going to change clothes and give you your dignity back." He got up, and picking up his ruined clothes, walked out of the room leaving a trail of water in his wake. He paused to give Brenna a quick kiss.

Callie and the healers immediately descended on her. After a short inspection and a couple of minor physiological adjustments, the healers left. Brenna asked Irina to get them all a drink.

Brenna came and sat by the tub. Rebecca's teeth had stopped chattering, and whatever the healers had done relieved the shock. It was starting to feel like a bad dream and not an immediate horror. She managed to lift the large glass of fruit juice the healers left and gulp some down.

"You're so lucky," Rebecca glanced up at Brenna. "He really is an extraordinary man." She slid down in the water up to her chin.

"I have a lot of very extraordinary people in my life," Brenna stroked her cheek. "That was quite a show you put on tonight."

"You're a hero," Irina blurted, walking into the room. "You saved my life."

Collin came back in dry clothes. He still kept his own room and closet. One of the rules was no outside lovers came to their shared room.

"Do we know what the hell happened?" Brenna asked.

"Yes," Collin said. "Betrayal by two of my men. They were posted at the main gate and another security post. All the men stationed with them are dead. They let in an outside snatch team. As I'm sure you've figured out, they came looking for succubi. It seems you're a very valuable commodity."

"Hey, baby, I'm worth every penny, too," Brenna joked.

"No, seriously. They were expecting to sell you in Europe for ten million euros each. If they'd known Rebecca was a carrier, she's worth two million."

"You're kidding," Irina said with an astonished look on her face. "See, Brenna, we need to capitalize while

135

we're still young. Why should we let a bunch of fat, old murderers get all the profit?"

Rebecca chuckled. Brenna and Collin looked at her in shock.

"Geez, I'm kidding. Mostly." Irina took a sip of her drink. "We really don't know each other that well yet, do we?"

Collin gathered her into his arms. "Are you okay? That must have been frightening."

"Kind of scary. If the bastard had ever taken the gun away from my head, I would have burned him out. But they never would have got me out of here."

"Oh?" Collin was surprised at the confidence in her voice.

"They were both half drained when Rebecca caught up with us. I was doing it slow so they didn't notice."

She surveyed their faces. "What? I'm not going to put up with assholes. I may not be trained to your standards, but my mom made sure I know how to protect myself."

She smiled and winked at Collin. "Be nice to me, boyo. I'm dangerous."

Rebecca lay in the tub with her eyes closed. She was so still they wondered if she'd drifted off to sleep.

"Are you all right?" Callie asked.

"Feeling better," Rebecca said, opening one eye and closing it again.

Brenna watched Rebecca with concern. "Is there anything I can do?"

"After I wash my hair again, you can hold me and help me feel safe."

"I can do that."

"I killed four men tonight."

"You're a soldier. You were protecting your own," Callie said.

They sat quietly for several minutes.

"Growing up, I never thought about being a soldier," Rebecca murmured. "I wanted to be a librarian."

~~~

They met with Seamus the next day to discuss the previous night's incident.

"Two of our own Protectors sold us out," Collin told them. "I have a thorough review started. Malcontents, those with records of problems with authority or other behavior incidents will get a complete psych review. It may not be fair to some of them, but I think this indicates our policy of tolerance may be too lenient.

"Seth and Pete were offered half a million dollars for access. George Mason brought a team of ten from England. They work for Lord Gordon, but this raid exceeded his instructions. We can't find anything in his mind to indicate Gordon ordered a direct assault on us."

"So we have two Clan chiefs involved with this succubus trade?" Seamus said, his mouth pursed with displeasure. He looked at Brenna. "Is that McDermott you captured still in the country?"

"Yes, we have him working with Charles Farrell. They've taken down a couple of prostitution rings," Brenna said.

"I want to talk with him. Can you bring him into the Baltimore house?" Seamus asked.

"Sure." Brenna pulled out her cell phone and made the call.

~~~

"What do you mean our team in the U.S. has been captured?" Lord Gordon roared, his face red as he erupted out of his comfortable chair next to the fire in his study. "What in the bloody hell were they doing to get captured?"

"It seems they invaded the O'Donnell estate and attempted to kidnap several succubi attending the New Year's festivities there," Gordon's chief of security told him. The man was not comfortable delivering this news.

137

"And who the hell told them to do that?" Gordon asked.

"No one. In fact, it was a direct contravention of their orders. I told them to maintain a low profile. I don't know why they decided to go on their own."

"Who was in charge of this team?"

"George Mason. He's evidently in O'Donnell's hands and most of his team are dead. I assure you, my Lord, I did not give any orders that would allow such an indiscreet operation. I specifically told him to stay away from O'Donnell. I can only assume that the bounty von Ebersberg is offering for succubi led him to take the chance on his own authority."

Lord Gordon cursed. "I hope you're telling your people about this, and that any further such stupidity will be punished." It wasn't a question.

"I've already sent out a general directive, my Lord."

"Foster, there have been too many cock ups on your watch. Make sure this situation doesn't happen again," Gordon said, looking his security chief in the eye.

Lloyd Foster felt a cold sweat break out on his face. "I shall control the situation, my Lord."

~~~

Sean walked down the street near Baltimore's Inner Harbor looking for the address he'd been given. A woman of medium height with blonde shoulder length hair, dressed all in black, walked toward him. Much more aware of people around him since his encounter with Brenna and Rebecca, he recognized her as a telepath.

"Sean McDermott?" the blonde said, stopping in front of him.

Cautiously he nodded.

"I hear you enjoy watching women's arses," she said with a grin. "Follow me."

He did, and enjoyed it.

They cut over two streets, then walked back in the direction from which he'd come. After another change of streets, they walked up the steps to a row house in the middle of the block. The door opened.

Sean stopped. "This isn't the address I was given." Immediately on guard, he covered himself in an air shield and poured power to his mental shields.

"We had to make sure you weren't followed. Brenna's waiting," the blonde woman said.

Brenna's mental voice in his head relaxed him, *It's okay, Sean. It's not a trap.*

Relieved, he entered the house.

"Thanks, Carly," Rebecca said, standing in the foyer. "Sean, hope you're doing well. If you'll come with me, please." He followed her down a hallway, taking several turns.

"Are you watching my ass?"

"Yes, ma'am."

"I'd think you'd learn."

"If you didn't want me to watch, you wouldn't wear your jeans so tight."

She chuckled. Opening a door, she showed him in and followed.

Brenna sat in a chair to the side of a large desk. A very large man with gray hair and beard sat behind it. Sean had never met Seamus O'Donnell, but it couldn't be anyone else. He sat in the offered seat, and uncomfortably watched Seamus.

Several minutes passed in silence.

"We've had an incident," Seamus said. "Lord John Gordon sent a team to kidnap succubi, and they invaded my home. I would like you to allow me into your mind so I can find out everything you know about this sorry business that's going on."

"Yes, sir," Sean said, dropping his shields. He knew Seamus didn't have to ask. There wasn't a person on the

139

planet who could keep the O'Donnell chief out of their mind.

He knew when Seamus entered his mind, but Seamus was so smooth that he didn't feel a thing. Over an hour later, Seamus withdrew.

"Thank you," Seamus said.

They invited him to stay for dinner, and afterward Rebecca led him to a room on the second floor.

"If you'd like some company tonight, let me know," she told him. "Someone will take you to the train in the morning."

He looked at her, eyes wide and mouth hanging open. "I thought you wanted to castrate me."

"You've changed. It's not just the construct. I can tell." She kissed him on the cheek, then walked away.

~~~

Chapter 11

*If you don't know where you are
going, you'll end up someplace
else.*
— *Yogi Berra*

Rebecca had primary responsibility for planning Brenna's trip to Ireland after the High Council meeting in April. After talking to Brenna's grandparents and their security, talking to Callie, and getting Brenna's ideas, the trip was planned to last two months. It would start with a week in London attending the meeting, then three weeks in Ireland, a tour through Amsterdam, Paris and Marseilles, ending with two weeks at Antonia's villa in Tuscany.

The first order of business was to send a team to Ireland to evaluate the O'Byrne and O'Donnell security capabilities there. No one had forgotten Lord Gordon or his unexplained campaign against succubi.

Antonia had some intelligence on that front. In addition to the money to be made by pimping exotic women, Gordon had lost a power struggle inside CBW and also lost a couple of large business deals, all to rivals with succubi working for them. He evidently felt eliminating that advantage would level the playing field.

Since both Seamus and Callie were going to London, the full resources and attention of Collin and Kallen were focused on their trip along with Brenna's. Adding in that Noel would be traveling from San Francisco, Todd Harwood from Dallas, and Caroline and Karen from the East Coast, Rebecca was just one of the security chiefs coordinating with Nigel in London.

The amount Rebecca was learning went far beyond what she had ever expected at her age. Between that, her training, and the normal security for Brenna's regular travel to Washington and Baltimore, she was falling into bed dead tired. She'd finally resorted to scheduling men to sleep with, glad the Protectors not only accepted her problem but seemed glad to help her out. She began to think about the advantages a steady boyfriend might bring to her life.

Her problem had made her life a living hell at times. As upset as she had been when Brenna explained the cause, it helped her come to grips with it and accept it. Her energy levels sliding out of balance were the cause of her undeniable urges. Understanding the problem finally allowed her to deal with them objectively.

Brenna and Irina had been helpful, learning along with her how to monitor her balances. As succubi, their skills with energy flows surpassed her own. They had been trying to find a way for her to shift the levels by herself, but so far it was out of reach. The discovery of how to prevent the succubi drain fueled Rebecca's faith that someday Brenna would figure it out.

Now she tried to arrange to have sex every night, knowing her cycle would allow her to get through the next day without any issues or loss of focus. That's where the scheduling came in. She hadn't slept in her own bed in over a month. She arranged for one of her friends to take her in each night and she visited her own room only to shower and dress, no matter which house they were staying in.

Although she didn't broadcast her problem to the world, for the first time since puberty, she felt as though she could face the world with pride in herself.

~~~

Brenna's travel party was a minor logistical nightmare. Past London, Rebecca would be solely responsible for the security of four succubi. She felt pretty good about her planning until she hit Paris. When she began to research hotels there and figure the costs for two weeks, she stopped, stunned at her calculations.

She went back and put all the costs for the trip, those not picked up by the Clan, into a spreadsheet. The total sent her into a state of despair. For thirty-six people, she was looking at hotel, food, and travel expenses of over two hundred thousand a week.

Callie, how much did the New York trip cost?

You don't want to know.

Yeah, I do. I'm working on the Ireland and Europe trip and I just can't accept the numbers I'm getting. Can I come see you?

She went down to Callie's office, where she was confronted with reality. The week in New York, not counting shopping, had run over two hundred thousand dollars.

"I need to figure out how to cut this down. It's just too much," Rebecca said.

"Rebecca, planes, hotels and restaurants are expensive, and when you add in all the personnel for security, the costs just balloon."

"Yeah, but I can't let her spend her money like this. I have to find a way to do it cheaper."

Callie looked thoughtful for a few moments then said, "Have you considered renting a house for your longer stays, like in Paris?"

"A house? You can rent a house for two weeks? It would have to be some house to hold this many people."

"Go see Antonia, tell her what you're trying to do and see what she thinks. She's lived all over Europe."

Rebecca called Antonia, and the next day drove to DC to meet with her. She showed the older succubus her problem and Antonia said she would make a few phone calls.

Less than twenty-four hours later, Antonia walked in with several sheets of paper. "Someone I know gave me a contact in Paris and I found this place for twelve thousand euros a week. It's on the southern outskirts of Paris, has twelve bedrooms in the main house, six bedrooms in the guest house and five bedrooms in the servant's quarters.

The family is on the Riviera for the spring and it's just sitting empty."

"Twelve thousand euros a week?" Rebecca squeaked.

"I'm sorry, is that too much? I don't know if I can ..." The rest of what she was going to say was cut off as Rebecca leaped from her chair and enveloped her in a bear hug.

"Oh God, Antonia, that's *great*. I've been looking at twelve thousand a *night*. And with a house, we can save on breakfast, maybe on some lunches. You're a life saver."

Antonia regarded the young, obviously flustered woman. "Have you ever done anything like this before?" Then a thought hit her, "Have you ever been to Europe before?"

Misery showed in Rebecca's eyes, "I don't even have a passport. I've never been out of the country before. I've only been on a plane once in my life."

"Il mia cara, do you need some help?" Antonia said, slipping partially into Italian as she often did.

"Well, Collin and Kallen are helping me. Sometimes. But they have their own stuff to do, and, well, sometimes they're kind of brief, and ..." she looked as though she was about to cry.

Antonia pulled up a chair. "Let's see what I can help you with. First, send an email to Callie telling her that you and Brenna and Irina need passports. I'm sure no one has thought of that simple item. Then tell me what you have and what you still need and we'll see what we can do to get it done."

Rebecca looked at her, face tight but trying to be strong and professional. "Thank you," one tear escaped and she brushed at it with her sleeve.

Antonia looked at Rebecca's preparations, then said, "Have you asked that man in London, what's his name, Nigel? Yes, Nigel, have you asked him about charter flights? Between Dublin and London and then from London to Amsterdam?"

"No, we're supposed to use our travel agency."

"Dear, you have thirty-six people and you're not shipping chickens. You have the most precious asset of the Clan in your charge. Send him an email. Ask about either O'Donnell aircraft or charter flights. Ask for his recommendation and get the costs. Also, ask if his travel people in London can recommend hotels in Amsterdam and travel to Paris. Then ask for recommendations for itinerary and hotels from Paris to Tuscany. Also, ask about a charter flight from Rome to Washington or New York."

"But I'm supposed to use the travel agency here. I'll get in trouble." The girl looked completely miserable.

Antonia came close to shedding tears herself. "Rebecca, you're arranging travel for Brenna, paying for it with Brenna's money, yes? Then, mia cuore, if anyone gives you any crap, tell them to take it up with Brenna."

Rebecca looked startled then smiled. "Yeah, let them deal with her. Antonia, that's brilliant."

Antonia nodded. "Our friend is very sweet, and very stubborn, isn't she? And very protective of you. If you do this and tell her you did it to save her money, and on my advice, do you really think Collin is going to put you in trouble?"

Smiling, Rebecca shook her head. "No one screws with Brenna. It's just not worth the grief."

Within a week, she had all her arrangements made and figured she'd cut well over half a million off the trip with Antonia's help and advice.

~~~

Brenna, Rebecca and Irina were spending a week in West Virginia relaxing and riding. Brenna also wanted to spend time with Collin. Callie found the young women in Brenna's room late one afternoon still wearing their riding

145

clothes and having a couple of beers. She set a stack of papers on the table, sorted them into three piles, and shoved a pile in front of each girl.

"There are a couple of things you need to sign and I need to explain a couple of things. Got an extra beer?"

Brenna jumped up and went to her fridge. "Light or dark?" She popped the top off and brought it to Callie.

"I'm a mother?" Rebecca asked, looking at the paper in front of her.

Callie smiled, "You and Brenna. I have plenty of time with Irina, but you're getting old enough you need to think about your future."

"I do?"

Brenna looked at the document sitting in front of her. "Aoife Brenna O'Donnell? Mother: Brenna Aoife O'Donnell? Callie, what is this?"

"In thirty or forty years, you ladies are going to need new identities. The easiest way to do that is set them up now. Then you can explain that your jealous bitch of a mother kept you locked in a closet all these years and you finally escaped when she died."

"Oh," Rebecca said brightly. "Yeah, that's a good place for kids. Thanks for the tip."

Irina piped up, "Why do I need two passports? And how do I rate an Irish one?"

"You especially need the Irish one," Callie said, "because Ireland is an EU country and that gives you the right to work in Europe. If you have to do any travel for Jayson, that will come in handy. The United States is not loved in some places. Traveling on an Irish passport may save you some grief. It also gives you access to Irish healthcare services. Only use the U.S. one to leave and enter this country and put it away safe the rest of the time.

"As to how you rate one, your grandmother was Irish, and with a statement from your great aunt, Siobhan's mother, I was able to establish your Irish citizenship. Brenna was born in Ireland, so hers was easy."

"I was? My birth certificate says I was born in West Virginia."

"Your parents smuggled you into the country as a baby and Dorothy signed a birth certificate to give you native status here. Rebecca, I had to take some liberties to establish your Irish citizenship. I made you Brenna's sister."

"Really?" She looked inside the green passport where her picture sat next to the name Aine O'Donnell. The birthdate was hers.

"If anyone asks, your parents were Jack and Maureen O'Donnell and you were born in Ballyshannon, Ireland."

"Where's that?"

"Where Seamus was born, County Donegal, we're going there," Brenna replied. "Where was I born?"

"At your grandparents' estate south of Dublin. Your mom plowed the north forty in the morning, popped you out at lunch, and plowed the south forty in the afternoon."

Rebecca choked on her beer, but managed to keep from spraying the table and the papers on it.

Brenna gave Callie a sour look.

"Almost," Callie told her. "Jack told me it was only an hour and twenty minutes from first contraction until she popped you out. Not me, fifteen hours with the first one and twelve with the second. I'd have given anything to have hips like yours."

Brenna chuckled and looked slyly at Irina, "You should reconsider that fetish you have for big men."

"Yeah," Rebecca chimed in, "You'll look really strange with a ten pound baby."

"You're the one who has to worry," Callie told her, "You've got hips like mine. Succubi can give birth to a water buffalo."

~~~

Rosie Thompson had become one of Brenna's close friends. An S-gene carrier, her sexual energies required balancing every three to four hours. It made her very popular among the men, to the religious Rosie's shame. Forty years old, she'd lived her entire life in the valley.

Noel Campbell, regional director in San Francisco, had posted a position as head of food service at his headquarters. Encouraged by Mrs. Doyle and Brenna, Rosie had applied and to her great surprise, Noel hired her. She came to see Brenna the next day.

"Brenna, I want to thank you for your recommendation, I hope I can live up to it and do the job."

"Rosie, Mrs. Doyle thinks you can do the job. All I did was tell Noel that you're a hard worker and a wonderful person and he'll be lucky to have you."

"Well, that's saying a lot. It's a big step for me, leaving the valley."

"You need to get out of here, need to be able to start fresh. Are you taking anyone with you?"

Rosie smiled, "Robbie's coming. You know, Robbie has probably asked me to marry him a hundred times, but I always said no because I didn't want him to have to live with my reputation. But I told him if he came with me I'd say yes."

Brenna jumped up and embraced her. "Oh, Rosie, I'm so happy for you. Congratulations!"

Rosie beamed. "Brenna, what I really came to talk to you about, well, I want to have a baby. When you told me what was really wrong with me, and that there's ways to keep my kids from having it, I talked to Callie, and she showed me how to pick an egg, you know, whether it has that gene or not. I can control that." She snorted, "Be the first thing about my life I've ever been able to control."

She sat down and said in a rush, "Brenna, I want to have a succubus. I want to have a daughter like you, like

Irina, a beautiful daughter, and if I pick the right man I can do it."

Brenna eyed her. "But Robbie isn't a carrier."

"No, he isn't, but he's okay with me having a baby with someone else. I told him, let me do this and I'll give you a son and a daughter that are normal, you let me do this and I'll love you till the day I die and I'll do anything for you. And Brenna, he loves me, he's always loved me, the fool. Ever since I took his virginity when he was fifteen he's followed me around like a motherless pup. Twenty years it's been, and it must be God's plan that we be together. So when I told him I wanted a succubus, he just smiled and told me that I could have a whole houseful if it made me happy." Her eyes misted. "He's such a good man. I should have said yes a long time ago."

"So who do you have in mind as the father?" Brenna asked timidly.

"Brenna, you know I was Collin's first, too, don't you? He's always been very kind to me, never made fun of me or said things behind my back. He never loved me, but he would help me out when I needed it, and I know for a fact he blacked more than one eye 'cause someone said somethin' about me.

"So that's what I came to ask you. 'Cause if it would cause you any upset, I'll just drop the whole idea. You've been so good to me, treated me like a friend. You know, I never really expected you to take me out, you bein' the Lord's granddaughter and all, but I had the time of my life goin' to DC with you and Rebecca. Damn, girl, you two know how to show someone a good time."

Brenna started to chuckle. "Rosie, why don't you just come out and say it? You've hinted like crazy that you want Collin to be the father."

Rosie turned scarlet red. "Uh, well, I, uh, I mean … I ain't never asked someone to screw their husband before. I mean, I've done it, and I ain't proud of it, but I couldn't do that to you if it would hurt you." Her West Virginia accent was becoming more pronounced the longer they talked.

Brenna got up and went to her sideboard. "Beer? Wine? Whiskey? I think I'll have a little fine Irish whiskey myself."

Rosie nodded and Brenna poured Midleton's into two glasses. Handing one to Rosie, she said, "This wouldn't be the first time you've done Collin since I moved here. Why are you asking me now?"

Taking a drink of her whiskey, Rosie squared her shoulders and looked up at her, "That was just fun, and I know both of you have fun. But this is different. Robbie would be her papa most all the time, but I'd want her real daddy to be part of her life, and I'd want her to know who her real daddy was. I want her to love Robbie, too, and I figure it's better for a girl to have two daddies than none at all. But Brenna, if it would cause you any hurt at all, God, girl, I'd crawl across broken glass rather than hurt you."

"You don't know who your father is, do you, Rosie?"

"No, my mama never told me. Had to be someone with that S-gene 'cause my mama ain't got it."

Brenna put her arms around her and drew her into an embrace. "Rosie, you have no idea how much it means to me for you to say that you wouldn't want to hurt me," she whispered into the shorter woman's hair. "If Collin is willing, then the both of you have my blessing, and you and your daughter will always be welcome in my house."

Rosie's eyes filled with tears, "Thank you."

"Don't thank me for anything, you still need to talk to him, and don't you tell him you and I talked. If he's going to be a daddy, it'll be because he wants to."

That evening when she and Collin went to bed, he said, "Brenna, I need to talk to you about something."

"Oh? Sounds important when you put it that way."

"Do you want to have children?"

"Are we talking about making a baby tonight? I want to have children, and I want to have them with you, but Collin, I'm nowhere near ready yet."

He chuckled, "No, I wasn't talking about tonight, but I was wondering if you knew when you wanted them."

She frowned at him, "Another decade or two. Do you mind telling me what this is about?"

"Am I the only man you want to have children with?"

Brenna took a deep breath and thought for a minute, carefully weighing her answer. "Collin, I want to have a lot of babies, spaced out, maybe two or three litters over sixty or eighty years. I've thought about this quite a bit, actually, and I want to have the first one with you, and the second one with Noel. And after that, I want to give you a son."

He smiled, "I assume the first two will be succubi?"

She nodded.

"Brenna, Rosie asked me today if I'd help her make a baby, a succubus."

"And what did you say?"

"That I'd have to talk to you about it, and if you were okay with it, I'd be honored, and if it caused you any discomfort at all, then the answer would be no."

"Come here, Mr. Doyle," she pulled him to her and kissed him until he pulled her down, rolled on top of her, and plunged into her, causing her to break the kiss with a gasp. He drove her over the top repeatedly.

When he finally spilled in her and they lay together panting, she said, "Make a good baby with her, Collin. Make her happy. And don't you ever let her or her daughter sorry you did, you hear me? It's a lifetime commitment to that little girl, and I'll cut them off if you don't do it right."

"I take it that's a yes?"

"It's a very definite yes, if that's what you want to do. Are you sure Robbie's okay with this?"

"Yeah, I know he is. As long as Rosie's happy, Robbie's happy. I haven't seen him so happy since we were kids."

~~~

Brenna and Irina were lying on her bed. She could feel the sexual tension in Irina, maybe not so much sexual, but rather a need to touch, to be closer to her. Irina was playing with Brenna's hair.

"Do you think I should grow mine out? Like yours?"

"I don't know," Brenna said, looking at Irina's shoulder-blade length golden locks. "It's an incredible pain to take care of, and you're so beautiful with it at that length. Why would you want to?"

"I just always hear people talk about your hair, how beautiful it is, how unique."

"Irina, don't grow it out. Men who like blondes aren't going to like you any better with it longer. You're perfect, Irina. If I was a man I'd go for you, not me."

"But you're not a man."

"No, I'm not. And I'm totally hetero."

"Yeah, I know. Does it bother you that I love you?"

Brenna thought about her answer for a while. She hadn't been ready for that statement. "Bother me? No, I'm flattered. I worry about hurting you." She sighed, "I've always worried that you'd tell me, and I'd say I don't love you in that way and that you'd be hurt."

Irina sat up and turned to look at her. "I'm not hurt, I know how you feel. I've always been afraid that if I told you, you wouldn't want me as a friend anymore. You're not mad? You aren't going to push me away? We can still be friends?"

Brenna reached up and pulled the smaller woman down, cradling her head against her shoulder. "How could I be mad that someone loves me? It's the greatest compliment you can get. I do love you. I'm just not

152

sexually attracted to you. You're beautiful, you're sweet, and I love you to death, but I don't want to screw you."

Irina sighed happily. "As long as you'll be my friend, and cuddle me like this, I'm happy. Thank you." She wriggled a little closer, and they lay like that for a long time, not speaking, just feeling each other's bodies and emotions.

Brenna reflected on how easy something she had been afraid of had worked out.

Irina asked, "Have you ever thought about taking money for it?"

"Sure, people tell me I could make a living as a succubus. A man offered me ten thousand dollars to go to bed with him once, before I knew what I was, before I met the family. I turned him down, but I think about it sometimes."

"Siobhan tells me I can make a lot of money in New York, like five thousand, ten thousand a night. I think about it. I mean, what's the difference between screwing strangers for free and screwing them for money?"

Brenna was quiet for a space then said, "Yeah, I wonder that, too. I guess I've always had a fear people would call me a whore. You know, in the society we grew up in, that's the worst thing people can think. You're a terrible person if you screw a lot of men for free, but you're a criminal if any of them give you money." Her face took on a look of distaste, "On the other hand, it's pretty much accepted if you're young and pretty and you can con an old rich man into supporting you. Weird."

Rebecca knocked on the door then entered when Brenna called out. She walked over to the bed and sat on it, not showing any surprise at the two women lying in each other's arms. "What's up? Can I have a beer?"

She went and got a beer, offering the others one. When they declined, she said, "Really, what's the deep discussion you've got going?"

"Rebecca," Brenna asked, "Have you ever thought about taking money for it?"

"Hmmm … interesting question. You know, when I was so uptight about being a slut, I still felt moral because I wasn't a whore. Isn't that strange? You talk to Siobhan and she'll tell you the condemnation of women selling their bodies is only because men don't want to pay for it. They want you to give it away. It makes sense. I really don't know what the difference is between doing strangers for free and charging them for it except the label."

Irina spoke up, "What about Solstice Night? What we did? What we were expected to do? How did you feel about that?"

Brenna considered, "I felt like I was playing a part, like an actress. Siobhan and Cindy say we're the celebrities, the rock stars of telepath society. Well, that's what I felt like. I was cast in a role, and I played it. I wonder if that's how my mother viewed it. From what I've heard, she screwed men for money, she screwed men for her own pleasure, and she screwed my dad for love. Either she was very good at hiding her feelings or she didn't have a conflict between those things."

"I just wonder if I'd feel different if someone was paying me. I wonder if I'd feel guilty or dirty or something," Irina said. "I was trying to count, the other night. I lost my virginity at thirteen, and I don't have any idea how many men I've been with. I don't even have a cheap necklace or pair of earrings to show for it."

~~~

Late that night, Brenna called Nigel, catching him first thing in the morning in London. "I hope I didn't call before you had your morning tea," she teased.

"Not at all, and it's coffee, just so you know. Actually, I've been up since four, the German bourse is doing strange things. So what's up? Just called to tell me you love me?"

154

She laughed, "You know I love you. As soon as Collin unties me from the bedpost I'll fly into your arms."

He returned her laughter, "The bounder, tell him I'm terribly displeased."

"Nigel, I have a rather strange question. I hope you won't be shocked or take it amiss."

He laughed, "Brenna, without any disrespect to your beauty or intellect, you're rather young and I've been working with Siobhan for a long time. I doubt you can shock me."

"Well, Irina and I were talking, you know, just speculating, and I was wondering if you know anyone who runs a high-end brothel or escort service …"

"And you were wondering what it might feel like to do it professionally?"

"Yes, that's what we were talking about."

"It so happens our main operative in Amsterdam, mine and Collin's, does run a high-end brothel, one of the most exclusive in Europe. Would you like me to make a discreet inquiry for you? What are we talking about, one night?"

"Yes, just one night. If you could, I'd be interested in finding out."

"Sure, I can ask Margriet if she'd like to market a succubus or two as a special. Would you mind sending me pictures of you and Irina? They don't have to be sexy ones. Just so she can see how beautiful you are."

"I can send a couple tomorrow and sexy isn't a problem. I can take pictures of us. Nigel, I don't know if I'm really willing to go through with something like this or if Irina is. We were just talking, you know? But I am curious."

"Send me the pictures, Brenna. I'll be discreet and I won't promise anything."

"Thanks, Nigel."

The next day, she spoke with Irina, then borrowed one of Callie's cameras that wasn't too complicated to operate.

She and Irina put on corsets, took pictures of each other and sent them to Nigel.

~~~

Standing in the middle of the room, Brenna turned to Collin with a lecherous smile. "Want to see some of the other things I've been practicing?" She teleported his pants to the top of the sideboard, and followed them with the rest of his clothes. More comfortable with her own clothes, she teleported all of them off at once.

He laughed. "Any other new tricks?"

"Not one I've practiced, but one I've wanted to try. Have you ever made love to another telekinetic? Do you think it would work to do it in mid-air?"

He floated up off the floor. "No, I've never tried it, but I'm game."

It was an interesting experiment, one that had both of them laughing as they tried several positions and discovered issues with keeping in synch with each other. They did manage to make it work until they reached their climax. That broke their concentration and they ended up in a tangle of limbs on the floor laughing. "Next time, we try it over the bed," Collin gasped.

~~~

Chapter 12

The two women exchanged the kind
of glance women use when no knife
is handy. - Ellery Queen

The flight to London was fun. Brenna discovered both
Rebecca and Irina had flown only once before and she
ensured they got window seats. Callie insisted Brenna take
one as well, and all three spent the time flying over Ireland
and England with their noses pressed against the glass.

The Council meetings were scheduled until three in the
afternoon, Monday through Thursday. Brenna was jealous
that her friends were free to sightsee and explore the city
while she was forced to attend the meetings. While Irina,
Rebecca, Siobhan and Antonia toured London, she had to
listen to boring presentations by each of the regional
managers for the first two days.

The bright spot, in Brenna's estimation, was meeting
Aislinn O'Rourke, regional director in Melbourne,
Australia. The Oceana region was the largest in area and
smallest in personnel. The office had been open only a
year. A forty year-old Oxford graduate and native of
Dublin, Aislinn had blazing red hair, a pale, clear
complexion, emerald green eyes, and a fit, curvy body. She
was very pretty but seemed very tired.

Her region seemed to be the only area of the company
that was struggling. Aislinn hadn't been to the holiday
gatherings at the estate. When they broke for the day,
Brenna sought her out and asked if she'd like to go for a
drink.

"So you're the new heir. I've been hoping to meet
you," Aislinn said wearily.

"I wasn't aware that had been decided yet."

157

"It's just a formality. Callie wants out and you're a convenient excuse. Everyone is tired of fighting her on it."

"It sounds as though you're tired of fighting a lot of things. What's going on in your area? Do we need a stronger manager there?"

Anger flared in Aislinn's eyes. "There's nothing wrong with my abilities. I could take any of the other offices and do as good a job as is being done there now."

"Oh? It sounded to me as though you were whining in there."

"Is that why you asked me out? To beat me up? To show me how smart you are?"

"No, I wanted to ask you what's really wrong, find out what it is you need that they aren't giving you, and to piss you off and see what you're made of. But I didn't ask you out for a drink to beat you up. There's something wrong that you're not saying, and I want to know what it is."

The redhead searched her face and probed her shields. Surprising her, Brenna dropped her first three shields and let her see inside her mind. "Good God! Oh … Oh my God …"

After a few minutes, Aislinn heaved a deep sigh, withdrew from Brenna's mind and took a drink of her beer. "You're scary. Jesus Christ you're scary. Do you have any idea …? Oh hell, of course you don't."

A bruised look appeared in Brenna's eyes, "People say that. I don't mean to be."

Hurriedly, Aislinn reassured her, "I don't mean I'm afraid of you, but your potential, what you're capable of, and I mean that in a good way, is incredible. Brenna, I'm going to trust you because I think you really want to help me, but if you ever think I'm in your way, let me know and I'll move.

"To make a long story short, Australia and New Zealand are small countries, not in land, but in population. Our Oceana operation will never be a major one like New

York or London or Hong Kong but there are a lot of natural resources in the area, raw materials that can feed other operations worldwide. What I need are human resources. I have a good core team, but there's no population to draw on. I can't even fill a position for an accountant, and the position has been vacant for six months."

"What about wilders?"

"Shit, what do you think I have now? Only twenty of my hundred employees came from the Clan or from other Clans. I've scoured for wilders and I've about tapped out. Besides, the learning curve for them is high and I don't have enough people to truly make up a society. We live with norms for the most part. It's like being in exile."

A bit of discrete questioning of various people revealed that Aislinn had been one of two candidates for that post. Callie and Jill had favored the other one, but Seamus had overruled them.

That evening, she sought out Antonia and presented her with the problem, hoping the older woman might have some suggestions.

"Brenna, sometimes there aren't any creative, innovative answers. And other times the answer is brute force. You say the west coast and Hong Kong are growing? Why aren't they including Australia in their plans?"

"We seem to have tunnel vision. Noel's operation in San Francisco is growing but there are almost a thousand Clan members in the Pacific Northwest and we don't have any facilities there. None of them work for the Clan."

"Then tell Aislinn to move her operations to Seattle. Set up a Seattle-Melbourne office. Market to Oceana, pull natural resources from there, but have the majority of her workforce in Seattle."

Brenna stared at her and then started laughing. "Interesting. Thanks Antonia."

The following day's meetings were primarily concerned with business planning and projections for the ensuing year. Brenna pulled Aislinn aside at lunch and explained her idea.

"They wouldn't let me," Aislinn said. "I've been assigned Oceana and the west coast is Noel's."

"I'm not saying you should pull out of Oceana, I'm saying you should expand into Seattle, especially for the business functions you can't find people for in Australia. Continue developing markets in your core region and developing the raw resources, but there are five times as many Clan members in Seattle as you have in all of Australia and Noel isn't doing anything with Seattle. He's focused on Tokyo."

Aislinn shook her head. "I understand what you're saying and it makes sense. It would take time to develop, though, and I don't have any allies that would support me."

"You will tomorrow."

Aislinn stared at her, understanding growing in her eyes. "You really think it would work?"

"I don't know. I think giving it a shot and finding out might be more productive than banging your head against the wall."

"And you'd support me if I made such a proposal?"

"I'm not suggesting that you make any proposal. I read somewhere that it's easier to get forgiveness than permission, and in my experience that's true. I'll make a proposal to spend my time attempting to help you straighten things out. They're all aware that I know nothing about business. They'll see it as a way to have someone other than them, namely you, train me. But I can request resources, which they'll give me as a sop."

Aislinn's eyes widened as Brenna spoke. "Some people think you'll be a puppet when Seamus retires. Succubus, scientist, young and not interested in the real world. I think they're in for a big surprise."

Brenna was silent for several minutes, her eyes unfocused. Then she asked, "What would happen to

Australia if there was a nuclear war in the northern hemisphere?"

"Probably nothing. We'd be cut off, but it wouldn't affect us. No trade, but the country is pretty self-sufficient," Aislinn said.

"Is land available there?"

Aislinn laughed, "That's the major thing they have."

That evening she asked Collin to run a database search on Clan and other known telepaths in the Pacific Northwest. She asked for all information about them, Gifts, education, job history, personal history. His search returned one thousand twenty-two adults in Washington and Oregon. What she hadn't expected was for him to expand her search parameters a little. It turned out there were another five hundred seventeen adults in Vancouver. He sent the file to her account and she took him to bed and thanked him.

~~~

With her party separated, Rebecca needed security for the three succubi playing tourist and another team to cover Brenna. Jeremy volunteered for Brenna duty, saying he had been to London many times. Rebecca suspected that a pretty brunette who was helping Nigel with the conference might have something to do with Jeremy's willingness to sit through boring meetings all day. When he showed up with the woman on his arm for breakfast on the second morning, she considered her suspicions confirmed.

Rebecca and Carly took a team of eight Protectors with them. Each of the succubi had two assigned to them and the others floated at the periphery of their group. The first day, they took the Tower of London tour, walked along the Thames, rode the Big Eye, and generally played tourist. A history major in college, Rebecca was in heaven. Irina's father was English, but she'd never been out of the U.S. She bounced around like a leprechaun on meth, laughing and skipping and trying to look at everything at once.

At one point, Irina flung herself at Siobhan, hugging the taller woman around the waist, and said, "Thank you so much for rescuing me. If I'd taken that job at the UN I'd be listening to a bunch of boring speeches right now."

The second day they took brief tours of Westminster and Parliament, then ate lunch outside along the river. In the afternoon they went shopping at Harrods. On the third day, they hit the British Museum. Rebecca could have spent a week there, but there was so much more the others wanted to see, Piccadilly, Leister Square, Trafalgar Square, Buckingham Palace and more.

Walking through Leister Square, they heard a woman shout in French, "My purse. Stop. That thief has my purse."

Looking around, Rebecca saw a young man running toward her clutching a woman's handbag. He dodged around her. She stuck out one long leg and the man flew through the air, skidding along the sidewalk when he landed. Pouncing on him, she grabbed the purse.

He twisted away from her and a knife flashed in his right hand. Without stopping to think, she spun and landed a roundhouse kick to the side of his head. Making no attempt to break his fall, he crashed face first on the street with a sickening crunch. Reaching out for his mind, she discovered Carly had already captured him.

"You know, you don't have to get physical," Carly said, shaking her head. "Learn to reach for your Talents first."

A middle-aged woman rushed up. Looking at Rebecca, she spoke in halting English, "Thank you," she pointed to the purse, "that mine."

Rebecca smiled and handed it to her. Speaking in French, she said, "You're quite welcome, Madame. I didn't think it was his, it didn't match his shoes."

The woman laughed, and launched into a long explanation in French of what had happened. At that point, two policemen showed up, and it took half an hour to sort

162

things out. The thief proclaimed his innocence and accused Rebecca of beating him up for no reason. Of course, none of the witnesses agreed with him. Irina, Siobhan and Rebecca all translated for the French tourist, often at the same time, and in spite of one of the policemen telling them several times that he spoke French. The poor policemen looked like they were about to lose their minds. Finally, they made a decision and the thief, bloody and scraped, was arrested.

Their party started to gather themselves when a woman holding a pencil, paper and electronic recorder stepped in front of Rebecca.

"I'm Dorothy Spalding, Daily Telegraph. That was a very brave thing you did."

Rebecca blushed, then registering that the woman in front of her was with a newspaper, her eyes widened in panic. *Carly! She's a reporter. What do I do?*

Carly was several feet away with her back to Rebecca. She whipped around and took in the scene in a glance. Although twenty years older than her friend, she hadn't been in such a situation either.

Smiling sweetly, Siobhan stepped between Rebecca and the reporter.

"She joost did wha' any gud Chrristian wou'ha doon in herr place," Siobhan said in a thick North Irish accent, "prrotected th' innocent frra' a' English brrigand." She took Rebecca by the arm and whipped her away from the reporter, walking away down the street.

We need to do something about your accent, Siobhan sent on a thread. *You, Brenna and Irina are traveling on Irish passports, but the minute you open your mouths, you're instantly identifiable as Yanks.*

That evening, Siobhan implanted small constructs with Irish accents in her three young friends.

~~~

163

Brenna had heard rumors that part of the reason Collin went to London so often when she'd first met him had to do with a lady who lived there. Rebecca, who was a gossip database, said they'd been in a relationship for over two years before Brenna came along.

Their third morning in London, Brenna eyed Collin with a lascivious grin, "I heard there's a pretty blonde you're rather fond of here. Have you seen her?"

"Pia? Yeah, I've seen her."

"Would you like to spend some time with her? I wouldn't mind."

He came out of the bathroom, took her in his arms and said, "Okay, Brenna, what's up? Do you have someone you want to spend time with?"

"Well, I would like to spend a little time with Nigel and Noel. You know, keep on friendly terms, network a little."

He laughed. "Network? Is that what you're calling it now?"

She blushed.

"Brenna, yes, I would like to spend some time with Pia, thank you for asking," he said with a chuckle. "But Saturday you're all mine. I'm taking you out to see the sights and I have theater tickets."

"You do? Great! I love you so much!" She kissed him, and one thing led to another and they were late going down for breakfast.

"I would like to meet her," Brenna said when they finally made it downstairs. "Will you introduce me?"

He led her across the room where the breakfast buffet was laid out. As they approached a group of three women, it became very obvious which one was Pia.

"Pia Lindstrom, I'd like you to meet Brenna O'Donnell."

Pia Lindstrom was six feet tall, around thirty years old though looking twenty, and gloriously blonde. Brenna wondered why she was in London instead of doing photo shoots as a member of the Swedish national bikini team.

"I'm so pleased to meet you," Brenna gushed. "Collin's told me so much about you."

Collin's face reddened.

"I'm pleased to meet you, too," Pia said, looking down her nose and hesitating before shaking Brenna's outstretched hand.

Brenna looked the tall woman up and down. "I'm sure you have many admirable qualities, but it's easy to see why he was first attracted to you."

Pia coldly replied, "I think I could say the same about you."

"And I'd take it as a compliment," Brenna smiled broadly. Almost reluctantly, a smile spread across Pia's face.

"I do hope we have a chance to chat while I'm here," Brenna said. "I'm sure we have a lot in common. Well, have to run. Collin, have a good time."

She picked up a glass of orange juice and crossed the room to where Nigel was pouring himself a cup of tea. "Do you have plans this evening?"

"Not unless you have plans for me," he smiled.

"Actually, I was hoping we could have a drink after dinner."

"I'd like that. I'd like that a lot."

On their way into the small auditorium where the Council met, she caught Noel's arm. "When are you going home?"

"On Sunday." He looked at Collin talking with Pia. "Do you have some time?"

"I was hoping you'd be free tomorrow night," she replied.

"Dinner? I know a nice place I think you'd like." They made a date.

~~~

After finishing the agenda right after lunch, Seamus asked if anyone had any new business to present to the Council. Callie stood.

"As you all know, I reluctantly accepted the designation as my father's heir after my brother died. At that time, there didn't appear to be another viable candidate. Events over the past year have caused me to reevaluate that, and so I am withdrawing my bid to succeed my father. Mr. Chairman, I propose that Brenna Aoife O'Donnell, your granddaughter, be named heir, to succeed you as chief of Clan O'Donnell."

Caroline and Karen both shot to their feet and Seamus recognized Caroline. "I second the motion."

"Miss MacIntyre, did you have something to say?" Seamus asked.

"I was going to second, but instead I would like to speak in favor of the motion," Karen replied.

In short order, Nigel, Noel and Jill rose, saying they also wished to speak in favor. Then William, with a look at Jill, rose. "Mr. Chairman, I would also like to speak in favor of the motion." Several gasps were heard from various parts of the room.

After Callie presented her reasons for nominating Brenna, the others took their turns, speaking of her in glowing terms. Finally, William rose to speak.

"I'd like to tell you a story about my boats," he began. Several groans were heard. "When I met Brenna at Thanksgiving, I asked to meet with her privately, and we had tea for about two hours. During that time, I asked her a few questions about her background, her views, and tried to get a picture of how she saw the world and her place in the Clan. But mostly, I talked about my boats. I talked about them for probably an hour and a half." Chuckles were heard.

"Brenna," he turned to her, "how many boats do I have, what kind, and how big are they?"

"A thirty-two foot sailboat and a thirty-five foot motor launch," she replied.

"And what was the last thing I told you at the end of our meeting?"

"That the boats were the second-most important thing in your life, after your family."

"Now, ladies and gentlemen, I defy any of you to tell me you would have still been paying attention after two hours of listening to me prattle on about my damn boats. I was beginning to bore myself."

Laughter erupted.

He turned to Brenna again, "What I learned that day was that while you might not agree with me, and I'm sure you don't on the wilder issue, you will listen to me. That, and you have the patience of Job." More laughter. "All I've ever asked of anyone here was to listen, and give me and my ideas a fair hearing. I'll follow someone who includes my input in her decisions, even if it's a decision I don't agree with. I've followed Seamus all my life, and there's not much we agree on, except our devotion to the Clan. But I know he listens to me with respect. I cast my vote to name Brenna the heir."

He sat down, and Brenna sent him a spear thread, *You were sandbagging me!*

Yes, and let that be a lesson, the easiest disguise to assume is that of a fool.

Lesson learned, thank you.

Brenna, Seamus is not a fool. Some people think I got my position by nepotism. But Seamus would keep an idiot close where he couldn't do any damage, not stick him out in the middle of nowhere to build a base on a continent we know so little about.

Second lesson learned.

I look forward to working with you, Lady O'Donnell.

The proposal was ratified unanimously.

Brenna rose to speak, "In fifty years, when I make a decision you don't agree with, or ask you to do something you don't want to do, remember that I didn't ask for this. But I will take my duty, my responsibility, seriously. I'm young, but Seamus says that's curable." Laughter.

"I am willing to listen and learn. I know the world in one hundred years will be vastly different, just as today is different from a hundred years ago, when Seamus' vision built this Clan into the power it is today."

She slowly scanned the faces of those in the audience. "I'm a very democratic sort of girl. I'll always listen, and I'm not afraid to change my mind. I've been wrong a lot, and I'm just getting started. I'm sure I'll get better at being wrong with practice." A ripple of soft laughter rewarded her comment. "But make no mistake. I'm an O'Donnell. When the decisions are made, I expect everyone to get on board. If you expect someone who's easier to manipulate than Seamus, I suggest you rearrange your expectations."

Letting a smile light her face, she assumed a low Glam. "Of course, since Seamus is going to live to three hundred, you probably won't have to deal with me for a long time." A ripple of laughter ran through the audience at the dismayed expression on Seamus' face.

Brenna's smile and Glam died. Her voice changed from silver bells to a cold north wind. The temperature in the room dropped noticeably. "I'm young, I'm naïve, and woefully ignorant in many areas. It's up to you to educate me. But don't ever think you can get away with ignoring me. I'll do everything in my power to earn your respect, but if you want mine, remember it's a two-way street."

Seamus looked around the room. With the exception of those who already knew her well, the look in their eyes was astonishment and wariness.

He chuckled, then spoke, "As she said, she is an O'Donnell."

The room warmed and Brenna resumed with a smile, "I've listened carefully to everything that's been said here the past few days. I'm very eager to start learning my new role, and I hope I can contribute to what you're doing very soon." She saw some people start to look a bit uneasy.

"It seems most of our operations are doing very well, but there are a few areas that could use some new ideas. I think I have a lot to offer, and sometimes a new perspective can work wonders. I mean, the same old stodgy business stuff can always use an enthusiastic boost, right?" The uneasiness spread.

"I think that, with the Council and Lord O'Donnell's permission, I'd like to lend a hand to our Australian operation to start, if that's all right."

Relief was palpable. She was soon promised a budget as Vice-Chair and a member of the Executive Committee, and a small staff. Those resources could be used to study the issues in Australia and she would have a free rein in trying out new solutions to help poor Aislinn solve her problems. Brenna made a note to herself to use some of that budget to hire a travel coordinator to take some of the burden off Rebecca.

I don't believe you pulled that off, Aislinn sent her.

After the meeting, she approached Aislinn. "Check your inbox. Collin found over fifteen hundred Clan members in the Pacific Northwest."

William sauntered over. "What have you got up your sleeve?"

Brenna smiled at him, "Uncle William, I don't have any idea what you mean."

"Don't bat your eyes at me. That was quite a performance."

"You're not the only one who can sandbag," Brenna said with a wink.

"So I see. Aislinn, if there's anything I can do to help, let me know."

Brenna stood on her tiptoes and kissed his cheek. "You wouldn't know any accountants that might like to relocate to Melbourne, do you?"

He smiled, "I might have a couple of resumes I could send over. Do you know if your friend Rebecca is busy tonight?"

"I'm not her social secretary, but the last I heard she was hopelessly dateless."

There's nothing hopeless about that girl," he grinned, "but if she's not feeling too picky, I can remedy her dateless condition."

As he walked away, Aislinn said, "Where did that come from?"

Brenna gave her a crooked grin. "Don't ally yourself too closely with him, but I think there's a lot more there than most people think. South Africa isn't that far away from Australia, is it? You don't suppose that two suppliers of natural raw materials might have some synergies, do you?"

Brenna smiled and batted her eyelashes, "Don't you love that word, 'synergy'? I read about it in a book Callie loaned me." Aislinn about fell over laughing.

~~~

During cocktails before dinner, Seamus approached Brenna. "What are you and Aislinn cooking up? She looked a little too happy to have your help when you were going out of your way to scare the pants off everyone else."

"Why do you think that?" Brenna gave him her best wide-eyed, innocent look. "No one else seems to have that impression."

"Brenna …," he eyed her with that 'don't bullshit me' expression she was becoming familiar with, his head slightly cocked to the side, one eyebrow raised and his lips pursed.

She smiled. "Well, except Uncle William. I think he suspects something. We're going to annex Portland, Seattle and Vancouver."

He stared at her, mouth open.

"Grandfather, did you know there are over fifteen hundred Clan members living in the Pacific Northwest? No? Collin ran a database search for me. And not a single one of them works for the Clan. I don't think Noel knows that either. He's more interested in Tokyo and getting in Jill's pants. Aislinn needs human resources, right? Well ..."

He looked at her for a long minute, then said, "I'd appreciate occasional updates. Informally of course." He walked away chuckling to himself.

~~~

Chapter 13

*...when she has on her clothes her
face is wondrous fair, and when
she has taken them off her whole
body appears as fair as her face. -
Lucian, Dialogues of the
Courtesans*

She met Nigel and he took her to a pub. Nigel
Richardson was an elegant man, sixty years old and looking
a boyish thirty-five, a trim six feet tall with immaculately
styled sandy blonde hair. He favored tailored Saville Row
suits and drove a Jaguar. Cambridge educated, he was as
far from Collin's homespun, laid-back West Virginia
approach to life as London was from the estate.

He told her he'd been living on the streets by his wits
and his Talents when he made the mistake of trying to pick
the pocket of a tall, gray haired gentleman one evening.
Seamus had captured him, cleaned him up, put him in an
Irish boarding school run by telepaths, and then sent him to
Cambridge. His loyalty was as fierce and complete as any
of Seamus' children.

"As you might guess, William's attitude toward
wilders falls a bit flat with me," Nigel said.

"Do you remember your parents at all?"

"My mum, she was a drunken whore, and I have no
idea who my father might have been."

"What bothers you most, that she was a drunk, or that
she was a whore?" Brenna leaned forward, anxious to hear
his answer.

He sighed. "I shouldn't have used that word. Not that
way, at least. Yes, she was a prostitute, but the drinking
was the real problem. Now that I'm older, and with
Seamus' help and the counseling I received at the boarding
school, I know the drinking was probably due to her not

knowing how to shield. It's a common problem with wilders."

He reached out and touched her hand.

"Brenna, I've been working with Siobhan the past twenty-five years, and knowing her has demanded an adjustment to my attitudes. I respect her immensely, as I do you. I don't consider a woman taking money from men who are eager to spend it a crime. With my mother, the money all went to booze. We lived in squalid conditions and she had absolutely no respect for herself.

"Most of the street prostitutes are in that situation, doing what they do out of desperation. It's entirely different from what Siobhan does, or any of the high-end escorts and courtesans I've known. Siobhan doesn't need to sell herself, rather she does it with a sense of joy."

"So how did you feel when I asked you to set me up with Margriet?"

"A flash that you're better than that, and then shame at the thought. Margriet herself is a succubus and has worked for the family since Callie recruited her in the sixties. Margriet would never take you on long-term. She finds wilders sometimes, trains them, but also insists they get an education. If they want to continue in the profession, she elevates them to an escort service she runs. The girls in the house are all norms, but beautiful and sophisticated. She pays well and treats them with respect. I have to admit, if I was a woman, a norm, coming from my background and with no education or skills, it would be tempting to make five thousand euros a week rather than five hundred working as a filing clerk."

"So, you'll still respect me if I sell myself?"

"Yes," he smiled. "I understand your curiosity. One thing Siobhan told me is she meets a better quality of man by setting her price high, men who treat her with respect, take her to dinner and can hold an interesting conversation.

173

The difference between that and draining men she picks up in a bar, well, if it were me, I'd prefer the finer gentleman."

"Irina wants to try it, and the more I think about it, the more curious I get."

"Well, I can tell you those pictures you sent have Margriet salivating. If you give the go ahead, she plans on offering you as a special, one night only, experience-of-a-lifetime deal to select customers. The prices she's talking about are astronomical."

"How much?"

"Twenty-five thousand euros for an hour."

Brenna was shocked. "Men will pay that kind of money to screw me?"

"So she says."

"Jesus, that's incredible."

"We're talking about the kind of men who think nothing of spending five hundred euros on a bottle of wine, or fifty million on a yacht. They have so much money that they measure their enjoyment by how much they spend."

"You have our itinerary, set it up."

They went back to the hotel and made love, with her feeding him his energy back. In a passionate hurry, he bent her over the back of the couch in his suite. She asked to change positions and they finished with her sitting on the back of the couch with her arms and legs wrapped around him.

Some time later, they came together again in a slow and gentle horizontal dance on the bed. Their third time, she mounted him and teased him with her muscles, barely moving on top of him while he worshiped her breasts with his hands and his mouth. She kept him just short of his climax for a very long time and when he finally exploded, the moment was delicious for both of them.

~~~

Collin and Pia came in the next morning early while Brenna was eating breakfast. He looked satisfied and

174

relaxed. She was happy and smiling until she saw Brenna, her smile fading. Brenna waved at them, and Collin, not seeing Pia's reaction, steered them to where she sat with Rebecca.

"Good morning, I hope you're doing well," she greeted them.

"It's a lovely day," he replied, "what are your plans today?"

"We're going out to see Windsor Castle this morning, then Oxford this afternoon. I'm having dinner with Noel this evening." She turned to Pia, "Do you have to work today?"

Startled, Pia answered, "No, I was planning on taking the day off."

"Is Seamus cutting you loose today?" she asked Collin.

"Yes, he and Callie are teleporting to Ireland to visit Lord O'Neill, so I have the day free."

"My great-uncle," Brenna mused, "I'm supposed to meet him while I'm there. Well, that's nice, isn't it? What are your plans? Are you going anywhere?"

"Pia and I are going riding and then dinner at a place she likes."

"What time do you want to meet up tomorrow?"

"Breakfast, about this time?"

Pia stood there, uncomfortably listening to this pleasant conversation and aware of so many people watching her. Brenna reached out and touched her hand. Meeting the tall blonde's eyes, she said, "It's okay, Pia. Have a good time, okay? I don't own him."

When they moved off to a table of their own, Rebecca said in a low voice, "It's never going to be okay. She loves him, head over heels in love, and sharing isn't on her agenda."

"Yes, I know. You can see it in her eyes. I'm going to try and catch her before I leave and talk with her, but I

175

don't know if there's anything I can say to make her feel any better."

After four days of boring meetings, Brenna enjoyed getting out in the English countryside and she approached her first trip to a castle with the enthusiasm of a child. Their itinerary was tight, and they didn't get to spend as much time at Windsor as she would have liked. She took pictures with the camera Callie had loaned her for the trip and vowed that the next time she would schedule a whole day to enjoy the castle.

Again, their time in Oxford was too short, and traveling with so many people was a bit uncomfortable on the narrow, crowded streets. She could have spent a whole day in Blackstone's bookstore alone.

"I hope you're enjoying yourself," Brenna told Rebecca.

Startled, Rebecca said, "Yeah, I am. Aren't you?"

Brenna grinned, "Just checking, because I want to do this all again, only slower."

Relaxing, Rebecca returned her grin. "Not a problem. I could spend a week here in Oxford. I wonder if there are tours of the libraries at the colleges."

Giving her a small puff of pheromones and watching her nostrils dilate, Brenna walked away with an exaggerated swish of her butt. "I'm sure we can get into any library you want to."

Laughing, Rebecca followed her.

Arriving back in London, she had to hurry to shower and dress for her date with Noel. He took her to a Russian restaurant, a new cuisine experience for her. Irina, sitting at a table across the room with Rebecca, Antonia and Siobhan, was happily explaining the menu to the other women.

"You don't have a lot of privacy, do you?" Noel observed.

"With fifty Protectors covering this restaurant, no, not really. After being alone for so long, it's quite an adjustment. But I'm discovering that I'm a bit of an exhibitionist, so it doesn't interfere with what I want to do."

As much as she liked Nigel and enjoyed him the previous evening, her attraction to Noel Campbell was much stronger and her feelings for him more complex. Born in Scotland to a family of telepaths, educated at Edinburgh and the Sorbonne, Callie said some in the Clan felt he was a candidate to succeed her as President of O'Donnell Group.

Going back to the hotel after dinner, she realized she was falling a little bit in love with him. Their lovemaking was as passionate as hers with Collin, but with more of an edge. He wasn't as tender as Collin, but not as rough as Kallen. She had lightly brushed his soul in West Virginia and they didn't resonate. She wondered if he was destined to be her Pia, someone she loved but to whom she could never commit.

He pulled her close and a pulse began between her legs. Placing her hands on his shoulders, she brushed her lips against his eyelids, touched his nose and met his lips. While they kissed, she ran her hand down his chest, past his belt and over the hard bulge in his pants. He kissed her face, her throat, parting her bodice with his fingers, following them with his mouth until he popped the clasp on her bra. Taking her breast in his hand, he ringed her nipple with his tongue, nipped it with his teeth, and sucked it. She squeezed him, her head thrown back as she pushed her breast into him, feeling electrical charges leap from her nipple to her clit.

Warmth flowed down to her stomach and lower between her legs. The ache to have him built and she tightened her grip around his waist, rubbing against him. She felt so empty and needed him inside.

Leaning her head back, he released her breast, his lips nibbling up her body until they found hers. She sucked his tongue into her mouth, hand entwined in his hair.
Fumbling, she managed to free his erection. He wrapped his arms around her and pushed her to the wall, bracing her back against it. Pressed against his body, his hands holding her bottom, she wrapped her legs around his waist. Taking his hard erection in her hand, she nudged aside her panties and moved it into her opening. He pushed inside her, filling her.

She cried out, clinging tight with her legs as he thrust hard and deep. His hard chest rubbed over her breasts and his rhythm increased, his hands cupped under her as he drove deeply. Losing all reason, bursting him with pheromones, crying for him to go harder and deeper, their minds merged and they lost themselves in shared sensation. It seemed as though a bright light exploded in her head as he shuddered and pumped his seed into her body. They soared, sharing their pleasure and energy.

Leaving their clothes strewn across the floor, they didn't make it to the bed before their passion brought them together again. She sat on the arm of the overstuffed couch, and he held her by the ankles with her legs in the air. He pushed into her slowly and deeply, setting a rhythm that teased as much as satisfied. Moaning, she felt as though she was drowning in the pleasure she shared in his mind. Savoring the slow, tantalizing feeling of him filling her, she gasped at his slow withdrawal and quivered as he hesitated before filling her again. She thought he'd drive her out of her mind, her climax temptingly just out of reach for a very long time. Then he quickened his pace and sent her over the edge into a shaking, screaming orgasm.

~~~

Collin took Brenna out on Saturday. It was a very romantic day, just the two of them with a couple of dozen Protectors. She finally got to tour the Tower of London, rode the Big Eye, took pictures of Westminster and Parliament, and ate fish and chips and oysters in an Irish pub off Trafalgar Square. That evening he took her to dinner and they saw *The Lion King* in the West End. Walking back to the hotel afterward, she hung on his arm and leaned against him.

"Do you know what I want more than anything?" she asked.

"Ice cream?"

"No, silly, I want to take a vacation with you. Go and see all the things I've only read about, just you and me, no Protectors, no succubi, no Rebecca. Take a couple of weeks, maybe even a month. Doesn't that sound great?"

He stopped on the street, pulled her into his arms and kissed her. "That sounds like the best idea I've ever heard. You know what your most attractive talent is? You build dreams for people. Now I finally have a goal in life."

"Don't laugh at me, Collin," she pouted.

"I'm not laughing, my love, that sounded like heaven to me. I'll see what I can do to make it happen, I promise." He kissed her again, and she forgot they weren't alone.

~~~

Brenna kissed Collin goodbye and walked with him to the van. Seamus and Callie rode in a limo with vans in front of and behind them. Most of the Clan who had gathered for the Council meeting were headed to the airport.

"Take care, my love. Write me if you can." He took her in his arms and kissed her again.

"Collin, is Pia all right? I mean, does she understand about you and me?"

He shook his head, "I think she understands, but she's not really all right with it. I do love her, but, it's different with us, and I don't think she accepts that. She wants the white picket fence and all of me, and I only have so much I can give her."

"And are you all right with things, with me?" Brenna searched his face.

"My love, my heart, you make me happy. You give me so much, and really ask so little. I can't imagine another woman who would understand about Pia, who wouldn't feel threatened. But you know there's no threat. I wish she could see that. Be safe, and have a good time."

He kissed her again and got in the van.

She went back into the hotel, and shortly thereafter said her goodbyes to Jill, Aislinn and Noel as well. Brenna's group would fly out the following day. Rebecca and a small team of Protectors would take a small corporate jet to Dublin at four the next morning, and then a larger plane with the rest of their party would follow, leaving at seven.

She returned to her room to pack, and found Pia standing at her door waiting for her. "Can I talk to you?" the tall blonde asked.

"Sure, come in." Brenna offered her a seat, then went to the wet bar and poured each of them a glass of wine. Sitting down, she said, "I was hoping we'd have a chance to talk."

"I know he loves you," Pia began, "but he says he loves me, too. I can't understand how he can say that, but when we're together, he almost makes me believe it. Do you love him? It seems you don't care sometimes, and yet you hold him. If you don't love him, can't you let him go?"

Brenna searched the other woman's face, seeing the pain in her eyes. "I'm not holding him, Pia. He's chosen to be with me, and I do love him very much. Our souls have merged and they resonate. We understand each other, our relationship and our needs. It's not a very conventional relationship, but we're not very conventional people. That in no way diminishes our love and commitment to each other. What we have is very special, I think.

180

"I do know he loves you, just as I love other people. I know being with you makes him happy, and I like to see him happy. But there's nothing I can do or say that will help you with what you're feeling."

A tear rolled down Pia's cheek. "I hoped he would be the one. I want to have a child with him."

"If you do, he or she will always be welcome in my home. I would do nothing to interfere with his relationship with any children he might have with other women."

"Don't you want children?"

"Oh, yes, I plan on having a number of children, and first with Collin. But I'm not ready for that yet."

"And would I be welcome in your home?"

"Yes, but I don't want you moving in. I hope we might become friends, but I'm not willing to let you into my relationship with Collin. You two need to define your own relationship, and if you can't agree on what that will be, I'm sorry, but it's not something I can help you with."

Pia stood. "Succubus," it was an epithet. "You just want all the men, don't you?"

"There's only one I'm willing to fight for. I'm sorry you don't understand, but don't mistake the freedom he and I give each other as not caring. Don't try to change my relationship with Collin. That will only drive him away and you'll have nothing of him. You can have his child, spend time with him and have him warm your bed, but don't stretch too far. Don't try and force more from him than he has to give."

Sadly, Brenna watched Pia go.

~~~

Rebecca stopped by her room at midnight, finding Brenna just coming in from hunting. "I see you have a fresh Glow on," she commented. "I would have thought you received enough attention this week to at least last you through the day."

181

Laughing, Brenna told her, "I didn't drain any of our men, well, one, but tonight I felt like I needed an energy boost. I just picked up a couple of guys at the hotel down the street and let them refresh me a little."

"God, you're turning into a real predator," Rebecca grinned. "Are you sure you collapsed that Samantha construct? Or did you decide you liked her better and dye your hair black to fool all of us?"

Sobering a bit, Brenna reached out and touched her friend on the arm. "Rebecca, I've never felt so comfortable in my life. For the first time, I feel as though I really know who I am and it's not at all who I thought I was. I don't know if everyone would think it's an improvement. I'm not conflicted anymore about being a predator. My morality has changed, not just my attitude and not just about sex."

Brenna went to the refrigerator and pulled out a bottle of juice. "I had a conversation with Pia today, and I knew for certain that if she crossed a line I would hurt her. I would dominate her and impose my will because she wants something I have. The old Brenna would be appalled."

Rebecca pulled her into a hug. "I love you, girl, don't ever forget that. I think we're going to need that attitude the way things have been going."

She pushed Brenna out to arm's length and studied her face, "When I first came to the Clan, when I decided to become a Protector, they told me the Clan has survived through the millennia by being stronger and faster than the people that want to kill us. Our continued survival depends on our willingness to fight.

"You're kind and gentle and sweet. That hasn't changed. But if a few men get sleepy and miss a couple of days out of their lives, you're not doing them any permanent damage. It's pretty obvious what they want when they look at you. I consider it a fair exchange if they give you what you want. "

Rebecca took her leave, and Brenna went to bed.

~~~

When Seamus prepared to leave on Saturday, he gave Brenna an envelope and told her to read it on the plane to Ireland. Once the plane took off, she retrieved it from her purse and opened it.

Brenna,

When I was a young boy, my great-grandmother gave me her Death Gift. It's unusual for such a gift to skip so many generations, but she was a succubus and a seer, precognitive, and I believe she wanted me to have that knowledge because the events she foresaw would happen in my lifetime.

The special Gift you have, called the Kashani or Succubus Gift, is the greatest Gift the Goddess gives to Her people. It is the Gift of Herself. In our past, those with this Gift were Her priestesses, Her link with Her people. In recent centuries, its meaning and importance have been misunderstood, even lost by many. I believe Siobhan has called it a curse.

The Goddess is a huntress, a predator, but also the Mother from whose womb all the blessings of the earth come to us. Her essence and Her power is what you hold. In our long-forgotten past, men made their obeisance by offering themselves to Her priestesses, who took the offering in Her name.

You need to understand this. You're not draining men of their life force because you're something evil. You're not a bad person. Sex with you is a holy sacrament, not an unholy debauch as the Christian Church would have you believe. The men who come to you in their moment of offering are held in the mind of the Goddess and She blesses them and enhances their souls. Even those who don't believe, the head-blind normal humans, are blessed by Her in that moment.

183

During the Middle Ages, the Church relentlessly hunted us and persecuted none so mercilessly as Her priestesses. As a result, what was once a fairly common Gift among our women has become a Rare Gift. But what my great-granddam foresaw was a rebirth, when our people would once again rise to strength through the love of the Goddess. She felt that a large amount of knowledge had been lost but that someday that knowledge would be relearned. She believed the number of women endowed with Her holy Gift would increase and lead us back into knowledge of Her.

You have rediscovered some of that knowledge and relieved the curse. I believe there is more to be learned. I remember when your mother was the only priestess to dance on The Longest Night, the only one to bless our people with the Goddess' smile. When you came back to us, I saw five, and believe the number will never be that low again. It is not an orgy, or a bacchanal, but a worship service in which we offer ourselves to Her, rejoice in the blessings of the earth and share each other the way She intended. The role of Her priestesses is to show us the way.

I know you're young and still unsure of yourself and your role, but from the moment you walked into my study in Baltimore, I knew you were the one who would do this. In my mind, you became my heir that night.

I have been called a visionary for leading our people out of Ireland and through the changes of the twentieth century. The days of my vision have passed and I am now passing into the next, and last, phase of my life. The only task remaining to me is to train you to take my place. Other than that, I plan to enjoy my new love and bounce babies on my knee. I hope before I pass from this earth I have the chance to bounce yours, but I'm not in a hurry for that, so don't feel a need to rush.

Be true to yourself, take good advice and reject bad, and always do what you feel in your heart is the right thing to do. You have an unerring sense of right and wrong and a spotless soul. I have no doubt the Goddess will someday welcome you back into Her arms and you will be remembered as the greatest Chieftain the Clans have ever known.

I love you, and feel blessed that you love me,
Your Grandfather, Seamus Hugh O'Donnell
P.S. Rebecca, I love you, too.

She read it over twice, then stared out the window at the green land passing below. When they crossed the coast and only the Irish Sea lay below them, she read it again. This time she smiled at the postscript. It was a blessing on showing it to her friend, but also an acknowledgement that Brenna would do so.

In some ways, it read like hokey religious mythology, but with what she had seen and learned since coming to the Clan, she had to wonder if myths still walked the earth. She had heard her Grandfather and others reference the Goddess and been curious, but right now she wished she had the O'Donnell library at hand. She remembered lists of Celtic goddesses, and how they seemed to overlap, and tried to figure out to which one her Grandfather referred.

~~~

185

Chapter 14

*A man is as good as he has to be,
and a woman is as bad as she
dares. - Elbert Hubbard*

When the plane landed, she sent out a spear thought. *Rebecca?*

That's me! <smile>

Her grandparents met her and walked her through passport control, the officer there staring off into space and stamping her party's passports like a robot.

Their motorcade drove the seventy kilometers south from the airport to Wicklow and from there to her grandparents' estate. Brenna and Rebecca rode with her grandparents and were entranced looking out the windows at the green countryside and the skyline of Dublin. After they left the freeway around Dublin, Caylin spoke to Rebecca, "I understand you're a half."

Rebecca colored, "If you mean that I carry the gene for the Kashani Gift, yes."

Caylin extended a piece of paper, "Here's a list, my dear. Nice men that are discreet and would be happy to accommodate you should you need it."

Rebecca's face flamed bright red. Brenna put her hand on Rebecca's arm, "My grandparents are both carriers, Rebecca."

Understanding flashed across Rebecca's face and she met Caylin's gaze. The older woman was still good looking at one hundred seventy. "My dear, I've lived with it all my life. We're not as stuffy as you Americans are, and my mother carried the curse also. Fergus has two daughters who have it, and the gene is fairly common, so you're not unique here."

"Are there any succubi at the estate?" Brenna asked.

186

"Oh, yes," Fergus answered her, "there are two girls living with us and three more Clan members in Dublin."

Amazed, Brenna told them she hoped she would have the chance to meet them. Caylin chuckled, "You won't have to go looking for them, they'll all be here for May Day and they're all interested, very interested, in that trick you discovered. Morrighan was ready to fly to America when she heard about what happened at the Solstice Ball, but I told her you were coming here. She's barely managed to rein in her impatience. It created quite a sensation."

When they reached the estate, Rebecca sent her a thread, *Masterpiece Theatre, anyone?*

It did look like a set from a British period movie. The stone mansion, not quite a palace, not quite a castle, was set amidst expansive lawns and lush gardens. The limo pulled up by the circular drive in front of the house and liveried staff poured out to assist them with their luggage and show them to their rooms.

As she was unpacking in the room she was to share with Rebecca, there was a knock at the door. Brenna admitted her grandfather.

"Do you mind if we talk while you unpack? I'd like a chance to brief you before you face the rest of the family and the staff," Fergus said.

"Brenna, this place is a cesspool of intrafamily politics. I don't know how much Seamus has told you about us, but Caylin and I had three other children besides your mother. All were killed in tragic accidents before Maureen's birth. But I have six children by other women, three men and three women, all of whom are still alive. Morrighan, the succubus that Caylin mentioned, is my youngest. She lives in Dublin and looks forward to squiring you about the city. Bridget and Aine live here and they are halfs, both married, and then there's Michael, Andrew and Brian, my sons. Brian lives in Paris, Michael lives in Dublin and Andrew lives here."

187

Fergus lowered himself into a chair near the window. Although he looked healthy, he always moved slowly, as though his joints hurt.

"Andrew is the oldest, and has always resented not being named my heir, but in the period before your mother was born and again after she died I named Michael. I don't think he will resent you, but expect some nastiness from Andrew, and he has his adherents."

He turned toward Rebecca. "I don't expect any overt action against you, but Rebecca, please don't relax your guard here. One never can guess exactly who is prepared to play the fool."

Dismayed, Brenna sat down on her bed. "Are you sure you want to designate me? I mean, wouldn't it be easier to name one of your other children?"

Fergus shook his head, "Michael will support you, as will Brian and the girls. Morrighan worshiped Maureen. The boys have always been at each other's throats and Andrew has just never been an option. You'll see why. The Clan would rebel if he were named."

Uneasy, Brenna squirmed, twisting her hands in her lap. "Grandfather, you talk as though my ascension is imminent."

"Brenna, I'm nearing the end of my run. I'm one hundred eighty-five, and we are a small Clan, wealthy in our way, but weak compared to O'Donnell. My alliance with Seamus and our location here in Ireland have allowed us to survive, but we made a pact when your parents married that we would choose one of their children to unite our Clans. Jack was Seamus' heir and Maureen mine. Normally you wouldn't have to worry about all this for another hundred years."

Her heart was pounding in her chest so hard she was sure the others could hear it. "I'm not ready to take over a Clan."

"My dear, I know you're young, and this past year has probably been overwhelming for you, but your modesty is only one of the qualities that make you most suitable. I don't think you realize just how impressive you are. I believe the Goddess has sent you to unite the Clans."

He told them what time to appear for dinner, then left.

Brenna showed Seamus' letter to Rebecca. "I'm sure hearing a lot about the Goddess today," she remarked.

Reading the letter, Rebecca exclaimed, "Oh, wow, now it makes sense!"

"That's nice," Brenna's voice was dry, "and exactly what the hell makes sense?"

"The Drain! Shit, Brenna, can I show this to Siobhan? She's been translating that book, *The Succubus Gift*, and there are some oblique references to this, but she's more convinced than ever it was written by someone in the Church. When the author refers to the Drain, it's always referred to as a perversion or heresy. The perversion we could understand but the heresy had us stumped. But if succubi are the priestesses for an older religion, it makes sense."

"I'm not sure about showing her the letter," Brenna said, the idea somehow feeling wrong, "but I can tell her what he said. And the rest of it? I mean, Seamus really believes this. It's not like he's telling me about a legend, he's letting me in on the mystery."

Brenna was frozen by the look on Rebecca's face. "Brenna, the things you and I can do with our minds are straight out of science fiction. I can't tell you how I know, but the Goddess and Her influence are real. Seamus *is* letting you in on the mystery, and if you haven't figured out by now that something other than pure random chance is directing your life, you're in denial."

Rebecca shook her head, "Seamus told us once you're not a goddess, but he says right here you're Her incarnation on earth. Get used to it, girl, you're nowhere close to

189

normal. It may be hard to accept, but at least stop trying to tell people you're not what they can plainly see you are. You confuse them when you do that."

"I'm so glad I showed you the letter, I feel soooo much better now." Brenna jumped up and walked to the window. "You think I confuse people? I must be projecting, because right now I'm the most confused person in the world."

She turned, and with a pleading tone in her voice said, "Rebecca, there are lots of succubi. Why do people seem to think I'm so special?"

Giving her an exasperated look, Rebecca said, "I guess we all consider obliviousness attractive."

~~~

After a discussion with Siobhan and some of her team who were familiar with Irish Clan culture, Rebecca informed Brenna in no uncertain terms that activities such as midnight visits to the kitchen or fraternizing with stable boys were strictly forbidden. She was only to socialize with her own class, and for God's sake, only screw her own class, except very, very discreetly. Brenna pouted but agreed to do as she said.

At O'Donnell, terms of address were very informal, but Siobhan and Antonia cautioned the three younger women that breaches of protocol were taken very seriously in most of the Clans in Europe. While Brenna could get away with addressing Fergus and Caylin as Grandfather and Grandmother, everyone else addressed them as Lord and Lady O'Byrne, and Brenna was Lady Brenna. Even her friends were required to address her that way.

Others she met had titles, but none of Fergus' children did. "They're bastards, acknowledged or not, and therefore not due a title of respect," Siobhan told them. "I'm sure that's part of Andrew's resentment of Michael, having to address him as 'Lord' all these years."

They dressed for dinner, Brenna wearing her mother's blue dress, as it was the most conservative evening attire she owned. For some reason, she was always slightly embarrassed of her succubus status around her grandparents. She guessed it was an unconscious assumption that due to their age they ascribed to Victorian morality. That feeling suffered a quick death at dinner.

As in the O'Donnell manor house, dinner was a formal affair at O'Byrne. What was different was the bawdy conversation and attitudes. Brenna and her friends might have dressed conservatively, but Morrighan's dress was more blatantly sexual than if the woman had showed up nude, and several of the others, especially the 'halfs', weren't far behind. Bridget was about eighty and Aine seventy in Brenna's estimation, brown haired with blue eyes, very pretty, and neither made any pretense of hiding their sexual activities. Their husbands didn't seem to mind, in fact, both acted completely besotted.

Morrighan could have been Brenna's older sister. Forty years old, raven haired with deep blue eyes and pale complexion, she was about the same height as Brenna. Placed side by side, a complete stranger would have labeled them kin. She laughed easily and had a constant spark of good-natured mischief in her eyes.

Brenna liked her immediately and Rebecca succumbed to her charms with hardly a whimper. Irina flirted with her shamelessly, and after a first appraising look, Morrighan returned the favor. Brenna dared hope the young succubus might have found a substitute for her infatuation.

Morrighan turned serious when she asked about Cindy. "She and I are very nearly the same age and I spent three summers with Lady Maureen and Lord Jack when Cindy lived with them. Dunany is not a large place, and we decimated the local men. There were times when the hunting became pretty sparse. Give her my best, will you please?"

"I will," Brenna said. "She's up and about now, recovering her strength. She's talking about going back to work this summer."

"Lady Brenna, Lady O'Byrne has told me you've discovered a way to prevent draining a man. I would be very interested in learning how you do that." The hunger in Morrighan's eyes belied the calmness in her voice.

Irina chimed in, "You can't really explain it to anyone. I think all of us have tried. You actually have to see someone do it. I could show you if you like."

"I would greatly appreciate it, if you don't mind," Morrighan said with a smile. "Do we need to find a willing lad for the demonstration?"

"Oh, yes," Irina responded, laughing. "It would probably work with an unwilling one, but I've never tried that."

"I'm sure an unwilling lad is rather difficult to find, looking the way you do," Bridget teased.

With Brenna being named heir, Michael was a Lord no longer. He was friendly toward her, though, and addressed her with respect. Brenna focused her Empathy on him, but couldn't detect a false note. Andrew, on the other hand, was almost openly hostile. After dinner, he approached her.

"So, *my Lady*," Andrew said with heavy sarcasm, "what plans do you have for O'Byrne? I assume we'll have to change all the curtains to match O'Donnell colors."

"I would have to study the business and other operations in some depth before I offered an opinion," Brenna said. "But I think the curtains are lovely. I don't think we'd have to change those."

She tried to turn away and speak to someone else, but Andrew was insistent on baiting her.

"What a novel idea. And would you conduct your studies by taking all the men to bed, and assigning duties based on their performance?" Andrew asked.

"Andrew, don't be so obviously stupid," Michael said. "It's embarrassing."

"I don't have to put up with you anymore, Michael," Andrew said.

Brenna appraised the two men. Michael was physically larger, more handsome and self-assured, and Rebecca reported he was the more powerful telepath. Though no longer the heir, he was President of O'Byrne's business enterprises.

"Don't you have something you need to do?" Morrighan asked Andrew with a sneer. "I'm sure you haven't pulled the legs off all the bugs in the garden as yet."

"Cow," Andrew spat at her.

With a dangerous smile, Brenna fixed Andrew with her eyes. "I'll evaluate everyone's role based on their value to the Clan and their loyalty," she said. "I'm sure some people will be more comfortable finding their own way in the world."

He sneered at her, then spun and walked away. Brenna was highly irritated with him and knew Rebecca was lovingly entertaining fantasies of castration. She vowed to avoid him whenever possible.

"I'm sorry about that," Michael said. "Please don't take Andrew's attitude to heart. The rest of us are quite happy to meet you."

"Thank you," Brenna smiled at him. "I would rather just ignore Andrew if I can."

"That would probably be the best idea," Michael said with a slight bow. "Father keeps him close so he can keep an eye on him. But someday we'll have to decide what to do with him."

"A grave would be the perfect place, don't you think?" Morrighan said, staring at Andrew's retreating back. Then turning to Irina, her face brightened. "Are you still up for a demonstration?"

193

Irina nodded and followed Morrighan from the room, trailing Darina and Fiona, the other two succubi attending the dinner. "Perhaps we should find several lads," Brenna heard Darina say, "so we can practice and make sure we get it right."

Brenna wished she could join them. A willing lad might help settle her nerves. The men of her own class were all over a hundred and not too appealing.

~~~

They arrived on April 29, just in time to observe preparations for May Day, the traditional Irish holiday of Beltane. It was the beginning of summer for the Tuatha De Danann, a springtime festival of optimism. It's considered a fertility ritual, connecting with the waxing power of the sun. At the Beltane celebration, this is symbolized by lighting bonfires and dancing around them in a sun-wise direction.

"What do you mean, fertility?" Brenna asked suspiciously. "Is this another dance of the succubi?"

"It could be," Morrighan told her with a soft smile, "but nothing so formal. I do guarantee the party will be quite wild."

On May Eve, the house was garlanded with flowers and two bonfires were lit that night using the powers of the mind. Cattle were driven between them in an ancient ritual to protect against disease. To the music of Irish pipes, fiddles and guitars, the revelers danced, leaping over the fires. Irish ale and whiskey were consumed in copious quantities, and as the night wore on, the scene began to resemble an even more ancient rite.

As Brenna suspected, the succubi were central to the celebration. When midnight approached, she and Irina were approached by Siobhan and Morrighan and told their presence was needed. Led away, they were brought inside a small barn where the other four succubi were already exchanging their clothes for filmy white robes. As they were changing, Antonia came in and began to undress.

"We are the priestesses conducting the ritual," Morrighan explained. "I've never done this with so much help. Nine succubi, what a luxury."

She went on to explain that at midnight, everyone would strip naked. Those who didn't want to participate would go home. Those who stayed would make an offering to the Goddess. The succubi would each have a bed of clean, fresh hay, the first cutting of the season, and she would lie on it and open her robe. "Don't use that reverse drain trick, not on this night," Morrighan cautioned. "The Lady would be deprived of her offering and it would be very bad luck indeed."

On this night, no woman could refuse any man who asked her. Tradition said if a woman were lucky enough, the man she wished for her husband would come to her. As a result, almost every unmarried woman was fertile.

When midnight struck, Brenna followed the others. Morrighan called out the Goddess' blessing on all who were there, asking Her to accept their offerings and grant the Clan a good growing season, large harvest, and fertility for the animals and people.

Lying on her soft, sweet smelling bed, Brenna spread her robe and waited, watching as lovers came together, seeing some women's faces light with joy and others turn sad with disappointment. But considering the options open to Clan women in preventing conception, she figured those who were disappointed would rid themselves of their waiting egg before morning.

She had feared a general orgy and expected to see a line of men standing before her, but it wasn't like that. Only three men came to her that night, and though they'd been drinking, they were polite and worshipful, making their offering to the Goddess, and she took their contribution. Looking at what she was doing in that light was rather interesting, a religious rite rather than a debaucherous revel, and when she rose to go into the house to bed, she felt an unusual peace in her soul.

~~~

Siobhan told them of an old tale. Even the plainest girl will be beautiful if she rises early on May Day and bathes her face in the morning dew at sunrise. If she's daring enough to undress and roll naked, her whole person will attain great beauty. The dew is also believed to bring immunity to freckles, sunburn, chapping, and wrinkles during the coming year. It cures or prevents headaches, skin ailments and sore eyes and, if applied to the eyes, ensures its user will rise every morning clear-eyed, alert and refreshed even after a very short sleep.

"Obviously this is something you did regularly as a young girl," Rebecca dryly remarked, referring to Brenna's notorious sleeping habits, rarely sleeping even four hours a night and waking bright and cheerful.

This tale, of course, led to a plan to roll naked in the morning dew at sunrise. An invitation to Morrighan to join them elicited a laughing response and a suggestion as to the best place. On the east side of the manor house was a swale hidden from view. As the sun rose, seventeen women stood shivering and waiting. Soon they were rolling in the dew, wet, cold and laughing. Then the play took on a different note as a number of young men showed up, tipped off by a member of the group the night before.

Lying on her back watching the sunrise, her skin tight and covered with goose bumps, her nipples hard and pointed, Brenna watched a handsome lad approach her clothed only in his confidence and armed with a hard erection. He walked up and stood between her spread legs, looking down on her. "My name is Brendan," he introduced himself.

196

"I'm Brenna, and that swelling you have looks painful. I'm a healer. Would you like me to do something about it?" she replied with a smile.

He knelt down, and placing his hands under her bottom, lifted her up and slid into her. Laughing, she arched her back and let him have his way. She waited a good five seconds after his energy started to flow into her before she triggered the loop, and when their mutual orgasm ended, he fell over and lay on his side, a happy smile on his face. "Pleased to meet you, Lady Brenna," he told her.

She had only drained him about ten percent, but the Glow made her feel marvelous. Wandering through the small glen, watching lovers on the grass, Brenna almost felt transported to a simpler, idyllic time. The beautiful Irish morning, the rising sun lighting the dew into a million diamonds, was like a fantasy, and she almost expected to see a unicorn. She smiled to herself, *But unicorns only come to virgins and I doubt I'll find any here past the age of puberty.*

Rebecca joined her. "Been dancing around a May Pole? You've got a Glow on."

"Oh, a willing lad presented himself to me, or maybe I should say exposed himself to me, and the pole looked so swollen and painful I felt obliged to apply my healing arts to its relief," Brenna answered gaily. "But I had a great Glow on from last night before he arrived. Isn't it beautiful?"

"Beautiful and cold. Aren't you cold?"

Brenna laughed, "My dear, how could such a lovely morning be cold to a cryokinetic?"

"Shit. God, am I stupid." Brenna felt the heat of Rebecca's body increase.

"That's what you get for daydreaming during class," Brenna told her smugly.

~~~

197

Chapter 15

*When women go wrong, men go
right after them - Mae West*

Brenna expressed a desire to see the sea, and her
grandmother immediately proposed a picnic at the beach.
Everyone went to their rooms to dress appropriately.
Brenna braided her hair in two braids, then wrapped them
around her head and pinned them securely. After putting on
their swimsuits under their clothes, she and Rebecca went
downstairs. The party gathered in front of the house and the
servants brought out food and blankets. Everyone piled into
several lorries, and off they went.

When they arrived at the beach, Siobhan said with a
smirk, "Now we're going to conduct an IQ test. Who put
on a swimsuit?" The three young Americans raised their
hands, but no one else did. Antonia shuddered.

"You'd freeze your titties off if you got in that water,"
Siobhan informed them. "No one in their right mind swims
in the Irish Sea, especially this time of the year."

Brenna, with a soft smile, began to take off her clothes,
revealing a skintight spandex bathing suit. "There should
be a law against looking that good," Siobhan muttered to
Rebecca.

"It wouldn't matter," came the reply. "Brenna's a law
of nature unto herself. She'd just ignore it."

Walking to the edge of the water, Brenna announced,
"Yes, it's cold all right," and without hesitation dived in
and began strongly stroking toward England. She missed
the look of total shock on Siobhan's face.

"Is she a good swimmer?" her grandmother anxiously
asked.

"Like a dolphin," Rebecca replied, squatting down and
putting her hand in the water, shivering at its icy cold.
Touching her Gift, she felt the water around her hand warm

to the temperature of a cooling bath, then stood and stripped down to her bikini and waded into the water. She knew she could never keep up with Brenna here, so she swam out a short ways and then turned, treading water and watching her friend. *Everyone's watching you, give them a show.*

Brenna stopped and looked back to the shore. She was about one hundred yards out, but those on the beach could see her smile. Taking a deep breath, she dove, and then turning upward used her telekinesis to hurl herself out of the water. At the height of her arc, she turned back down, knifing cleanly into the waves. She turned the maneuver into a series of jumps like a dolphin. When she leapt up and did a full backward loop in layout position, Rebecca sent, *Showoff!*

<exultant> This is fun!

After a few minutes, Brenna sent a general broadcast to the party, *Does anyone know if there are sharks in this water?*

Sharks? <alarmed> Rebecca answered.

There's something out here bigger than I am.

Entering Brenna's mind, Rebecca saw a ghostly form drawing gradually closer and then becoming clear.

Well, hello, aren't you a pretty girl! Brenna sent to the seal, not in words, but in images and feelings. Awed, hitchhiking in Brenna's mind, Rebecca was able to follow the strangest conversation she had ever imagined. *Yes, I think it's a fine day for swimming, are you enjoying this sunny morning?*

~warm human~swim like dolphin~curious~

The seal swam up to Brenna, almost touching nose to nose, and studied her. Turning and brushing against her, turning again, *~play~swim~chase~*

Her mind bubbling with delight, Brenna played, chasing and being chased, *I can't go as deep as you can, my beauty, nor hold my breath as long, we'll have to play here near the surface.*

Suddenly, the seal darted off, faster than Brenna could keep up even with telekinetic help. With a mental shrug, she went back to swimming and jumping, luxuriating in the feeling of freedom and power she felt in the buoyant medium.

And then the seal was back, nudging her to the surface. Breaking water, she stared at the seal, holding a fish in its mouth and shoving its face toward hers.

~friend~like~fish~give~

A feeling of pure joy ran through her. Laughing, she sent, *I've been invited to lunch! Sushi! <laughter>*

Thank you, darling, but I just had a meal and I'm not hungry.

The seal flipped the fish into the air and swallowed it cleanly when it came down. Two more seals appeared.

You brought your friends to meet me? Oh how wonderful!

Brenna played with the seals another hour, Rebecca joining them for a short time, then swam to the beach. Walking up onto the sand, she asked Rebecca, "Will an air shield float? Will water penetrate it?"

"I don't know," Rebecca created one and nudged it out into the water. "It floats," she announced. "The water molecules are too large to get through."

"Wonderful," Brenna cried. Casting an air shield around Irina, then wrapping it in a telekinetic blanket, she started pulling it and the tiny blonde succubus toward the water. "I've got some friends I'd like you to meet."

"What are you doing? Brenna? Noooooo!" Irina shrieked.

Paying no attention, Brenna swam back out to where the seals were watching curiously. To those on the beach and to the seals, the air shield was invisible and it appeared as though Irina was floating along the surface of the water, standing and fully clothed. Reaching the seals, Brenna invited them to check out the air shield, and soon they were pushing it around the waves, playing with the human in the invisible ball. Irina's shrieks of laughter echoed across the water. Linked to Brenna's mind, she could hear the communication between the seals and Brenna.

Brenna brought her back after about fifteen minutes, disheveled and a bit bruised from bouncing around the inside of the air shield, giggling like a drug addict in a pharmacy.

"My God, that was the most fun I've ever had with my clothes on!" Irina bubbled. "Absolutely incredible!"

Caylin stepped close, an intense look of longing on her face. "Brenna, can you take me out there? Please?"

Searching her grandmother's face, seeing such a strong need there, Brenna nodded. She cast an air shield around Caylin, closer than the one she had set around Irina so the older woman could brace herself against it with her arms, carefully crafted a seat for her, then towed her out into the sea. *I have brought my old one, my mother's mother, please be gentle with her,* she sent to the seals.

They gathered round her, gently pressing against the shield at three corners of a triangle, holding it steady. Brenna felt her grandmother send, *It has been very long since I have played with the selkies, I used to play with your mother's mother's mothers. Well come, and may your hunting always be good.*

Listening to Caylin's conversation with the seals, Brenna learned as much about communicating with animals in fifteen minutes as Seamus had taught her in all his lessons. Caylin had an incredible affinity for the sleek hunters, but her frail, aging body had kept her from her friends for many years.

A seal's head, larger than the others and almost white with age, burst from the water and swam to the bubble, nosing it. Caylin bent down so that she was looking the ancient seal in the face and gave a cry of joy. The communication between two old friends made Brenna want to cry.

When Brenna towed her back to shore and dissolved the shield, Caylin leaned against her, hugging her and crying. "I thought I would never see them again, they never come into shore here. Thank you so much."

Walking back up the shore supporting her grandmother's frail weight, Brenna looked up at the people watching them. The looks on their faces made her falter and stop. Some, such as Rebecca and Irina and her Protectors looked amused. Some, and she noted these, looked angry enough to spit nails. But the majority looked at her with awe on their faces, some almost to the point of worship.

Morrighan stepped forward and took Caylin's arm on the other side. Softly, she said to Brenna, "You *are* the chosen of the Goddess. Fergus told me, now I believe him."

"I just have a few Gifts, that's all," Brenna answered, feeling uncomfortable.

"It's not what you have, but how you use them. You live your life with such joy, and you share that joy with everything and everyone around you. You make the trees glad to be alive. That Gift has nothing to do with telepathy, or if it does then it's the twenty-sixth Gift. I shall follow you, Brenna. I'll give you my fealty when your time comes, and stand beside or behind you as you deem my place."

Caylin stopped, turned to Morrighan and kissed her on the lips. "Daughter of my soul, that is the second gift of joy I've received today. Bless you, Morrighan."

Embarrassed to her toenails, Brenna helped her grandmother back up the beach. She dressed, then sat and ate her lunch with the others. She wondered how just wanting to have a good time could become a quasi-religious experience for those who watched her.

~~~

County Wicklow encompassed one of Ireland's best fishing harbors and its highest mountains. From anywhere on the estate a person could see the green mountains rising amidst the clouds.

Fergus' daughters took them to the estate of Powerscourt, where a Japanese garden had been created, complete with flowering cherry trees that were currently in bloom. Brenna had taken Irina and Rebecca to the Cherry Blossom Festival in Washington that spring, and Powerscourt didn't have anywhere near as many trees, but the surrounding garden was beautiful and peaceful, and she didn't miss the million-person mob they had dealt with in DC. Powerscourt also boasted the highest waterfall in Ireland, cascading from the highlands beyond.

That night the nice weather broke and it rained. Brenna was sitting in bed reading when she received a spear from Rebecca. *Are you in our room?*

Yes.

Are you alone?

Yes, what's the problem?

I've got a guy and nowhere to take him. It's raining lions and wolves outside.

O'Byrne was nowhere near the size of O'Donnell and Brenna's party, plus all the locals wanting to meet her, had stretched them to overflowing. Brenna only had to share with Rebecca, her Protector, which was a testament to her status. Siobhan, Antonia and Irina shared a room with only two small beds and a cot.

You can bring him here if you're not bashful, won't bother me.

Do you want one?

<laughter> How many do you have?

Three, and trying to figure out which ones I want to throw back.

Brenna thought about it a minute, then, *What the hell, bring all of them.*

A few minutes later, Rebecca ushered three men into the room. There was a bit of uncomfortable shuffling, but finally Brenna broke the ice by pulling her t-shirt over her head and giving the room a burst of pheromones.

The women each enjoyed all three men, and sometime around midnight she found herself sitting on the bed watching Rebecca take all three men at once. Watching them together and being in her mind as all four reached orgasm ruined Brenna for porn movies forever.

Lying with Rebecca after the men had gone, Brenna marveled, "It didn't hurt. It's always hurt for me."

Rebecca took a moment to understand what she was referring to, then, "Oh, well, if you tried it with Collin, no wonder. He's too big. You notice I had the smallest one go there."

They fell asleep in each other's arms, enjoying the closeness and the warmth on a cold, rainy Irish night.

~~~

Morrighan asked Brenna if she'd like to go riding. Brenna knew her mother, Maureen, had bred horses at the estate Brenna inherited at Dunany, so she wasn't surprised Morrighan shared her interest. Rebecca and Jeremy went with them.

The day was sunny but cool. When they stopped to eat their picnic lunch, Rebecca surrounded them with an air shield. She and Brenna then heated the air inside the shield. Morrighan broke out laughing.

"My God, you two are wonderful," she said. "Do you just sit around dreaming up uses for your Gifts?"

The Americans looked at each other.

"It just makes sense," Rebecca said. "If you have a Gift, why wouldn't you use it to make your life easier? I mean, so many of the talents we have are only good to hurt people."

"I'm not arguing with you," Morrighan said, lying back on their blanket and popping a grape in her mouth. "I've just never seen anyone do this before."

Jeremy spotted the riders first. Soon, Andrew and five companions rode up and stopped, looking down at them. One of the men with him, named Liam, had been in Brenna and Rebecca's room the night before.

"It's the whore squad," Andrew said. "You must be one hell of a man to take on all three of them," he said, looking at Jeremy.

"Andrew, I'm on holiday and not in the mood to put up with you. Go away," Brenna said. Her O'Neill shields covered her party from mental attacks and Rebecca's air shield covered them from physical attacks. Brenna threw an air shield around their horses, tied to a tree twenty feet away.

"I live here," Andrew said. "Why don't you go away and not come back?"

Brenna, don't let him bait you, Rebecca warned.

Don't you think he'd look good merged with one of these trees? Brenna responded.

Rebecca and Morrighan cracked up. Jeremy's eyes widened in alarm.

"Pass me those smoked oysters," Brenna said to Jeremy. She put one of the oysters on a cracker and ate it.

Andrew tried baiting Jeremy next. "Your girlfriend fucked three men last night. A real man wouldn't put up with that."

Jeremy eyed Rebecca. "At the same time?" he said with a grin.

"It was really hot," Brenna said, reaching for the grapes. Rebecca blushed.

"Oh, I see," Andrew persisted, "he's a fancy boy, only interested in men."

205

"They weren't very good," Liam said. Almost immediately, he began to sway in the saddle, his eyes closed, he slumped, then fell off his horse.

"Delayed succubus reaction," Brenna told them. "He's so damn stupid he didn't realize he'd been drained until now. It happens sometimes."

Morrighan burst into laughter.

"Bitch! What did you do to him?" Andrew's face was red, veins standing out in his forehead.

Brenna and her party ignored him. Rebecca picked up the wine bottle and refilled everyone's glass. Andrew spurred his horse forward, evidently intending to ride through their picnic. His horse bumped against the air shield and stopped.

One of his companions dismounted and knelt over Liam. "He's drained, Andrew. His life energy is dangerously low."

Andrew wheeled his horse and charged toward the tied horses. This time his horse hit Brenna's air shield, stumbled and fell. Andrew hit the ground hard, and lay still after the horse heaved itself back to its feet.

"If I was you," Brenna looked up at the three men still awake, "I'd cut my losses. Take your asshole buddies and get the hell out of here before I lose my temper."

It took them some time to hoist Liam over his saddle and to get Andrew up and mounted, but they left, riding back in the direction of the manor.

Grandfather, Brenna sent to Fergus, *Andrew and some of his friends attempted to assault us. They're heading back to the manor now.*

How badly did you hurt them? Fergus responded. Brenna appreciated the calmness in his thought.

I drained one of them, and Andrew fell off his horse when it hit my air shield, but we didn't do anything to them otherwise.

<chuckle> Damn. Don't worry, I'll take care of it.

206

By the time they rode back to the manor, Andrew had been sent off to Dublin and told not to come back until Brenna had left.

~~~

Chapter 16

*It is always surprising how small a
part of life is taken up by
meaningful moments. Most often
they are over before they start
although they cast a light on the
future and make the person who
originated them unforgettable. -
King Chulalongkorn, Anna and the
King of Siam*

As comfortable as she felt with most of the people,
when it came time to take their leave, Brenna was ready to
go. As they rode in a luxuriously appointed bus toward the
west coast and Limerick, Antonia told her that if she held
multiple Clans, she should consider finding trusted
stewards to act as her managers.

"Not necessarily locals, Brenna, but people who above
all are loyal to you. If they are local and have the respect of
the local people, and the power to hold off any
insubordination, then all the better. I don't see that
happening here unless you have a violent purge at the
beginning. And that also has its dangers. Starting your
reign by showing strength is good, but it must be strength
with fairness and mercy. Cruelty and retribution only build
resentment, and mercy without strength is too often seen as
weakness."

As they crossed Ireland, those who had never been to
the country before were fascinated and the bus windows
were filled with faces the whole way. They spent one night
in Limerick, then traveled up the wild Atlantic coast, past
the breathtaking Cliffs of Moher. Finally arriving in
Ballyshannon, they took over a small hotel. After a short
rest, Siobhan took her friends to a village on the outskirts of
the town to meet her mother.

208

A tall blonde woman of middle age, still beautiful with a voluptuous body, opened the door of the house where they stopped. She smiled at them and gave Siobhan a hug, then stood hands on hips studying Irina.

"You took two turns in the pretty line and missed the height line altogether, didn't you?" Sinead O'Conner said. "Welcome, niece, I thought I'd lost my sister forever, but here a piece of her shows up on my doorstep." She shook her head, and then enveloped the young succubus in a hug. "It is so good to see you, come in, all of you come in."

Inside the tidy cottage, Sinead fussed over them, served them tea and sandwiches and finally settling herself made Irina tell her everything she could about her mother and herself.

"You and my grandmother were twins. Did you look alike?" Irina asked. "I've never even seen a picture of her."

Sinead pointed to pictures above the fireplace. "As alike as two peas," she said. "No one could ever tell us apart, even our mother."

She pulled some pictures out of a drawer and gave them to Irina. "For you and your mother," she said.

At one point in the evening, Siobhan asked her mother, "Do you see Da very often?"

"Oh yes, he comes around every month to be drained. He would like to see you Siobhan. You haven't visited him the last three times you've been here."

Siobhan's face showed distaste. "He hasn't made any move to come see me, or write me either. I'm not going to see him under his conditions. It's humiliating to have him tell people that I've come for counseling, as if there's something wrong with me. He's the one with the problem."

Seamus had been born near here and O'Donnell Group ran a factory here as well as two more between Ballyshannon and Donegal. This was part of the traditional O'Donnell holding and the area was full of Clan. The village Sinead lived in was all Clan and there were two more in the area, feeding workers to the factory.

"I'm getting ready to retire," Sinead told them. "I've spent my whole life in this village, and a hundred years is enough. My sister had the wanderlust and wanted to see the world. She saw it and it killed her, but now I also feel restless."

She went to a cabinet and pulled a double handful of picture postcards from a drawer. Setting them on the table, she waved her hands at them, "Mairead sent me these from everywhere she went, almost every country in Europe. Russia, Turkey, the Middle East, Egypt, over thirty years of post cards. I'm going to take a year or two and go to each of these places and then I'm going to settle down in Paris and become a courtesan to rich old men."

"You've never even been to Paris," Siobhan protested. "How do you know you'll like it?"

"It's close to Ireland, it's full of rich old men and it's warmer than Donegal. What's not to like?"

"Have you considered London?" Irina asked.

Sinead looked at her young niece. "London? Why in the devil's name would I want to go there? It's full of *English*, the worst of all the trash in the world. I might as well go to Dublin and live in the sewer."

Brenna laughed, "Not a fan of the English, eh?"

"The people who invaded my country, killed, tortured and subjugated my people? Burned innocent Clanswomen at the stake? And their food?" she leaned forward and confided conspiratorially, "I think that's what makes them so mean. If I had to eat what they do, I'd be angry all the time, too."

Before they left Siobhan extracted a promise from her mother to come to New York after her retirement and spend a month before embarking on her tour.

On the way back to their hotel, Brenna asked Siobhan about her father. "He's a Catholic priest. I'm glad she's

210

getting out of here. He's been stringing her along for sixty years, telling her he's in love with her but he's dedicated his life to God. Well, his vows have never stopped him from warming her bed, or knocking her up. He can go to hell, which if he's right about his God, he will."

~~~

They drove along the coast under gray skies, turning off the highway and then turned again and yet again onto increasingly smaller roads and away from civilization. They came to a gate in a high fence, electrified and topped with razor wire. Rebecca sent out a broadcast that was nothing but letters and numbers, and in less than five minutes two Protectors showed up carrying assault rifles.

"State your business," one said in a deep brogue.

I am Brenna Aoife O'Donnell, and I have come home.

When she had asked Seamus about her castle, he made a wry face. "Your father always called it The Castle, but Brenna, it's not like what you'd picture from that description. It's more of a fortified manor house. Yes, there's a wall with battlements, but it wouldn't withstand a two-hour siege, not even in the sixteenth century. The wall is only eighteen feet high, not sixty, and the house is not a castle. It has about forty rooms, two stories tall with a basement."

Seamus' eyes seemed to focus on something far away. "It's in one of the most beautiful places on earth, but it's a wild and stark beauty. Donegal is not like most of Ireland. It's mountainous and rocky and a hard place to live. The population is small and it's out of the way. We've located several factories there, but that's to provide work for our people. The factories are marginally profitable, but the logistics reduce what we could make if they were located elsewhere."

His attention shifted back to Brenna. "What I do ask is that you don't sell it, at least not in my lifetime. If you

211

don't want it, let me know and I'll figure out a way to take it off your hands."

He had shown her pictures, so she knew what to expect. The outer wall did remind one of a castle, though lower and narrower. The house sat at the back of the compound, surrounded by a rough lawn with grazing sheep.

They drove to the house, the Atlantic before them. Pulling in through the main gate, she disembarked and stared up at the house. Several people, mostly Protectors, came out the front door and a man who reminded her of Seamus approached her.

"Good day, mi' lady. I'm Darwin O'Donnell, steward. Welcome, it's good to see you and to have people here again."

While their luggage was carried in, he showed her about. A large two-story foyer formed the entry, with wide curving staircases on either side leading to an open landing. Beyond the foyer, a wide short corridor ended in the main hall, a large room but only a quarter the size of the ballroom at the West Virginia estate. It contained several large tables and Darwin told her that was where her party would dine.

To the right were the kitchen and storerooms, laundry, and other areas for the support of the house and its occupants. He took her down a narrower hall, opening doors to show her first the main parlor, then various rooms used as offices, an entertainment room with a billiards table and wet bar, a small theater and a smaller parlor. The rooms had twelve-foot ceilings and were spacious but not huge. The walls and decorations were elegant and tasteful, the overall impression definitely nineteenth century. It was in this house that Seamus had been born.

Upstairs were twelve bedrooms, the two largest, as in West Virginia, at the opposite ends of the hall. Shown to her room, it was about the size of the room she had shared with Rebecca in Wickford, but the view through the wall of windows took her breath away. Looking over the outer wall, she could see that the house sat on the edge of a cliff falling away to the ocean. The coastline was rugged, but she could see a sandy beach a bit to the north. Black-faced sheep grazed along the edges of the cliffs. The area was spectacular but there was nothing soft about its beauty.

Sitting in the main parlor with Darwin and Rebecca, he explained that he was Seamus' younger half-brother. The estate was fairly large and he lived in a small village, comprised mostly of his family, about a quarter mile north of the manor. The estate was self-sustaining, raising sheep and cattle and growing grain, mostly for the animals and people living there. The estate also owned two fishing boats that berthed in Killybegs around the bay and some of his family ran those.

She owned it all, but neither Seamus nor her father had ever taken anything out of the place. All the money earned went to sustain the people living there and maintain the estate. Darwin had a fund set aside to support the infrequent visits of his relatives from the States. She told him she had no plans to change any of that, except that she would transfer money to him to pay for their stay. His relief was apparent.

~~~

The next day they toured the area around the bay, going up to Donegal and having lunch at a pub in Killybegs, where she had a chance to see her boats. Fishing mainly for herring and mackerel, they were large enough to venture north at times for the more lucrative white fish in northern waters. Before heading back to the manor, she was given two large coolers full of fresh fish to take back for their night's dinner.

They spent a week and the sun shone one day. She and Rebecca walked along the cliffs and in the woods, sometimes accompanied by her other friends. She was told the beach was popular with the locals at the height of

213

summer, but Siobhan told her the Irish thought seventy degrees Fahrenheit was a heat wave. Nonetheless, she and Rebecca went swimming that one sunny day, and she was delighted when she discovered gray seals and again had the chance to play with them. This time, however, there was no audience save for a few Protectors and she didn't have to deal with any weird reactions.

Touring Donegal Castle was fun, but it wasn't the same structure her family had once held when they ruled Donegal. Red Hugh O'Donnell had razed it to keep it out of the hands of the English and the castle had been rebuilt by later lords after the English conquest.

~~~

They bid goodbye to the O'Donnells and the castle, heading next to the O'Neill estate in County Tyrone, sightseeing on the way.

At the ring fort at Grianan Ailigh, Brenna had a startling experience. Built by the Tuatha De Danann four thousand years before, it was an impressive structure, perched on the top of a high hill. Legend said it was destroyed in 1101 A.D. and reconstructed in the 1800s. Once it was the seat of power of the Niall, King of Ulster and ancestor of the O'Donnells and O'Neills.

When she first saw it, she had a moment of déjà vu, a slight disorientation. But when she walked inside she felt the world spinning and then she blacked out for an instant. Opening her eyes, she was standing in the middle of the fortress, but it was different. Dark-haired people with blue eyes wore richly colored robes with sparkling metal jewelry. Fine wooden buildings three stories high filled the space. Streets radiated from an open center. A woman in a gauzy white gown that did nothing to hide her body floated – literally floated – across the compound wearing a definite Glow and a smile. Everywhere Brenna looked, the people were using Gifts.

214

Down one street, two women had a large pot hanging over an open fire, next to two men who were skinning a deer. Naked children ran playing and laughing. In an alcove between two buildings, a young man and woman were making love, in full view of everyone, but no one seemed to notice and the couple didn't seem to be in any hurry to finish.

Something very hard hit her in the butt, and she found herself sitting on the ground in the present time, Rebecca turning toward her with a startled look on her face.

"What happened? Are you all right?" Confused, Rebecca looked around, then knelt beside her. "Brenna, are you all right? Did you slip?" Her concern deepened, "Did you faint?"

Feeling the vision flee, her mind clearing, Brenna looked up at her friend and said, "Did I go anywhere? Have I been here the whole time?"

"Yes, you've been here. We walked through the entrance and I turned around for a moment. When I turned back, you were going down. Good thing you've got a lot of padding back there."

"So as far as you know, I just decided to sit down all of a sudden?"

"Sit down rather hard."

"Wow, what a trip! I … I think I just had a postcog vision. Either that or I've been out in the sun too long."

Glancing at the leaden sky and the drizzle that had been their constant companion all day, Rebecca discounted the second explanation. "What did you see?"

"This place on a bright sunny day, but populated by people dressed in fine robes, using Gifts. A priestess, a succubus, was floating along, not touching the ground. They all had black hair and blue eyes." She brightened, feeling excited about what happened. "I had a feeling of disorientation and then it felt as though I blacked out, just for a second, and I was standing right here. There was a

215

village all around me, inside the walls, people doing things, wooden buildings like row houses, people cooking, kids playing, a couple making love. They were civilized, Rebecca, not savages. Wow! I saw my ancestors!"

~~~

Chapter 17

What we can or cannot do, what we consider possible or impossible, is rarely a function of our true capability. It is more likely a function of our beliefs about who we are. - Tony Robbins

The O'Neills and O'Donnells shared a common heritage and had been neighbors for thousands of years. Feuding, fighting border skirmishes and raiding each other's cattle, they weren't opposed to trading their women in marriage, and were staunch allies against the English. Following the Flight of the Lords in 1607, the O'Donnell Clan had settled in exile in France, Spain and Austria, but after a couple of generations the O'Neill head had returned home, bowed before the English monarch and regained lands and prominence.

Tyrone was now part of English-held Northern Ireland, while bleak and poor Donegal was the only part of Ulster remaining with the Irish Republic. The families had kept their ties, and the alliance they had forged against the English had never wavered.

Brenna's grandmother O'Byrne was Corwin O'Neill's younger sister, and Brenna's mother had been Corwin's heir. Brenna anticipated another uncomfortable situation such as the one at O'Byrne. Corwin was almost two hundred years old, and had named several heirs over his lifetime. His own legitimate son Hugh was currently heir, but at various times Fergus and Caylin's son who had died in World War I had been heir, another of Hugh's sons who was now dead had been named and then Maureen. Hugh had been heir for the past fifteen years.

Corwin showed his age. He moved slowly and tired easily. His body might be giving out, but Brenna found his mind was strong and clear. He had built a solid empire, controlling a sizeable amount of the business in Northern Ireland, with interests in banking, hospitality, shipping, agriculture, and manufacturing. He wasn't as rich as Seamus, but his fortune was counted in the billions.

While Brenna was unpacking, her cousins Darcy and Aine O'Neill arrived. They were the daughters of Hugh's younger brother, and had come to Washington to help with the operation to capture the monster who tried to kill Cindy. She spent some time chatting with them and they spent some time comparing notes on their shared O'Neill Gift of Super Shielding.

As at the other Clan manors, O'Neill dressed for dinner. A maid was sent to help Brenna with her clothes, her bath, her hair and if Brenna hadn't stopped her, her toilet. The air of nineteenth-century class distinction and noble entitlement was firmly in place. The *Masterpiece Theatre* theme kept running through Brenna's mind. She had almost gone to Hugh when she discovered Rebecca had been given a small, cramped room connecting to hers, assuming she was Brenna's servant. Rebecca was not expected to sit at the table for dinner.

Rebecca stopped her. "Let me play Protector here. There are undercurrents I've already picked up that are rather uncomfortable. Calm down and let me do my job, okay?"

Of course, thinking about it, when they had shown up at the estate, Brenna and the other succubi had all been wearing dresses while Rebecca was wearing jeans and giving orders to Protectors. Brenna wished she was wearing jeans, with wool long underwear. Without her Gifts, she knew she'd be as cold as Irina, who swore she would freeze to death before they escaped Ireland.

The maid looked at Brenna's evening dresses and immediately pulled the teal, the most revealing dress she'd brought.

"Why that one?" Brenna asked uneasily.

"It's a Donegal color, of course. Besides it best shows your figure. You're a succubus aren't you? You want to attract the men."

Brenna had brought it for Paris, and just looking at it caused her to kick her body temperature up a little more. A sleeveless, strapless, almost backless corset top with a deep, wide V cut between her breasts and a slit to the point of her hip, it left little to the imagination and did little to cover flesh in a cold, damp climate. Only Alice's wizardry and tight spaghetti straps attaching to the side of the bra, running under her arms to the small of her back, kept the top in place.

Almost a hundred people were seated in the main hall for dinner. She sat with Corwin at the head table across the front of the room. Three long tables ran away from them toward the rear. Brenna sat on Corwin's right side, where his wife would be if she were still alive, with Hugh on his left. She could detect that there were many conversations about her, but couldn't catch the gist of them.

Siobhan sent her a spear thread, *Brenna, everyone is talking about where you're sitting. Protocol says that Hugh, as the heir, should be on the right side.*

Brenna relayed that to Rebecca, standing behind her wearing a mid-calf LBD with lace over the shoulders, paneled deep V-neck, long sleeves and deeply cut back. The skirt from mid-thigh down was also lace. It was the most conservative thing she had brought that wouldn't be construed as dressing above her station. Conservative being relative. She had worn it to go clubbing in London. She played the lady's attendant to perfection, but still projected an air of danger.

Brenna knew there was a small Beretta strapped to the inside of her thigh and at least two knives concealed somewhere on her person. God and Alice alone knew where in that dress, but Alice was a wizard and accustomed to clothing dangerous women. After the New Year's Eve fiasco, Rebecca had hauled her entire wardrobe to New York for modification and went nowhere without being armed.

Throughout the meal, Brenna was aware of Finnian O'Neill, Hugh's son. He never took his eyes from her, as if staring at her might make her disappear. He made her uncomfortable enough that she constantly checked her shields.

If looks could kill, Rebecca sent on a thread, *Finnian would have already sliced and diced you. Can I kill him for dessert?*

Involuntarily, Brenna glanced back at her. Rebecca's face was perfectly placid, staring straight ahead. She stood at attention but her body appeared relaxed.

When the meal was over, Finnian threw one last murderous look toward Brenna before leaving the room. Several men fell in beside him.

Hugh gave them a tour of the estate and the surrounding countryside the next day. It was very beautiful and a major contrast from the wild and unruly lands of Donegal. He offered to give them the tour on horseback and Brenna had enthusiastically accepted, but Rebecca vetoed the idea. There weren't enough horses for her Protector force and she wouldn't bend.

When they got back, Antonia came to Brenna's room for 'tea', a deep red vintage they drank out of long-stemmed crystal glasses.

"Brenna, I have never spent more than two days in a row in Ireland before, and now I remember why," Antonia said. "I spent a warmer winter in St. Petersburg."

Rebecca shrugged, "It feels like a soggy San Francisco to me. I'm not cold so much as I'm afraid I'm going to rust."

"Rebecca, what are you hearing?" Concern was obvious on Antonia's face. "I've heard some disturbing

220

things here, although no one talks freely in my presence. Things don't feel right."

Rebecca let her own concern show. "There are deep divisions in this Clan. I screwed a guy yesterday who let his shields get a bit sloppy during a moment of passion. What I picked up there confirmed the picture we'd started to put together."

She looked at Brenna, "Make no mistake, my Lady," Rebecca's lips twitched and her eyes sparkled when she addressed Brenna with the honorific, "Jeremy and I have all of our people on high alert. There's murder in people's thoughts around here, both the committing of it and the fear of it. Finnian is evidently a right bastard, in the figurative sense, and plans to take control of the Clan when Corwin dies. A large number of people wouldn't be happy about that."

Rebecca paced, shoving her hair back from her face.

"Then there's Hugh's faction, which basically espouses the philosophy of 'why can't we all get along?' Eat, drink and be merry is evidently his motto. Now you showed up, fresh off being named O'Donnell heir, right after being named O'Byrne heir, right after Seamus and Callie's visit. You're a wild card, and it's stirred up the hornets' nest. The seating arrangements last night have everyone talking."

"You don't seriously think someone would be stupid enough to attack me here and risk Seamus' wrath, do you?" Brenna asked.

Rebecca shrugged. "Evidently, a list of Finnian's virtues puts intelligence near the bottom, along with kindness, charity and humility. He's attracted a bunch of followers almost as smart and virtuous as he is, and who knows what people with a bully mentality will do?"

When her maid came to dress her for dinner, Brenna tried to subtly check some information. A mention of Lord Finnian's name brought an involuntary shudder, but she

221

steadfastly refused to talk about her 'betters'. On a question about late night activities, she was more forthcoming, suggesting that a woman, even one of high station, might find refreshment and entertainment at a pub on the edge of the village.

"Do you ever go to the pub, Aileen?"

"Oh, my Lady, I've been known to step out an evening. I'm not much older than you are and haven't found a lad that suits me as yet. But a girl does have needs you know."

"And you think there might be lads at this pub willing to help with the needs of a wee lassie from America?"

"Oh, Lady Brenna," she answered with a gay smile, "I'm sure such a lassie could easily find one or two who might be somewhat friendly."

After another deadly boring dinner, Brenna solicited her friends who didn't have dates to check out the pub. Rebecca and Siobhan joined her with the Protectors on duty. It was larger than she expected, with a rock band playing and a mix of people she recognized, from kitchen and household staff to Protectors to members of the O'Neill family. Rebecca said her intelligence indicated the clientele might include almost anyone who lived on the estate.

There were three rooms and the two smaller ones had patrons wanting a quieter experience. One had games, people playing billiards, darts and dominoes when she looked in, and the other held booths with either serious drinkers, serious lovers, or serious discussions. Looking around at the place as a whole, she pulled on Rebecca's arm, "Wouldn't this place go great in the valley?"

Rebecca surveyed the pub, then said, "Just as long as I'm one of the patrons. You aren't getting me to wait tables just to prove one of your bright ideas."

They danced and flirted and Brenna did find a friendly lad who asked if she'd like to 'walk out' with him. Signaling Rebecca, she allowed him to lead her out of the pub to a soft, grassy place nearby, past other couples in various stages of getting to know each other better. He laid her down and treated her as gently and sweetly as she could ever want. She drained him halfway and sent a spear asking her Protectors to take care of him and take him someplace safe out of the morning dew.

On the way back to the manor house, they were passing a copse of trees when one of her Protectors lurched and fell. *Attack!* Jeremy broadcast, and Brenna extended her O'Neill shield to the others in her party. Jeremy threw up an air shield around them.

Casting her mind out, Brenna found over a hundred people in the close vicinity, and the mixture of emotions made it difficult to separate someone attacking them from a woman angry at her boyfriend.

I can't isolate them, she sent.

Rebecca sprinted away from them, *Jeremy, let me out of your shield.* He shrunk the shield so that it covered them from the front.

Seeing movement in the trees, Rebecca sent a bright stream of fire into the air. It lit the area and they could see several men in the light. A fireball shot toward her and she put up an air shield to block it. The scene dissolved into chaos with flames and fireballs lighting the area.

Brenna pinpointed one of their attackers, shattered his shields, seized his mind, and read who they were and why they were there. *I have one captured,* she sent to her party. She made her captive drop to the ground behind a tree.

Rebecca, Jeremy and Siobhan unleashed their Rivera Gifts, sending streams of disruptive neural energy toward their foes. Two men fell and the others paused. But this was O'Neill, and someone on the other side had that rare Gift, shielding their attackers as Brenna shielded her own party.

Siobhan, Brenna sent, *can we drain them?*

Yes, the response came. They both reached out and started draining everyone they could feel in front of them.

223

It would take too long to disable a large force that way, but it would weaken them. They fed the energy they pulled into their comrades.

Rebecca scuttled farther away, intermittently dropping her air shield to light the area with flame, then forming the shield again and sending Neural Disruption energy through it.

Don't go too far, Brenna sent, frantic that Rebecca might go too far, past the range of her mental shields.

One more attacker fell, victim to a Protector's mind fist, and the rest ran. *Let them go,* Rebecca sent. Brenna sank to her knees, shaking. The others heaved sighs of relief as it became apparent they weren't under attack anymore. Jeremy and one of his men ventured into the trees to find the fallen enemies.

Brenna's captive slowly climbed to his feet and stumbled toward them. Jeremy cuffed his hands and Brenna knelt to attend to the Protector who had fallen. Donny was conscious, victim of a mind fist but not seriously injured. He had a major headache, but that would pass in a couple of days.

Brenna sent a spear to Hugh O'Neill, and a force of Protectors came out from the manor to meet them. Taking the captured men to Hugh, she presented his mind to Thomas O'Neill, the Clan's security chief, and went to pack. Rebecca wanted them out of there, and Brenna agreed.

Hugh promised to take care of the problem, but his demeanor wasn't promising. Brenna got the feeling he was incapable of dealing with his son. She had no desire to get mixed up in O'Neill Clan politics, especially when her attackers were sent by Finnian O'Neill. She made a mental note that the Finnian issue would probably need to be dealt with in the future.

At six o'clock in the morning, Rebecca herded everyone onto the bus and their vans. But before they could leave, Brenna received a spear thought from Corwin, asking her to see him. Surrounded by armed Protectors, she made her way to Corwin's suite.

Hugh greeted her courteously upon her arrival and conducted her to his father. She spent almost three hours with the old man. Much of their conversation was carried on mentally. Corwin obviously wanted to prevent eavesdropping.

Corwin told her that while Hugh was a good man, he was uncreative, of but average intelligence, and uninterested in business. He preferred to hunt, fish and ride, leaving responsibility and decisions to others.

Corwin frankly told her, *Finnian is a cruel, ambitious, ruthless man. I wouldn't give a tin shilling for Hugh's chances of surviving a week after my death. Of course, Finnian wouldn't last a fortnight himself. The Clan would never tolerate him and he's not strong enough to stand against them. But a civil war would be damaging, and with both Hugh and Finnian gone, there would be a vacuum in leadership. I prefer not to do that.*

Brenna, it's not easy being chief of a Clan. It's like having thousands of children. You love them, but occasionally you have to spank one. Unfortunately, when dealing with grown men holding telepathic powers, sometimes that spanking must be rather forceful.

She considered what he was asking, studying his aged face.

Uncle, I haven't asked to be named heir of either O'Donnell or O'Byrne. To be honest, I gain no pleasure from telling people what to do. I don't feel qualified to run anyone's life. I'm still trying to figure out my own. But if you're asking me if I would rather take on a responsibility I don't want, or see good people come to harm from a poor leader, I guess you've got me.

She took a deep breath, pacing the room and considering the situation.

Come in, Uncle, see what's in my mind, my soul. Make sure I'm what you want. To be honest, I hope you change your mind.

She dropped her shields and welcomed him in. He spent longer in her mind than anyone ever had, save Collin or Rebecca. When he finally withdrew, the door opened and Hugh entered the room.

I'm going to give you some peace, boy. I'm naming Brenna my heir.

The look on Hugh's face might have been the look of a condemned man given a reprieve.

What do we do about Finnian? Hugh asked.

I believe she will deal with him appropriately. But when I die, if she isn't here, you must find a safe place, and call her immediately.

Yes, Father. Brenna, I pledge you my full support.

Uncle, you need to exile Finnian. I won't accept your offer otherwise.

Corwin called Thomas, who must have been waiting outside the room. Rebecca entered with him.

"Finnian's gone, my Lord," Thomas reported. "We can't find him or any of the men who participated in the attack last night. Several of his close friends are also missing. I've alerted our people across Ulster."

"He's exiled, Thomas. Post an announcement immediately. Include those you've identified from the attack. Anyone harboring him or giving him aid is also exiled," Corwin said.

"What do I do with the men Lady Brenna captured?"

Corwin looked at Brenna.

She took a deep breath, then looked at Rebecca, who nodded.

"O'Donnell doesn't execute people, especially our own," Brenna said. "We burn out their Gifts and strip them of their memories. In extreme cases, we implant a construct that creates a new identity, with compulsions in case their

226

souls manage to overcome the constructs. Then we exile them. It's not a matter of mercy, but of preserving our own souls."

Corwin nodded, a look of satisfaction on his face. Thomas looked relieved.

"Lord Thomas," Brenna said, "Do you have someone who can take care of the matter?"

"Yes, I do, my Lady," he answered. "I've never been fond of murder, and I'm glad you feel the same."

As they were leaving, Corwin stopped her.

Brenna, I hope you forgive me for this someday. I don't have long, and I know you'll curse me to every god and goddess in heaven when I die. I will try to send for you. I want to pass my Death Gift to you. Perhaps that will ease the transition.

Everyone in Brenna's party returned to their rooms as Brenna agreed to stay two more days. Brenna called Seamus and Rebecca called Collin.

Seamus told her to hang up the phone and then contacted her through a spear thread.

Grandfather, I'm not ready for this. Corwin is on his last legs, and Fergus isn't far behind.

Seamus projected calm strength through their link. *I assume you plan to merge both of those Clans into O'Donnell?*

Yes. That's what you and Fergus want, right? I see no reason to leave O'Neill separate.

Then here's what we need to do ...

Their mental conversation lasted thirty minutes, an extremely long discussion when conducted mentally. At the end, they had an interim plan in place. Seamus dispatched fifty Protectors to O'Neill under the command of one of Collin's senior team leaders, James Coughlin. Siobhan would be left at O'Neill to oversee the formation of a liaison team that would be sent to West Virginia to begin preparing for the transition. Twenty Protectors would be sent to O'Byrne with her cousin Jared Wilkins, Callie's son, to work with Fergus to prepare for the transition there.

When they finished, Seamus told her he would contact Corwin and Fergus to inform them of the plan.

Grandfather, what is a Death Gift? You mentioned it in your letter, and Corwin said he wanted to give his to me.

The tone of Seamus answer was very somber. *At the moment of death, when a telepath's soul leaves their body, they can pass the contents of their mind to a living person who is in physical contact with them.*

If Brenna hadn't been sitting, she would have fallen down.

All of it?

Yes, Seamus answered, *all of it.*

Her mind raced, trying to process that.

You said you received your great-grandmother's Death Gift. If I received yours, would it contain hers as well?

Yes, and those before.

How many before? She tried to keep a rising surge of panic under control.

In my mind? Over fifty. I received my father's as well.

Overwhelmed, Brenna asked, *Going back how far?*

Almost two thousand years.

And I'll ... someday ... know how you see me?

You don't have to wait that long. Seamus pushed a thought package through their link. It exploded like fireworks in Brenna's mind. *Take care, Brenna. You're precious to me.* And then he was gone.

Brenna lay on her bed for almost an hour before she could pull herself together, then called Collin.

"What do you think about pulling McDermott and putting him to tracking Finnian and Andrew O'Byrne?" Brenna asked.

"Sounds smart to me. Sean is probably compromised with Siegfried. He's helped Charles take down half a dozen prostitution rings, and if he sticks around here much longer he'll probably end up dead."

Brenna called McDermott, gave him her itinerary, and asked him to meet her in Dublin.

~~~

After dinner, when tea and cordials were served, Corwin made his announcement. The quiet in the room was total. He didn't stand, but when he began to speak the hall was totally silent. Everyone knew of the attack on Brenna the previous evening.

"For those who have not yet met her, we have a guest, Lady Brenna O'Donnell, heir to the Clans of O'Donnell and O'Byrne. Her grandmother is my sister, Caylin, Lady O'Byrne. You may be seated near some of her party who are also with us tonight."

Corwin's voice took on a hard edge. "Last night, Lady Brenna and her party were attacked. Those responsible have been exiled. That includes my grandson Finnian. There are formal notices in all O'Neill facilities worldwide. Anyone assisting those on that list are also subject to exile."

Corwin paused to gather his strength and took a long drink of his wine.

"Earlier today, my son Hugh came to me and expressed his deep desire to abdicate his position as heir to my position as Chief of this Clan. Regretfully, I have accepted his decision, agreeing with his reasons, and feeling that it is in the best interests of the Clan.

"I'm old. I was born in 1815, in a very different world than the one we now live in. I've tried to ride the significant and often violent changes that have happened. Currently, we're the strongest we've ever been, but the world continues to change, and when compared to people who split the atom to make war, our power is insignificant. People no longer burn witches, at least not in County Tyrone, but the challenges and dangers to our people have

229

not diminished. It will take a strong leader to steer you through the murky tides that are coming.

"As many of you know, among my Gifts is precognition. I won't say I've always seen clearly, but when I've been smart enough to listen to what that Gift tells me, I've at least been able to avoid disaster. A little over a year ago, I had one of the clearest visions of my life." He turned and said quietly, "Stand up, Lady Brenna."

Turning back to those assembled, he continued, "This is what I saw. I didn't know who she was, and at first I thought I was dying, seeing my beloved niece as she welcomed me into the arms of the Goddess.

"Then Seamus O'Donnell contacted me and told me that Maureen O'Neill O'Byrne O'Donnell's lost daughter had been found, and I understood. Tonight, I name Lady Brenna Aoife O'Donnell my heir, to inherit my wealth, my position, and my power when I die. She has agreed to lead and protect this Clan for as long as she is able and has life. Please welcome her and make her glad she has agreed to this sacrifice."

He paused for the polite applause to die. Looking out at the crowd, Brenna saw a full range of emotions on people's faces, from smiling to blankly stunned, to worried, to angry. She wished she was anywhere else.

"And let none of you think it is not a sacrifice," Corwin continued. "She has agreed to put your health and safety over her own, your happiness and prosperity over her own, your interests ahead of hers. Such is the task a leader faces. May she, at the end of her life, find it in her heart to forgive me for asking her to assume such a burden."

He turned to her, folded her into his arms and kissed her on the forehead.

Numb and feeling the room spin, Brenna sent, *Uncle, please hold me a minute more while I get myself under control. I don't want them to see me cry.*

He looked down at her, and turned with her slightly away from the people in the hall. *There's a handkerchief in my sleeve. Wipe your eyes and put it back.*

She did as she was told, looked up at him and smiled, then turned back to her awaiting audience. Butterflies the size of seagulls bounced around inside Brenna's stomach as she faced the people in the hall. Bracing her feet, she started to speak but her voice caught in her throat. She put her hand on the table in front of her to steady herself and cleared her throat.

"I was stunned when Seamus O'Donnell named me his heir. I told him I didn't want it and wasn't qualified. My reward for that protestation has been to be named the heir to O'Byrne and now O'Neill. Obviously I've angered the Goddess and this is my punishment."

The general laughter lightened the mood and helped her to relax.

"Hopefully, my grandfathers and my great-uncle will live for three hundred years. I'm hoping the Goddess will at least grant me that. But if I am called to lead O'Neill, I pledge I will be a fair and impartial leader, tempering strength with mercy, power with kindness. I know little about your businesses, or your lands, I don't know any of you. I won't be able to spend as much time as I probably should here in the near future, but I will be here when I can. I'm a good listener and a fast reader, so please, help me get up to speed. And thank you for the kind, warm welcome I and my party have received."

She sat down, and the stunned silence stretched.

~~~

"My Lord, Finnian O'Neill has contacted us. It seems he has been exiled."

"Really?" John Gordon raised an eyebrow. "And what does he think I can do about it?"

"He has some interesting news," Security Chief Foster answered. "It seems the O'Donnell girl has been named heir of all three Irish Clans."

Gordon lost his indolent look, sitting straighter in his chair. "The succubus?"

"Yes, my Lord."

Gordon cursed. Standing, he paced the room. "Get Geoffrey in here. I assume they plan to unite the Clans under O'Donnell?"

"That seems to be young O'Neill's take on it."

Geoffrey McCarthy, the Gordon Clan's President and Chief Operating Officer, came into the room and at a nod from Gordon took a seat. Foster briefed him on the new developments.

"From a business perspective, it creates a juggernaut," McCarthy said. "We have a difficult time competing with O'Donnell now, and O'Neill has a commanding position against some of our businesses in Northern Ireland and Scotland. Right now, they compete with each other, and us, in several important markets. We'd be at a significant disadvantage against the combination."

"Not to mention the military power they'd be able to wield," Foster said. "O'Donnell has become increasingly aggressive in the States. If they decide to consolidate their power here in England, it would be very uncomfortable for us."

"Yes, and the merger will free them to strengthen their efforts in France and northwestern Europe," McCarthy said.

Gordon shifted uncomfortably in his chair. "Seamus is relatively young," he said. "O'Neill could die any day, and O'Byrne isn't much younger. This isn't something we have the luxury of time to see how it works out." He fixed Foster with his eyes. "I want a complete profile of this heir on my desk by day after tomorrow." Turning to McCarthy, he told him, "And I want an analysis of the business ramifications by next week. Assume O'Neill and O'Byrne both fall to O'Donnell by this time next year."

His lieutenants nodded. After they left, Gordon picked up the phone and made a call. His side businesses, the illegal ones, were a minor part of his empire, but very profitable. He ordered one of his top operatives to find the O'Donnell heir and put a small team to tracking her.

~~~

Chapter 18

*To the moralist prostitution does
not consist so much in the fact that
the woman sells her body, but
rather that she sells it out of
wedlock. - Emma Goldman*

On the way south, just before reaching the town of Dundalk, they took a side trip to see Proleek Dolmen, a so-called capstone tomb. A gigantic forty-ton boulder sits perched on three large upright stones. At Summer Solstice, its opening aligns with the peak of a nearby mountain and the sun at sunrise. This area included Newgrange, an ancient winter solstice temple and was a center for the Druids thousands of years before the birth of Christ.

Tramping across a field to view the huge monument up close, someone made the comment that they didn't understand how such a huge formation as this or Stonehenge could ever have been built by ancient peoples.

Brenna walked around it and said, "It wouldn't really be that difficult if you had several powerful telekinetics. I could probably lift one of those smaller stones and hold it up by myself, and with just a few more people … The difficult part would be setting it in place and balancing it there. I'll bet they didn't get it right the first time and people were cursing like Rebecca on a bad-hair day."

Several people chuckled, but most were staring at her. Jeremy nudged Rebecca, "You and I think about how in the hell you'd get a crane across this soft ground, or what kind of levers and machines you'd be able to build three thousand years ago. She thinks, 'I could do that'." He shook his head. "It's not just a matter of thinking outside the box, she's in a completely different box than the rest of us."

"Jeremy, have you seen her snowman out behind the manor house?"

"Snowman?"

"Yeah, she built it out of boulders, three of them. The largest is about four tons."

He looked back at the dolmen, then at Brenna.

"She's twenty-three, Jeremy. Seamus told her not to lift anything larger than that until she reaches thirty so she doesn't strain herself. It's not even a box. I think it's some kind of round-sided dodecahedron with an opening into a different dimension. Sometimes I think her whole purpose on earth is just to blow my mind on a regular basis."

~~~

With the help of the Clan travel agency, Rebecca had reserved an entire Inn near Dunany. Brenna's mother's estate sat near the coast, and though the house was rather large for a 'country cottage', it wasn't large enough for a party of thirty-six.

County Louth was as welcoming and pretty as Donegal was rough and forbidding. Brenna understood why her mother would have preferred this place to her father's. Arriving at the house, she was met by the resident staff of five. John Stewart was the steward, running the estate and its stables where racing horses were bred and trained. The O'Byrne Clan had used the house at times over the past fifteen years, especially Caylin. Seamus and Fergus shared the expenses for the estate and the stables. Now this was all Brenna's.

The house was simple in design and looks, the architecture of an Irish cottage rather than of an English manor. Two stories tall, it was a rectangular box with no wasted space. Entering directly into the living room, the dining room was to the left and the kitchen beyond that. A morning room beyond the living room on the right faced the rising sun and the Irish Sea. The back of the house had several smaller rooms on the sea-facing side that could be used as offices, workrooms, or possibly an extra bedroom.

On the other side behind the kitchen, pantry and laundry were rooms for the staff.

Upstairs were twelve bedrooms, eleven with their own small baths, and the master suite with a bath rivaling the one in Brenna's room in West Virginia. The inn was twelve miles away and they had reserved all twenty rooms.

This was the first time they had almost enough rooms for everyone to have privacy, but it wasn't a big deal. Indeed, their party consisted of twenty men and sixteen women and the Protectors worked shifts. But considering the number of pubs within easy driving distance, there was always the chance someone might want to take a break from the sleeping arrangements they'd had for the past weeks.

They arrived several days early due to their early bolt from O'Neill. But as with their other hotel reservations, Rebecca had booked the week prior to their arrival to allow her advance team to vet the place and install their security. Since Brenna would not be staying at the Inn, they did their scans quickly and moved in. The area had a lot to see, restaurants and pubs, and the large towns of Dundalk and Drogheda. Brenna told Rebecca to leave their itinerary for arrival in Dublin as originally scheduled.

She went down to see the stables and her steward introduced her to the horses. He and the stable hands were surprised but pleased that she shared their Gift. Several people volunteered to take her riding and show her the surrounding area. Making arrangements to go riding the next morning, she went down to the beach and walked along the sand, enjoying the illusion of solitude. She could feel the Protectors, but they were unobtrusive.

Brenna called Collin that night. They talked about West Virginia and how much they missed each other, then she asked him if he had any news on the O'Neill situation.

"Our Protectors arrived about the time you pulled out," Collin said. "Siobhan reports there have been two incidents involving Finnian's supporters. One fool tried to assault her last evening."

"Assault Siobhan?" Brenna was horrified.

"I don't think anyone will try that again soon," Collin said.

"Goddess," she breathed. "Did she kill him?"

"He probably wishes she did," Collin said grimly. "The woman has obviously spent too much time with Kallen. Otherwise, James reports things are going smoothly. He's getting good cooperation from Thomas O'Neill and Siobhan has been given access to the Clan and corporate books. It seems a lot of people there are happy Finnian's gone and relieved that you've been named."

"Collin, I'm going to have to spend a lot of time in Ireland over the next few years."

"Yes, I know."

"What are we going to do? I don't want to be in Ireland with you in West Virginia."

He chuckled, "Well, I do a lot of traveling in my job, checking with my security chiefs around the world. The work I do here at the estate can be done in any of our offices."

"So you'd come here with me?"

"Darling, I'd follow you anywhere. You should know that."

She hung up feeling a lot better about the world.

~~~

Rebecca, Antonia and six Protectors showed up at the stables after a hearty breakfast of sausages and porridge. Two stable hands, Harry and Del, had their horses saddled and took the Americans out to show them the surrounding countryside. They rode along the sea for a couple of hours then cut inland and climbed a hill that gave them a view of the entire area. They ate a picnic lunch atop the hill as their guides pointed out the sights.

By the time they took their leave and headed back to Dublin, Brenna had fallen in love with her country cottage. Dunany was almost exactly halfway between Belfast and Dublin, an hour and a half to each, quiet and secluded with a nice beach and horses to ride. Amenities and a quiet nightlife were readily available, and cities close enough but also far away enough.

If she had to spend a lot of time in Ireland to deal with the two Clans, this would be a good, neutral place. She placed a call to Jack Calhoun and asked him to send someone to Dunany to evaluate what would need to be done to create an Irish headquarters for her.

~~~

Sean McDermott was sitting in the hotel lobby when they walked in. Brenna asked Rebecca to take care of checking her in and getting her luggage upstairs, then motioned with her head toward the bar. Sean followed her.

Sitting in a private corner, she told him about the problem of Andrew at O'Byrne and Finnian at O'Neill.

"So what do you want me to do about them?" he asked.

"First, find Finnian. Once you do that, I can inform O'Neill and we can arrange for someone to keep track of him. After that, try to figure out what Andrew is doing. I don't trust him and I'm wondering how bright he is. I just don't understand people like him, or why they act like that."

Sean smiled, "That's why you have me. I'm dumb enough to understand them. Is there anyone local I can trust to help me?"

"Yes, my Aunt Morrighan. I'll give you her cell number and let her know you might be contacting her."

"No might about it," Sean said. "I can't keep track of two men unless they're together. But if they get together, it'll be easy."

"If they get together, we have real problems. But you're right, it would be easy to take them out."

She called Morrighan and arranged to have dinner with her. She and Rebecca took Sean and introduced them. Morrighan reported that Andrew was back at the O'Byrne estate, acting somewhat chastised after his short exile. She said Fergus had trusted Protectors keeping an eye on him.

The next day, Morrighan took Brenna to the O'Byrne Enterprises' corporate office in downtown Dublin. They breezed through the lobby and got on an elevator that required a key code, which Morrighan gave her. Arriving at the President's office on the top floor, Morrighan introduced her to Michael O'Byrne's secretary and she showed them into his office.

"Thank you for stopping by," Michael said with a smile, jumping up from his desk and coming around to give her a hug and a kiss on the cheek.

They chatted for a while, then Michael gave her a tour, explaining their operations and the businesses they owned. When she prepared to leave, he took her hands and looked down at her with a slight smile on his face.

"Brenna, don't ever doubt that I'm behind you. I loved Maureen, and it gave me no pleasure to assume the role of heir when she died. You are so much like her, and I don't just mean the way you look. If you ever decide to take Andrew out, let me know. I'll attend to the matter personally."

On the elevator, she turned to Morrighan. "I can't believe he made that offer so blatantly."

Morrighan shook her head. "If it wasn't for Father, he'd have done it already. He hates Andrew, and Michael has the power to do it. Andrew has five Gifts, Michael has twelve, not to mention being about ten times as smart as Andrew."

As they made their way to the car, Morrighan put a hand on Brenna's arm and stopped her. "When Michael said he loved Maureen, he didn't mean brotherly love. He was deeply in love with her from the time they were children. If he wasn't her half-brother, I'm sure he would have tried to court her. After she married Jack, he and Michael became very close friends. Don't worry about his loyalty. He'll back you every step of the way."

~~~

Back in London, Brenna confirmed with Nigel that her adventure with Margriet was set.

"Margriet is expecting you," Nigel informed her and Irina. "She said the response to her advertised special was over-subscribed." He chuckled. "I think she used the pictures you sent me, and I must say, the two of you are spectacular dressed only in corsets."

Brenna and Irina both blushed.

Amsterdam was a delight. The weather was wonderful, the people friendly, the architecture amazing, and the gardens incredible. Irina was in heaven walking down the streets hearing dozens of languages in that most cosmopolitan of cities. They had only scheduled three days there as a halfway point between London and Paris, and Brenna wished she'd set it for longer.

Their second night in Amsterdam, Brenna and Irina went to work for Margriet. Jeremy and a team accompanied them to her stately mansion in one of the better parts of the city, well away from the red light district. Antonia took Rebecca out for what she called 'more respectable and elegant entertainment'.

Margriet was a hundred year old succubus, blonde haired and large breasted, dressed in an expensive evening gown. Her front reception room looked as elegant as the parlors at the manor houses they had seen. Indeed, the wallpaper was a copy of that in Brenna's bedroom in West Virginia, though made of nylon instead of silk and not hand painted. The rooms where they would entertain clients were tastefully decorated, with a queen-sized bed, small table

240

with a pretty tablecloth and nice chairs, and a small bath. There was nothing Brenna would call tawdry or dingy.

Brenna's outfit was a black corset with white piping, matching garter belt and panties, with black lace-topped hose and four inch stilettos. The corset was from Alice's shop and fit her like a glove. Irina wore a similar outfit in red.

Margriet explained she had set up two rooms side by side for each of them. They each had eight appointments and the men would be shown in on schedule every hour. They had about forty-five minutes to seduce and drain each one. Brenna's clients all spoke English, none of Irina's did. When they finished with each client, they would push a button by the door, then go to the room next door to get ready for the next customer.

"We don't have to completely drain them. It doesn't work as well with norms, but we found a trick that allows us to reduce the drain to about half their reserves," Brenna told Margriet.

"I'd like to learn that trick, but these men expect some drain. In fact, it was part of my marketing. But if you can leave them awake, the tips will be better," Margriet answered.

"Tips?" Irina asked.

"Marketing the drain?" Brenna asked.

Smiling, Margriet showed them the color brochure she had sent out to select customers. "These are all men who have purchased specials from me before. I'm sure they were skeptical about this, but as one of them said, my promises have always proven good before."

The brochure showed Brenna and Irina in their corsets and had their measurements and ages, but the headline and descriptions stopped them cold.

SUCCUBUS
For one night only, the legend is available

241

The Succubus is the ultimate in providing intimate pleasure
When a Succubus rides you to climax
It will be an experience such as you have never known before
Few men ever have the chance to savor this legendary delight
You can be one of them

The other side of the brochure with the details explained a succubus was not a demon or a minion of the devil, but a woman, trained in the sensual arts in an ancient tradition. It further said that the succubus experience was so intense many men reported feeling as though their life energy had been drained, but there was no danger to anyone.

Brenna stared at her, "You didn't!"

"I did," Margriet smiled.

"But ... but ..."

"Brenna, these are wealthy, educated men. They don't believe in succubi, but they are curious enough to check it out, and wealthy enough to indulge their curiosity."

"So what was that about tips?" Irina asked.

"Although they pay for your time, which I will split evenly with you, they may also give you a tip. Normally, the tip might range from twenty to one hundred percent of the fee."

Brenna could almost see the cash register totaling up sums in Irina's head.

"Use your Glam, use your pheromones. You're selling a fantasy and you've got less than an hour. Take them quickly but make it seem slow," Margriet said with a smile. "I assumed you didn't want to use your real names, so I'll be calling you Brandy and Iris."

Brenna went into her room and sat on the bed to wait. Her stomach felt a bit queasy and her hands were sweaty.

She wondered what she should say to the men who would come to her.

The door opened and Margriet showed a tall dark haired man in an expensive suit into the room. Brenna kicked her Glam up to high. "This is Brandy," Margriet said. She closed the door and left them together.

Brenna stood. "I'm so glad you came to see me," she purred, sending a burst of pheromones into the air of the small room. "Do you have a preference, straight or special?"

His eyes were fixed on her as she stalked toward him. Stepping into him, her breasts pressed against him, she reached up and started pulling on his tie. "Why don't you get a little more comfortable so we can get to know each other, very, very well," she said in a slow sultry voice.

She took a short step back, giving him some room, dribbling pheromones at a fairly high rate. He quickly began to undress, and when he was finished, she turned and walked back to the bed. Stopping and keeping her legs straight, she bent at the waist and pulled her panties down, skimming them down her legs. From practicing in front of a mirror, she knew that her bottom looked like a perfect valentine from that angle. What she was selling winked at him from its center. She straightened and turned to face him. Slowly, she began to undo the front closures on the corset. When she was finished, she dropped it on the carpeted floor and lay back on the bed, her legs spread, watching him.

He joined her on the bed and half an hour later she drained him, flipping the switch on the energy loop immediately when his energy started to flow into her.

She and the other succubi had discovered that the loop, while working almost perfectly with another telepath, was far from perfect with a norm. They just weren't able to hold the energy she returned and it cycled back into her again. It did cut down on the drain and the men were left awake but

243

extremely lethargic. However, they did feel the Glow and the cycling energy extended their climax and heightened their pleasure.

He rolled off her and stared at her with drooping eyes. "That was the most incredible thing I have ever experienced. My God, you really are something special."

"I'm glad you enjoyed it, sweetie. I know I did," she purred, leaning forward and kissing him.

She began to get up and retrieve her clothes. "Wait," he called, "where are my pants?" He made an effort to rise.

Brenna retrieved them and handed them to him. He fumbled out a wallet, opened it and pulled out a sheaf of bills. Handing them to her, he collapsed back on the bed. "Thank you," he said.

She gathered her corset and panties and went to the door. Pushing the button as Margriet had instructed, she stepped out into the empty hallway and went into the room next door. Cleaning herself in the bathroom, she dressed and glanced at the clock. She had five minutes until the next customer. The tip was ten thousand euros.

When Margriet showed the next man in, Brenna gave him a burst of pheromones and purred, "I'm so glad you came to see me. Do you have a preference, straight or special?"

It was like an assembly line and by the end of the night her memories were clear for only three of the men. She remembered the first, and a very large German man who reminded her of Seamus. He was a tender lover and tipped her twenty-five thousand euros. The other was a small, overweight man with a bad comb-over and glasses. It had been very difficult to get him hard, even bathing him in pheromones, and it took him forever to climax. She felt like she earned her money on him, and was so frustrated and irritated by the time he finished that she didn't care about a tip and drained him completely.

Sitting in Margriet's parlor with Jeremy and Irina drinking a glass of wine, Margriet handed each of them one hundred thousand euros and thanked them. "If you ever feel like doing this again, let me know, it's been very profitable." She smiled, "Brenna, your mother used to use me as a broker to set up dates for her in Amsterdam. I'd be happy to provide the same service for you. Let me know if you're interested."

In the car on the way back to the hotel, she asked Irina, "How did you do on tips?"

"Fifty thousand. God, Brenna, I can't believe it; I just earned my yearly salary in one night! How were your tips?"

"Sixty-five thousand. Two guys were very generous." She paused, studying her friend. "How do you feel about it?"

"Well, it's kind of boring after a while, but I could see doing it once a month. Hell, look at the money!"

Brenna reflected that she didn't really need the money.

"Other than bored, how do you feel?" Brenna asked. "Are you okay?"

Irina thought about the question, then said, "I don't feel smutty or dirty. I guess I don't feel any different. It was a lot more comfortable than doing a bar crawl. How about you?"

"I feel wonderful -- the Glow." Brenna tried to decide if her conscience or her soul felt anything. "I don't feel guilty. I don't feel dirty or cheap. But you know, if I had a choice, I think I'd rather have her set me up on a date. If I could spend the night with a nice man, have a nice dinner and a pleasant conversation, I'd be fine with the Glow from one man."

Irina nodded, "Yeah, that would be nice. I haven't been out on a real date in a long time. You know, I like having sex with telepaths, but other than Jared, they never take me anywhere except to bed."

When they got back to the hotel, the Protectors there reported Antonia had returned with a man but Rebecca was spending the night at another hotel. They would retrieve her in the morning.

It was five o'clock and Brenna fell into bed. Waking at nine, she ordered a room service breakfast and sent a spear to Antonia who soon joined her.

"So I guess you and Rebecca did okay last night?"

"Oh yes, we ran into some old friends of mine. A rather more elegant setting than where you spent the night, I expect."

Brenna had seen them dressing and going out to dinner before she and Irina left for the brothel. Evening dresses and updo hair aiming for, as Antonia put it, 'a higher class of men.'

"So Rebecca decided not to bring him back here?"

Antonia smiled, "His rooms were quite a bit fancier than these."

Brenna looked around at the sumptuous suite in the five-star hotel they were staying in. "So he has a palace or something?"

Antonia laughed, "Yes, but not here in Amsterdam. He's in the penthouse of the one hotel in the city that is more exclusive than this one. She had a very successful hunt last night and bagged a dukeling."

"Huh? A dukeling? What's that?"

"The younger son of the Grand Duke of Lichtenstein, who is partying hard here in Amsterdam. The man who holds his purse strings is an old friend of mine. He's currently sleeping in my room as a matter of fact. We'll take him home later and retrieve Rebecca."

Brenna rousted a sleepy Irina around noon. *Come on sleepyhead, we need to retrieve Rebecca and meet her dukeling.*

Does he quack?

<laughter>

246

Did anyone ever tell you that you're disgustingly cheerful in the morning?

It's not morning, Irina. It's noon.

Too early.

Okay, we'll just leave you here and you can catch up to us in Paris.

I'm coming. Do you have coffee?

A couple of men showed up and bundled Antonia's date into a limo. Brenna and her friends followed them and found Rebecca waiting for them in the lobby of the hotel.

"Where's the dukeling?" Irina asked. "The only reason I got out of bed was to meet him."

Rebecca chuckled, "You'd be good for each other. He's still in bed. Of course, to be fair, I think I wore him out. And for good measure I drained him a little bit in your honor."

"You drained him?" Brenna asked, mockly aghast. "God, talk about greedy."

Rebecca laughed out loud. "Just a little bit. He was all hopped up on coke and a bit too enthusiastic so I figured I'd even things out a bit, cool him off and give me a little more oomph."

~~~

247

Chapter 19

Being powerful is like being a lady.
If you have to tell people you are,
you aren't. - Margaret Thatcher

The chateau Rebecca had rented in Paris was quite
nice, but looking around, Brenna could tell it was built
fairly recently. Some of the décor screamed *nouveau riche*
as compared to the nineteenth century elegance she had
seen so much of since rejoining the Clan. It was on the
southern edge of the city so they had to drive in to the city
and find parking. They couldn't even take the subway
because of security concerns.

The first day they just wandered around the city, had
lunch in a sidewalk café and dinner at one of the finest
restaurants in town. Antonia knew the city well and in fact
kept a flat there. She was in her element, and at the
restaurant seemed in heaven.

"Forgive me, but more than a month of eating English
and Irish food …" Antonia shook her head. "If Dante had
ever been to England the food would have rated one of his
levels of hell."

"Do succubi gain weight?" Brenna asked, "Because if
they do, you'll have to bury me in a piano crate if we eat
like this every night."

After dinner, they strolled along the Seine, viewed the
Louvre and Eiffel Tower and the Cathedral of Notre Dame.
Paris at night was a wonder and the young women were
very impressed.

The next evening, Antonia ordered them to dress in
their best cocktail dresses and took them out to a nightclub.
The clientele was decidedly upper class and in their thirties
or older. The music wasn't rock and roll either, but there
was dancing.

"This place is rather unique," Brenna observed.

"Yes, it's a very exclusive club. I haven't found anything like it in the States."

"There are a lot of telepaths in here."

Antonia laughed, "Brenna, it's a telepath club!"

Brenna scanned the crowd and was stunned to discover almost all the patrons were telepaths. She also felt at least a dozen succubi. The maître'd showed them to a table and seated them. He looked at Brenna and Irina, then at Antonia with a rather stern look and Antonia nodded, "They'll behave."

Startled, Brenna turned to Antonia as the host left, "What?"

"You'll notice the ages of people here?"

Brenna looked around then grasped the issue. She had initially thought the crowd was thirty-plus in age, but if they were all telepaths, that meant the youngest were in their forties or fifties.

"People your age usually frequent the same type of clubs you normally go to. The only people your age here will probably be the dates of older men and women, and perhaps a few succubi. Discretion is important. No pheromone bursts. It's considered rude. At most, you might use a bit of leakage directed at someone who's receptive. No Influence. That would also be considered rude. But notice my Glam?"

Antonia was wearing a medium Glam, and the two young succubi immediately increased theirs to match hers. "You do want to stand out, after all," she told them.

A waiter took their drink orders and left menus. They sat watching the scene with interest. Rebecca seemed a bit uneasy and Brenna asked her why.

"How many non-telepaths have tried to kill you?"

"Oh."

Antonia leaned forward and spoke to Rebecca, "Brenna has you covered with her shield and I have Irina covered. We have four Protectors inside and another eight outside. If anyone tries to start something in here, well, it would be a very foolish thing to do. Murder and mayhem are considered rude, and the bouncers here are more than a little Gifted. We just need to be very alert when we leave."

Rebecca nodded and relaxed a little.

Dinner was quite good, the wine Antonia ordered was superb, and the cocktails were mixed to perfection. When they finished eating, men began to approach their table and ask them to dance. In spite of their Glams, or perhaps because of them, the most popular woman at their table seemed to be Rebecca. She was a very good dancer, and she spent a lot of the evening on the dance floor. The funniest pairing was the man close to six and a half feet tall who was enamored with Irina, asking her to dance several times. She looked like a child in his arms, her head barely reaching his chest.

As the evening wore on, each of them made a decision as to a man to go home with. Rebecca called in the Protectors who were off duty to provide enough coverage for each of them. It was inconceivable they would bring someone back to their chateau. The Protectors would have had a fit at such a security breach. Irina left first with her tall companion and then Antonia with a man who was well over a hundred. She told them on a thread he offered her fifty thousand euros to spend the night with him.

Rebecca shook her head, watching them leave. "I just don't understand why someone would pay to have sex. It's something both people enjoy, both receive a benefit."

"I've been thinking about that a lot," Brenna said. "In some cases, I think they do it because it's convenient. They don't have to spend time building a relationship and don't have to deal with the other person in the morning. It keeps it on a purely physical level."

Rebecca made a sour face, "You know, I'm tired of it only being physical. I want to wake up with the same man two mornings in a row." She looked at Brenna with longing in her eyes, "I want someone to love me, dammit!"

A gentleman asked Brenna to dance, and as he guided her around the floor, asked if she was looking for someone to warm her bed. Rather startled at such a blunt approach, she answered, "And if I am, I take it you're willing to volunteer?"

He chuckled. "I am prepared to make it worth your while. You are very beautiful."

She realized he was offering to pay her.

"Monsieur, please understand that while I may be easy, I am not cheap."

"Would one hundred thousand euros satisfy you?"

It was difficult to maintain her composure. "And exactly what do you propose?"

He wanted her to accompany him to his chateau outside the city and spend the week with him. She turned him down, and he seemed baffled.

Back at their table, she told Rebecca of the offer. "What I don't get, is why would he want me to spend the week? He's going to be out of it after the first night."

"Maybe he expects you to service his whole entourage," Rebecca said with a chuckle, then broke into full laughter at the look on Brenna's face. "Hey, take him up on it. If he's really rich, you can drain everyone and then we'll pull up the moving van and haul everything away."

Brenna ended up going home alone, to her Protectors' great relief. Rebecca left with a young man who said his flat was within walking distance.

They spent the next day at the Louvre, taking a break for lunch and then returning in the afternoon. Rebecca told her that before they left Paris she wanted to go back again. That night after dinner Brenna told them she wanted to go hunting in a hotel bar and Irina decided to join her. Antonia declined, heading back to the club they had been to the night before. In a stretch of four luxury hotels in close

251

proximity, the two young succubi put on quite a Glow, arriving back at the chateau not long after midnight.

The following days Antonia showed them more of the city, including Versailles, they did some shopping and basically took it easy.

A trip to Castle Margaux and its famous winery put everyone in a good mood. Rising early the next morning, they made the two hour trip to the Loire Valley where they spent the day at Chenonceau, sometimes called Le Chateaux de Femmes or Castle of Six Ladies, reputed to be the most beautiful castle in France. Built across the Cher River and once the home of Henri II's mistress Diane de Poitiers, the Americans were awed by its magnificent architecture, the spectacular entrance hall, the art museum and the bedrooms of its famous owners.

"Now this, my dears, is what a courtesan of the sixteenth century could aspire to," Antonia told them. "Of course, when Henri died, his widow Catherine de Medici forced poor Diane to trade for a lesser castle. Such a fall from grace, it is to be pitied." Her eyes sparkled with ironic humor.

Irina stood in the huge kitchen, looking at a fireplace with a spit large enough to accommodate an entire cow. "Antonia, how much can a succubus, a courtesan, expect to earn nowadays?"

Chuckling, Antonia told her, "It depends on how good you are at your craft. A true courtesan has skills beyond the bedroom. She must be educated, cultured, entertaining. She devotes herself to her patrons, whether it be one or many. It is a lot of work and the income flows are often very sporadic. The overhead is high -- clothes, jewelry, a luxurious place to entertain her patrons, being seen in all the right places such as the theatre, Cannes for the Festival, Monaco, other places where the rich go to play. It takes some time to establish yourself and acquire introductions into the best society.

"But all that said, my daughter clears a couple of million euros a year. Nice, but nowhere near enough to support a lifestyle such as this."

She put her arm around Irina's shoulders. "Irina, you are young and very bright and capable. You do something you enjoy, and you have a family who loves you. If you want to enhance your income by taking on patrons occasionally, no one will object. But I would not advise you to try and live such a lifestyle. You are much too sweet and naïve, il mia cara. Get some life experience and seasoning before you decide you want to do something like that. Victoria was in her thirties before she was able to establish herself, and even with my assistance it has taken her ten years to get to the point she's reached."

As they walked down the hallway, she said, "I can teach you, but I've always made better money as a lawyer. I entertain only patrons who interest me and who I find attractive. If you approach it that way, it's far more enjoyable."

~~~

By the terms of the treaty ending the Silent War in 1959, Paris was designated an open city, neutral ground. No Clan could claim it as its territory, and no hostilities could take place within fifty kilometers. All of the Clans had offices there, including those from Asia and Africa, which were not signatories to the treaty. It was the common meeting ground, where business deals were negotiated and telepaths from all over the world socialized.

Before they left the States, Antonia told the young women of a ball scheduled during the time they would be in Paris. An annual affair, it was hosted by the de la Tour Clan, the last of the major French Clans and an O'Donnell ally, whose power was based in Marseilles.

Brenna wore the teal dress, the most revealing and formfitting of the evening gowns Alice had made for her. Rebecca wore the maroon off-the-shoulder dress she'd

253

worn at Solstice, and Irina wore a pink number with ruffles and lace that made her look even younger than usual.

"My God, are you trolling for pedophiles?" Rebecca said.

Irina dimpled and curtseyed. "Daddy, you're such a naughty man," she purred, then burst out laughing at Rebecca's aghast reaction. "I'm in the mood to wear it," she said. "Sometimes I like to play games."

"You're a Goddamned enabler," Rebecca muttered.

Held at an exclusive hotel, so exclusive it wasn't advertised or open to normal humans, the ball was an expensive affair, tickets running five thousand euros apiece. Seamus was paying the tab for the four ladies. The hotel and its vicinity swarmed with Protectors, or as other Clans might call them, Warriors, Guardians, or Watchers, but only one was allowed with each ticket inside the ballroom.

Siobhan and Antonia had attended this event many times and had told the young women about it, but it was the first formal occasion for any of them outside the O'Donnell manor. Brenna was nervous and Irina looked like she was about to bounce out of her skin, smiling and laughing and looking around, her blue eyes huge in her face.

As Brenna scanned the crowd, the only visual clues that a person was a bodyguard were the expression on their faces and the cut and quality of their clothes. O'Donnell's Protectors didn't give themselves away on the latter score. Carly wore a designer gown and the men wore quality wool-silk tuxedos. Seamus insisted that O'Donnell uphold a certain image, no matter what the occasion.

Brenna identified almost thirty succubi. Antonia introduced her young charges to her daughter Victoria and several other succubi. Victoria's friends were younger, others were middle-aged as Antonia was, and two women who were graying. The younger women struck Brenna as somewhat arrogant, but the grace and elegance of the two

254

older women was incredible. Both were courtesans in the nineteenth century tradition, a time when royalty gifted incredible jewels and estates on their mistresses.

One of them, Olivia de Montespan, fixed Brenna with a hard stare, making her feel uncomfortable. Just as she was about to either say something or turn away, the woman said, "Turn around. Slowly. Now, walk away from me. Take ten steps, then turn and walk back."

Brenna shot a look at Antonia, who gave an almost imperceptible nod. Brenna did as Olivia directed.

"Incredible," Olivia said. "Antonia, she is just divine. She reminds me so much of that friend of yours. The one you used to hang around with in the sixties." Turning her attention back to Brenna, she smiled and said, "Darling, do come visit me in Geneva sometime. I'd love to have you."

Brenna had never met Victoria Federicci, but had heard a lot about her from Antonia. The family comparison was evident in their faces, but where Antonia was Brenna's height and build, Victoria was even taller than Rebecca, and her hourglass curves less pronounced than Antonia's. Long, straight black hair fell almost to her waist.

It soon became apparent that Brenna had been identified as the O'Donnell heir. Michel de la Tour, Clan Chief of the O'Donnell ally hosting the ball, escorted her around the room and introduced her to three other Clan Chiefs and half a dozen heirs. Brenna was proud of her memory, but she met so many people they became a blur. She met people from at least a dozen Clans, including at least one person each from China, Africa and the Middle East. The way many of them looked at her made her feel like a horse at an auction.

Antonia had dozens of men she knew asking for introductions to her three young friends, and Brenna found herself beset with men asking her to dance. Drinking champagne and flirting with admiring men, she felt like Cinderella. Taking a short break, she looked around and

255

saw Rebecca dancing with a tall man who said something to make her laugh. Rebecca's face was flushed, her eyes sparkling. She looked happier than Brenna had ever seen her.

It was almost midnight when a short, thin man with a French accent approached Brenna and asked for a dance. He introduced himself as Pierre la Fontaine as he pulled her into his arms. It became apparent that in her heels she was the same height he was. Dark haired with a pencil mustache, he wasn't a very good dancer, and Brenna wasn't very experienced. She usually depended on her partner to keep her from looking like a total klutz. He stepped on her feet a couple of times, and she stumbled once.

That didn't bother her too much, but his groping her butt did. He also unnecessarily brushed her breast a couple of times. His clumsy flirting was barely short of offensive, blatantly making comments about her physical charms and suggesting she should go home with him. When the music ended, she briefly thanked him and turned away.

He grabbed her arm. "Where are you going, Mademoiselle? We fit together so well. Stay and dance with me."

"I'm a bit tired," Brenna said. "I need to sit for a while."

"Oh, no, you cannot be tired. Dance with me and you can rest later while I pleasure you."

Taking a deep breath, Brenna said, "I don't think that's going to happen, Monsieur. I have no plans to leave with you."

Fontaine's hand tightened on her arm, almost to the point of pain.

"I do not wish you to go. What, do you think I cannot pleasure a succubus? Do you think I'm too short, perhaps? I assure you, I am not short where it matters."

"Please, Monsieur, I don't wish to make a scene. I'm sure someone else would be glad to dance with you. Please release me."

His hand tightened further, and he jerked her toward him. "I do not wish you to go," he repeated.

Brenna slapped him. "Sir, you're offensive, and you're hurting me." She jerked her arm out of his grasp and turned to walk away from him. She ran into an invisible wall, an air shield. Whirling, she saw his scowling face was red, his eyes bright and focused on her.

Immediately, she threw a close air shield around herself, inside of his, and threw power to her mental shields. *Rebecca, Carly, I think I have a problem.* She sent to her Protectors.

"Do you think you're too good for me? Putain! O'Donnell chienne!" he yelled at her. The words weren't in the phrase book Irina had given her, but she figured they weren't flattering.

An older man stepped forward. "Stop. There is no dueling here. Take your dispute elsewhere!" He jerked and reeled backward.

Fontaine sent a thin stream of Neural Disruption toward Brenna, not strongly enough to burn her out, but enough to hurt and do some damage. Her O'Neill shields deflected it. She needed to be careful, there were too many innocent people close. Brenna always needed to be mindful of not revealing too much of her Talents to strangers.

His air shield disappeared and he hurled an electric bolt toward her. Fontaine might be a jackass, but he was also a powerful telepath who obviously meant her harm.

Drain him, Rebecca's thought came through their link.

Brenna began to drain him, pulling energy from him as fast as she could. It was one weapon completely undetectable to anyone. He threw another electrical bolt and another stronger thread of neural energy. She blocked

257

both and he staggered. His own efforts were helping her to drain him.

Fontaine's energy levels dropped abruptly, and she knew someone else was draining him also. He stumbled, swaying like a drunk, then fell.

Back away, let's get out of here, Rebecca sent. Trusting her, Brenna began walking backward, keeping her focus on the man on the floor. Allowing some input to filter through her first level shield, she heard Rebecca mentally sending Irina and her Protector out of the hall. Out of the corner of her eye, she saw Antonia head toward the door holding her daughter's arm. Her daughter's friends followed them.

Several men descended on the man on the floor, checking him over. A couple of them stood and began walking toward Brenna. Rebecca touched her elbow and the two of them continued backing away. Carly and Jeremy circled around behind the men approaching her.

The way to the door is blocked, Antonia sent to them. *Irina is safe. If you need me to clear the way for you, I'm here.*

Brenna, and she was sure every succubus in the place, felt electricity being drained out of the hotel systems. The idea of Antonia unleashing the amount of power she was capable of in that small space was horrifying to think of.

Sweat trickled down her ribs and Brenna placed her feet carefully. High heels weren't made for walking backward.

Suddenly, there were walls around them and she realized Rebecca had steered them into an alcove where the coat check was located. Rebecca stopped, throwing an air shield over the entrance. Brenna's triple-strength mental shields covered them both. Rebecca stepped in front of her and held out her hands, electricity dancing between her fingers on one hand, a ball of fire in the other. Facing them were at least a dozen men, and none of them looked friendly.

"There's no dueling here. You've broken the treaty," a handsome man who looked around forty said with a German accent.

"Miss O'Donnell has done nothing," Rebecca replied. "She was attacked and defended herself. If there was a duel, he'd be dead, and he's unharmed."

Brenna couldn't see Rebecca's face, but the man who had spoken flinched and took a step back.

"There's no need to be hostile. We're just here to escort you out of here," he said, his voice quavering a little. His confident arrogance was slipping.

"If you aren't from de la Tour, then you have no right to escort us anywhere," Rebecca said. "I suggest you get the hell out of our way, Herr Stiegler."

You know him? Brenna sent.

I've seen his picture. He's one of Siegfried's top lieutenants.

Shit.

"I'm afraid you have the advantage of me, Fraulein," Stiegler said.

"In more ways than one, Mein Herr. If you don't get out of the way, I'm leaving here over your dead body," Rebecca said. "Your choice. Personally, I don't care, but I'd prefer not to get any blood on my dress."

"You've taken on more than you want to, Jurgen," Jeremy said from behind them. He and Carly stood there, faces hard and grim.

Stiegler's head whipped around. A small smile played about his lips. "Kallen's side man," he said. "Where's your boss?"

"On holiday. We have plenty of firepower here, Jurgen. Let the young ladies go or I guarantee we will leave bodies. And yours will be the first to fall," Jeremy said, his voice level and calm.

Jeremy, Carly, get the hell out of here. We'll meet you at the vans, Rebecca sent.

We're not leaving without you, Jeremy replied.

Damnit, don't argue, Rebecca sent.

With a shrug, Jurgen moved aside, motioning for the men with him to create a path for Brenna and Rebecca. Brenna leaned over the coat check desk and spoke to the woman cowering behind it. She jumped up, and began gathering their coats. Brenna put hers on and handed several to Rebecca, gathering the rest into her arms.

"I'm not walking through a gantlet," Brenna said softly in German. "If you don't clear our path completely, I'll have my Protectors clear a path. And if that happens, my grandfather will clear a path all the way to Herr von Ebersberg's bedroom. O'Donnell does not bow to intimidation. You have overstepped yourself."

Her eyes locked on Stiegler's and the blood drained from his face.

"Jurgen, I'm not telling you again," Jeremy said. "You have ten seconds to move before we kill you and everyone with you."

"You don't know how many are with us," another man said.

"One hundred sixty-two," Brenna said, her voice devoid of emotion. "We'll leave one hundred sixty-two bodies. I don't know how many of them are involved in this disgraceful scene, but we won't discriminate. Everyone connected with CBW will die."

"You have a rather inflated opinion of your power," a third man said. Brenna turned her eyes toward him. He clutched his chest, face turning red, and fell to the floor.

"Your friend needs a doctor," Brenna said calmly. "He just had a heart attack. Too many sausages, perhaps."

Stiegler and his companions stared at the man on the floor. Several of them moved back and a couple knelt by the stricken man, checking on him. Brenna and Rebecca started edging out of the alcove.

What did you do to him? Rebecca asked.

When Elsie teaches you to use your Healing Gift, she teaches you everything. Some healers don't have another weapon. I interfered with the neural nexus that regulates heartbeat. It's mild, he'll recover.

Stiegler staggered, stumbling backward, hit by a projected air shield. His nose started bleeding.

"I said move," Rebecca speared him with her eyes. All of the men moved away from the two women, who slipped away from them toward the door. Managing to make it into the lobby, they were joined by Antonia and surrounded by the rest of their protection team. The group moved out of the hotel and loaded into their vans.

"We have to wait for Jeremy," Rebecca said.

"Where is he?" Brenna looked around. "Did he make it out?"

"He said he needed to tie up loose ends. Just wait."

Inside, Jeremy took advantage of having everyone's eyes following the women out the door and made his way to the room off to the side of the ballroom where Brenna's original antagonist had been carried. Shouldering his way past the men outside the room, he walked in and looked at the sleeping man lying on a couch. He walked over, saw that the short Frenchman was still breathing.

"Is he one of yours?" he asked a Watcher of von Ebersberg that he recognized.

"Ja."

Jeremy leaned down and put his finger to the man's temple, then sent a tight stream of neural disruption energy into his brain. The man jerked, shuddered, then was still. Jeremy turned and walked out of the room.

When they got back to the chateau, he and Carly followed Brenna and Rebecca to the room they shared.

261

"Goddess, you scared the shit out of me," he told Rebecca. "When I looked in your eyes and saw you riding the killing edge, I ordered everyone out. I thought we were going to have bodies everywhere."

Rebecca laughed. "I guess I put on a good bluff."

"Bluff?" His brow furrowed in confusion. "What do you mean bluff? Goddamn it, you don't bluff in a situation like that. Either you're ready to blow everyone away, or you don't threaten. What the hell would you have done if they'd called your damn bluff?"

"Rebecca was a diversion, but she's strong enough to take all of those guys," Brenna said. "I wasn't worried about us losing. Antonia was holding enough electrical energy to blow the roof off. But you can't be selective with their Gifts. If they'd cut loose, it would have been an indiscriminate slaughter."

"I don't understand," Jeremy said.

"Brenna was isolating the hostiles," Rebecca explained, "and targeting them with her O'Donnell Gift. Why didn't you leave when I told you to?"

"I can't leave you to fight your way out of that kind of situation," Jeremy said. "I don't give a damn how tough you think you are."

Brenna chuckled. "We really weren't planning on fighting. Once all of you cleared out, we'd have gone to plan T."

"Plan T? What's that?"

"Brenna's a teleport," Rebecca said. "We could have left any time."

Jeremy stared at them, then put his hands over his face and turned away. Brenna and Rebecca weren't sure if he was crying or laughing hysterically. Carly stared at them with her mouth hanging open.

~~~

Chapter 20

*Accidents ambush the
unsuspecting, often violently, just
like love. — Andrew Davidson*

The weather had been beautiful through their entire
stay, and after a month of rain and cool temperatures in
Ireland, it was very welcome. In spite of the ugliness at the
ball, the next two days had been uneventful and it receded
in the minds of Brenna's party.

Their party was strolling beside the Seine on the Left
Bank when Brenna sent a spear to Rebecca and Jeremy.
*We're being followed ... no not followed, there are some in
front of us, too.*

Jeremy sent three scouts out to reconnoiter. Rebecca
asked Brenna, who had the longest range, to alert the
Protectors back at the chateau. They continued to walk,
Brenna stopping at one point to purchase a painting from an
artist showing his work on the sidewalk. While Irina
bargained with him, Brenna concentrated on trying to
figure out exactly what was going on.

What are you seeing? Rebecca sent. *Let me in, show
me.*

Brenna brought her friend into her mind and showed
her the minds she had isolated as being together and
showing hostile intent toward their party. Rebecca's
reaction was immediate.

*Jeremy, they're bracketing us. Protective formation
and high alert.* She showed him what she had seen in
Brenna's mind.

Antonia, we have stalkers, Brenna sent.

*So I have noticed. Brenna, I have covered Irina with
my shield. How far can you extend yours?*

I'm not sure. I can cover all of us if we're close together, but I'm not sure how far out I can go. I know the farther out, the fewer I can protect.

If we are attacked, I will cover those close, Antonia told her. *You cover Rebecca and Jeremy no matter what, any more if you can.*

Brenna relayed that to Rebecca, who responded, *Antonia, Brenna, link with me. I need you to coordinate with me. Brenna and I will provide air shields. Jeremy is taking a tactical force out and will shield them.*

Irina finished her haggling and the artist wrapped Brenna's purchase. As Brenna paid him, she saw Irina was pale as a ghost. "Are you okay?"

"Yes, but I'm scared. Antonia says I need to do exactly what she tells me and I'll be okay, but I don't like this." Beneath the fear, Brenna could sense the youngest of them gathering her determination.

"We're all afraid, but it will probably just be for nothing. I doubt anyone will attack us out here in front of all these people," Brenna said.

Looking around at the hundreds of tourists and Parisians out on a bright sunny day, Irina nodded. She took Brenna's painting and went to stand beside Antonia.

They continued on and their mysterious companions moved with them. Jeremy reported his scouts had spotted several visually. Their party consisted of the three succubi, Rebecca and seven Protectors. Jeremy and three more Protectors were somewhere close. Brenna was pulling electricity from the lines under the street and filling her reserves. She could tell someone else was doing the same thing and looked at Antonia, the woman who had been called a Storm Queen.

Is that count of thirty still good? Rebecca asked.

Yes, Brenna replied.

Rebecca scanned the surrounding streets and buildings, trying to see a route to safety. *Any chance of going back the way we came?* Brenna shook her head.

Rebecca steered them to an intersection where things were most open. *Antonia, you've been in more battles than the rest of us combined. Any advice?*

Rebecca, urban battles are something most telepaths avoid. There are so many people here, innocents who could be hurt. She took a deep breath. *Form in a circle, me and Irina in the center, you and Brenna at opposite ends. Use the weapons you're most comfortable with. Brenna will cover you and herself, I'll cover everyone else and feed both of you energy. I'm your reserve, just pay attention to what's in front of you and I'll worry about everything else. Irina, if anyone not ours gets close enough, drain them hard and fast and completely. Be ready to feed anyone who needs energy, you have a good Glow from last night, right?*

Pale but looking determined, Irina nodded.

Brenna heard a cry of pain in her mind, coming from one of the Protectors out with Jeremy. She felt Jeremy respond with neural disruption and the thirty islands of hostility she was tracking became twenty-nine. Calmness enveloped her as she set herself in a karate ready stance and cleared her mind as her sensei had taught her.

It's started.

Brenna scanned their vicinity looking for threats. Without warning, she felt something hit her shields. It took her a moment to realize the assault had started with projections of raw mental force, what the Protectors called a mind fist. It was a weapon any telepath could use and was the only one most could employ. She reached out to try and find the source of the blows.

A man dressed in black stepped from between two buildings and struck at her with neural disruption. She sent a bolt of electricity in return and he flew backward, hit a building and slid to the ground lifeless.

265

Then all hell broke loose. Men emerged all around them, trading mind fists with the O'Donnell Protectors, sending neural disruption at them, and an electrokinetic sent a bolt that was deflected by the O'Donnell air shields.

Brenna responded with electric bolts and three men fell. An air shield appeared in front of the men advancing toward her and she hurled the spear of her O'Donnell Gift toward the man who had formed it. For the first time using that weapon she didn't pull back, and the bolt of mental energy shattered both his shields and his soul. His head jerked back and he fell. As the air shield dissolved, she sent lightnings at the men he had been protecting and five more men fell.

Brenna sensed one of her Protectors get hit and fall, neural disruption finding its way through a weakness in Antonia's shield. She extended her own shield to augment the older woman, but couldn't give too much without uncovering Jeremy and the other Protectors out with him. They were at the extreme end of her range, and if they stretched her any further she would have to surrender one of them.

On the other side of their circle, a Protector jerked and fell senseless to the ground. Rebecca stepped over the body of her fallen comrade and sent neural energy toward five attackers advancing on them, burning them out. Another turned to run, and the Protector next to her hurled a fireball to strike him down.

Brenna noticed two of the enemy lurking around the corner of a nearby building, and sent a bolt of electricity into the alley. She felt one mind go out and the other, diminished, retreat. It met an O'Donnell mind in the alley and only the O'Donnell Protector survived.

She had expended a lot of energy but still felt strong, appreciating Antonia feeding her.

More men advanced behind an air shield, hurling fire and electricity before them. Brenna took out three with her

O'Donnell Gift, the air shield dissolved, and a shower of electrical bolts arced past her from Irina and Antonia.

Searching for targets, then checking on Jeremy and his men, Brenna realized she couldn't locate any of the enemy. Jeremy emerged from a street a block in front of her, heading toward them at a dead run.

Brenna turned and looked down at a female Protector lying twitching on the street. She knelt next to the injured woman. Using her healing gift, she entered Cherise's body and began strengthening the myelin in her brain, attempting to sooth and anesthetize her wildly firing neurons. Antonia's shield had prevented her from taking a direct hit and the man who had assaulted her wasn't as strong as Rebecca, but the damage was bad enough. At the periphery of her consciousness, she heard Rebecca wail, "Oh my dear God," and become violently sick.

"Brenna, we need to get out of here. We've got a containment problem." Jeremy's usual calm was tattered.

She looked up and surveyed the carnage. "Gee, ya think? What the hell do you want me to do, Jeremy? Heal her, or discuss containment with you? I'm only good for one miracle at a time, Goddammit!"

He looked down at the very young woman with tears in her eyes hunched over his fallen friend. "I'm sorry. I'll take care of things."

She stabilized Cherise and turned to look for others. Alan, their other healer, was working on another man. She went to the Protector that had fallen next to Rebecca and scanned him for damage. He had taken a blow from a mind fist. His soul was bruised, but he'd suffered no permanent damage and would recover.

She went to Rebecca, who was on her hands and knees retching. It didn't appear there was anything left in her stomach. Irina knelt next to her, projecting soothing feelings with her empathy. Brenna entered her mind attempting to find out what was wrong and jerked back,

267

appalled. She lay a Comfort on her then helped Irina pull her to her feet.

"Jeremy, are we ready to roll? We have our wounded ready to travel?" Brenna asked.

They moved with all the speed they could toward where their vans were parked. Antonia directed everyone who was whole to project confusion to all they met. Hundreds of people had witnessed the battle, far too many for their small force to modify their memories. Brenna prayed that none of the tourists had taken pictures.

She looked at Irina, "How long?"

"About three minutes. It seemed like an eternity, but I looked at my watch just before it started." Irina was still pale, but was holding up. "I can't believe she did that," indicating Rebecca with pity in her voice. "Even I know better than that."

Brenna agreed. Some strange impulse had prompted Rebecca to touch the mind of one of the men she'd burned out. His last thought, before the disruption of his neural circuits ended his thinking forever, was of his three-year-old daughter.

Somehow, they got back to the vans and managed to make it back to the chateau without being stopped by the police or having news reporters follow them. Taking their wounded inside, Brenna put Rebecca to sleep and dulled the memory of the little girl almost to nonexistence.

After making sure everyone was all right and the house was settled, she went to the bathroom and threw up. She felt someone come in behind her and pull her hair back and hold it. The look on the face of the man she had first killed with her O'Donnell Gift, no, her O'Donnell Weapon, at the moment she shattered his life crossed her mind and she threw up again.

She rocked back on her knees and Antonia handed her a glass of water. She drank it down then threw it up. Refilling the glass, Antonia handed it back to her. She shook her head but Antonia was insistent. "It hurts more if you don't have anything in you. Drink it."

She did, and only when the next glass stayed down did Antonia wipe her face with a damp washcloth, tender as a mother, and handed her another glass. Brenna looked at the amber liquid, took it and downed it. It was brandy. It burned all the way down and hit her empty stomach like a bomb. For a minute she thought it was going to come back up, but it didn't.

"Thank you," she said weakly.

"After my first pitched battle, looking at all the death, I was sure I'd never be able to eat again," Antonia told her. "Such a waste," she shook her head, "I wonder what they wanted, who they were."

~~~

"Lord Gordon's men," Jeremy told them later. "I've talked to Nigel and Collin. We are to sit tight and wait for reinforcements. Nigel will have men here tonight."

A dozen people sat in the living room. Rebecca had joined them and sat next to Brenna, both holding snifters of brandy cradled in their hands.

"What happened out there?" Brenna asked in a quiet voice. Several TVs had been set up, gathered from throughout the house. The French stations were filled with the disaster on the Left Bank and it ran in the main news loop on English-language CNN Europe.

Brenna's prayers had been answered and no pictures of the battle had been discovered, but there was plenty of news footage of the aftermath. Pictures of bodies, many with scorch marks on their bodies, lay on the pavement. A cameraman had captured video of men on stretchers drooling and twitching, their minds gone.

Eyewitness accounts were confused and contradictory, but several agreed they had seen a black haired woman with lightning shooting out of her head. Others said that a coven of black haired witches with their followers had

269

struck down the victims. Still another said the battle was over possession of a blonde haired child.

"Out of your head?" Rebecca asked, snickering. "God, how inelegant. You need to direct it through your hands. Haven't you seen any science fiction movies?"

"I don't know what happened, Brenna," Jeremy said. "Gordon has violated every stricture the Clans have lived by the past fifty years."

"So what happens next?" Irina asked, huddled next to Antonia, the older woman's arm around her shoulders.

"War. Seamus has ordered three thousand Protectors into England and put a bounty on Gordon. Collin said he's never seen him so angry, not even when Cindy was hurt."

"How many men did I kill today?" Brenna asked in a voice so quiet that only those closest could hear.

Jeremy stood and closed the short distance between them. Taking her arms in his hands, he said sharply, "Brenna, look at me. John Gordon killed those men. We were attacked by a force that outnumbered us two to one and we survived. That's the important thing. O'Donnell doesn't count kills, and I won't stand for you doing it. We protected ourselves. Those men attacked us without warning. They didn't come to talk. Their first move was to strike."

He straightened and went to refresh his drink, then sat back on a couch. "Everyone conducted themselves with honor today. You showed strength and dignity." He looked at Irina, "Everyone. I'm told the men who attacked Rebecca's position were staggering a bit, almost as though someone had drained them, and my people said someone kept feeding them energy. What's your range, Irina?"

Irina shrugged, uncomfortable with the attention. "Antonia said to drain anyone who got close enough. Not too many got close."

"About thirty meters, I think," Antonia answered for her, "quite remarkable for one so young."

All of the protectors were astonished. "That's remarkable for anyone," someone said.

A quiet smile crossed Antonia's face as she looked down on the blonde girl. "Succubi are more than a pretty package. When we're described as predators, most people only think of sexual predators. Our Talents are far beyond that. When attacked, a succubus will react like a bear with cubs.

"This one has a strength of will even she doesn't understand. She lets herself dwell on her fear and seeks people to protect her, but if left on her own she'll surprise everyone, even herself. There's a core of steel in her."

Nigel's security chief arrived that evening with two hundred Protectors. A plane had been sent to fly Brenna's party to Washington in the morning. No one got much sleep that night, whether due to packing, or finding a place for everyone out of the light rain that started at sunset, or the memory of the terrible events of the day.

~~~

In West Virginia, Seamus waited for a connection on the secure line set up by Collin's technicians. When someone came on the other end of the line, he spoke in German, "Gunter? Seamus. I assume you've seen the news out of Paris. Those were my people attacked and they say the people who attacked them worked for John Gordon. He's out of control, Gunter, and I'm not going to sit still for it any longer.

"You and I have always understood each other, even when we don't agree, so I thought I'd call and explain what's about to happen. I have three thousand Protectors on their way to England and I'm going to clean Gordon out. When they finish there, they'll move to the Continent to finish the job.

"I hope you'll pass this information along. I'm not ordering a general offensive, but anyone who stands with

271

him will be treated as an enemy. Keep your head down and tell your people to stay out of our way."

Gunter Schiller hung up the phone in Dusseldorf, more shaken than he'd been in fifty years. O'Donnell was moving in force into Europe? What was that madman Gordon thinking? He pondered the warning he had been given for several minutes, then picked up the phone and made some calls of his own.

~~~

Collin arrived on the plane from Washington and Brenna was as happy to see him as she had been that day in Spencerville.

She was cuddled up with him in the back of the plane when Rebecca approached. "Collin, I'm sorry. You put me in charge and obviously I'm not up to it. You can have my resignation if you want it, otherwise I expect you'll be putting someone else in charge of this team, and I understand."

"What in the hell are you talking about?" Collin's face showed his confusion.

"I fell apart when the fighting was over. When I should have been organizing our retreat, I was out of it. People had to get me out of there like someone wounded."

Jeremy surged out of his seat, strode down the aisle and placed his hand on her shoulder. "I was going to do this privately, but since you raised the subject ... Collin, the people responsible for her training really screwed it up. Who in hell forgot to warn her not to look in the mind of her kills? That's Goddamned basic."

Collin shook his head. "The blame would have to go to Kallen and me. Rebecca, it's not your fault. My screw up and you paid the price."

"But I should have handled it, even if I did something stupid," Rebecca protested.

Jeremy spun her around and the look in his face silenced her. "You led a team facing two to one odds, ambushed in a place with no cover. You organized your force, set up your protection, and stood tall protecting the body of a fallen comrade while eliminating at least six hostiles yourself, all while holding an air shield and coordinating my attack team. You walked off the field with all of your force alive and the enemy eliminated.

"You're young, you made a mistake, but your mistake didn't get anyone hurt and you didn't fall apart until after the action was over. I puked my guts out the first time I killed someone, and so did Collin. Quit trying to play the martyr and shut up and soldier.

"And you," he turned facing Collin, "clean up your damned training regimen or you and Kallen can turn your trainees over to me." Looking disgusted, he went to the galley and got himself a drink.

With a faint smile, Brenna told Collin, "Something I like about you is you're willing to take criticism from your subordinates."

Collin shook his head, "He was the one who trained me. Kallen and I took on Rebecca as a special case to train ourselves. I guess he's still training me."

~~~

Chapter 21

"Grandfather, do you have some time to talk about a couple of things?"

"Of course, Brenna, come in. Are you doing okay?"

"Yes, it sort of seems like a bad dream, but …"

She flopped down in a chair. "You know, a year ago the most complicated thing I had to deal with was my research. Now I'm looking at being responsible for eighty thousand human beings. To say I'm feeling overwhelmed would be an understatement."

"I'm not planning on retiring any time soon, so you don't have to worry about O'Donnell," Seamus said.

"And how long until Corwin dies?"

"It could happen any time. He's had one major stroke and two minor ones. His health isn't good."

"How about O'Byrne? Fergus seems healthy enough, but he moves like he hurts."

"Your grandfather has arthritis. Otherwise he's fine." He pursed his lips and looked away. When he looked back at her, he said, "It's your grandmother whose health is fragile. Her heart is very weak, and without Caylin, I doubt Fergus will stay in his position. They've been married for a hundred and fifty years. I was a child when I attended their wedding. I have the feeling it will devastate him if she dies."

"So what are we going to do if they die or step down?" Brenna asked. "I'm still your granddaughter, I'm loyal to you. They might make me head of those other Clans, but you're going to be calling the shots."

Her face, her entire being, radiated hope that he would agree.

"Yes, Brenna, I'll call the shots. We'll figure out a strategy to fold the other Clans into O'Donnell, and you can wait awhile before you have to grow up."

Tears ran down her face as she jumped up and rounded the desk. She hugged him and he pulled her into his lap. "Thank you, Grandfather."

~~~

Brenna was sitting in her room in West Virginia sorting through the pictures she'd taken on her trip when Rebecca burst in and strode to the seldom-used TV, turning it on and changing channels until she found the one she was looking for.

The picture was of an elegant manor house, a palace actually, on fire and blackened with smoke pouring through the windows and a huge hole in the roof. The voice of the British announcer was saying, "… it is believed that Lord Gordon was in the house. Witnesses say that he had arrived shortly before and his party was in the house only a short time when the explosion occurred. Authorities have not given a reason for the massive explosion, but the smell of natural gas is strong in the area and until the leaking gas is controlled, fire authorities are not sending any personnel into the home."

"That wasn't us, was it?" Brenna asked, staring at the TV.

"No," Rebecca replied. "We had surveillance on the house, but it was a surprise to us when it blew up. Our Protectors on the scene say that Gordon entered the house and it blew sky high about two minutes later. Some men were seen leaving the area shortly thereafter. We've been following them."

~~~

Seamus picked up the phone and a man spoke in German, "Herr O'Donnell, we have taken care of your problem. I hope you will hold off on your plans until we can reorganize our English operations. I assure you, there will be no further attacks on your personnel."

###

Look for Book 3 in the Telepathic Clans saga, *In Succubus We Trust*.

For more information about BR Kingsolver, The Telepathic Clans, and background on Brenna O'Donnell's world, please visit my web site. I'm also on Twitter and Facebook.

brkingsolver.com

~~~

The Telepathic Gifts

(* Rare Gift)
(# Part of Succubus Complex)
GIFT: Telepathy
COMMON LABEL: Telepathy
Read minds, project thoughts into the minds of others, shield their thoughts from others - telepaths have additional awareness and ability to understand their own minds and bodies and the minds and bodies of others. Telepaths can, for example, detect and eliminate pathogens, poisons, and other foreign substances in their own bodies. One example is the ability to detoxify alcohol. Women are able to control ovulation and conception. Telepaths mature and age very slowly. Average physical maturity occurs in the early 20s, but mental development isn't complete until the mid-30s. Complete development and command of their Talents is not complete until then. Natural life expectancy is 160 - 220 years. Mental acuity and Talent don't begin to decline until the person is in their last 10 - 15 years of life.

~~~

GIFT: Charisma #
COMMON LABEL: Charisma
Influence others, project an impression of a person so that others' perceptions of the person are enhanced. A very short-range projection, i.e. "wrapping" oneself in Charisma, can simulate the Succubus Talent of Glamour. Part of the Succubus complex.

~~~

GIFT: Empathy #
COMMON LABEL: Empathy
Feel the emotions of others. The person with the Talent can feel other people's anger, joy, fear, hope, anxiety, etc.

~~~

GIFT: Bernard #
COMMON LABEL: Empathic Projection
Project emotions into the minds of others. Change the way people feel and manipulate their emotions.

~~~

*GIFT: O'Donnell **
COMMON LABEL: Domination (Strong dominance)
Ability to penetrate or destroy another telepath's shields and take control of their mind. This is a rare and extremely powerful talent. It cannot be blocked.

~~~

*GIFT: O'Neill **
COMMON LABEL: Super Shielding
A complex Gift that provides the telepath with stronger, deeper shields, with 17 shield levels in the mind rather than the normal 9. Shields can be extended to others, even without physical contact. Shields can be projected onto others without their permission, blocking them from using their talents. Shields can be so strong that the telepath can mask their telepathy from other telepaths, and can even become invisible to others - telepaths and norms. A defense against any mental attack except the talent of Domination. The only complete defense against Neural Disruption.

~~~

*GIFT: De la Tour **
COMMON LABEL: Telekinesis
Manipulation of physical objects, including animate objects.

~~~

*GIFT: Murphy **
COMMON LABEL: Teleportation
Instantaneous relocation of an object or person. They can relocate an object or their person to a remote location. How far or how large an object is dependent on their strength. Some adepts can take another person or object

*with them, and some can relocate other objects or persons
from remote locations.*

~~~

*GIFT: Kilpatrick
COMMON LABEL: Power Shielding/Shield Projection
Stronger than normal shielding with the ability to
extend their shields to others with whom they have physical
contact (the attributes of this Gift are part of those in the
O'Neill Gift). May deflect or diminish an attack by Neural
Disruption.*

~~~

*GIFT: Christopoulos
COMMON LABEL: Aerokinesis/Air Shielding
Manipulation of air molecules - an air shield will
harden air into a transparent, solid shield that will block a
physical object, such as a bullet or car. This is the only
talent that can block attacks of Electrokinesis,
Orgonekinesis, Pyrokinesis, and Cryokinesis. Diminishes
and deflects Neural Disruption. A strong aerokinetic can
manipulate air currents and wind.*

~~~

*GIFT: O'Byrne
COMMON LABEL: Dominance (weak domination)
Ability to penetrate another telepath's shields and take
control of their mind. This Gift is not as strong nor does it
have the range and power of the O'Donnell Gift, and
cannot penetrate the shields of one with the O'Neill Gift
(the attributes of this Gift are part of those in the O'Donnell
Gift).*

~~~

*GIFT: Lindstrom
COMMON LABEL: Construction
Creation of mental constructs inside the mind of a
person that create a strong illusion that the person is a
different person, masking the underlying real personality,
memories, etc. The person carrying the construct may or*

279

*may not be aware of the overlying construct. Compulsions
and other kinds of control can be built in if desired.*

~~~

GIFT: Shamun
COMMON LABEL: Precognition/Clairvoyance
*Awareness of an event prior to it happening - may
range from a "feeling" to clear "visions" of the event - may
occur immediately prior to the event, days to weeks prior,
or in some it manifests as visions of far-future events. The
ancient Druids used various plants to enhance this ability.*

~~~

GIFT: Lubomudrov
COMMON LABEL: Postcognition/Psychometry
*Perceive information about events that have already
occurred. Psychometry is another form of postcognition
which enables a person to perceive information about
events that have already occurred by being in close contact
with the area or object where the event took place.*

~~~

GIFT: de Filippo
COMMON LABEL: Magnetokinesis
*Manipulation of magnetic fields. An adept can erase a
computer hard drive by removing its magnetic charge or
cause complex machinery, such as a car engine, a pistol or
a lock, to freeze by magnetizing the parts so they can't
move. Putting a super magnetic charge on a piece of metal
could cause it to attract other objects. The adept must be in
contact with the metal to affect it.*

~~~

GIFT: Sivakumar
COMMON LABEL: Pyrokinesis
*Manipulation of fire, including starting fires, shielding
from fire, and hurling fire. An adept can create fire out of
the air by super exciting air molecules and using heat from
the friction created.*

~~~

GIFT: van Serooskerken
COMMON LABEL: Cryokinesis
An adept can manipulate the temperature of an object or person to immediately drop to -20C. When applied to a person can put them into immediate hypothermic shock. Can condense moisture from the air or other source into ice. Can thaw frozen objects within seconds. A person with the Gift can regulate the temperature of their immediate environment (for several inches around them) to allow them to be cool in hot weather or warm in cold weather.

~~~

GIFT: Hakizimana
COMMON LABEL: Healing/Biokinesis
Healing and manipulation of a body to cure injury or disease. The method used is similar to micro-telekinesis, moving pieces of broken bones or sealing blood vessels, then using energy infusion to accelerate the body's own healing mechanisms. This ability is enhanced in those having the Petrescu Gift.

~~~

GIFT: Jalair
COMMON LABEL: Animal Telepathy
Telepathic communication with animals - this is more of an empathy-influence communication. An adept can usually feel the "thoughts" of primitive creatures, such as reptiles, fish or insects, but can truly communicate only with mammals. Communication with birds isn't as clear as with mammals.

~~~

GIFT: Krasevec
COMMON LABEL: Distance Communication
Telepathic communication over long distances - often hundreds of miles. This can't be blocked by physical means but strong electro-magnetic fields may interfere. There is evidence this Gift may enhance other Gifts, such as the O'Donnell, Hakizimana, Murphy, etc.

281

~~~

GIFT: Rivera #
COMMON LABEL: Neural Disruption
Neural energy from the wielder is projected into the neural network of a victim, disrupting their neural network. Depending on the strength of the projection, can be used to shock/stun a victim, or can burn out the neural synapses causing permanent damage. At its most extreme completely burns out the mind of the victim. It can also be used surgically to burn out a telepath's Gifts or select neural areas, or even in weak doses to deaden pain. A weak talent must be in physical contact with the victim. A strong talent can strike several victims at once, and at a considerable distance. This type of attack cannot be blocked by mental shields except by one having the Super Shielding talent. It can be deflected or diminished by one with the Power Shielding talent. Without strong focus and direction, everyone in the vicinity of the wielder is at risk.

~~~

GIFT: Simsek #
COMMON LABEL: Electrokinesis
Channeling of electrical energy. The wielder can drain electrical circuits, store the electricity in their own neural network temporarily, and discharge the energy into another object or the air. Care must be taken by the wielder as too much electricity, such as trying to channel a lightning strike, may overload the wielder's own neural circuits. As a weapon, the channeler may be able to discharge the energy for a considerable range, both distance and breadth. Without strong focus and direction, everyone in the vicinity of the wielder is at risk. As a weapon it cannot be blocked by mental shields.

~~~

GIFT: Petrescu #
COMMON LABEL: Orgonekinesis (life energy)

Projection of life energy into another person or animal. A person possessing the Talent always also possesses Energy Draining. Depending on the strength used by the wielder, this can be used to restore a person's life energy after being drained or wounded, or as a weapon. This type of attack cannot be blocked by mental shields except by one having the Super Shielding talent. It can be deflected or diminished by one with the Power Shielding talent.

~~~

GIFT: Farooqui #
COMMON LABEL: Energy Draining (human or animal)
Drain a person's life energy from them, similar to the Drain a Succubus effects during sex. A weak talent must be in contact with a victim. A strong talent can drain several victims at once at a considerable distance. This type of attack cannot be blocked by mental shields except by one having the Super Shielding talent. It can be deflected or diminished by one with the Power Shielding talent.

~~~

GIFT: Kashani #
COMMON LABEL: Succubus
Found only in women (X-linked trait). The Succubus Gift includes both mental Talents and physiological attributes. The genitalia have several internal and external differences from normal female genitalia. Specialized glands in the groin, breasts, underarms, and throat contain strong sexual pheromone attractants and the release of these chemicals as an invisible aerosol is under the wielder's control. Spectacular physical beauty is considered part of the manifestation of this Gift. Other attributes include specialized modifications of Charisma (Glamour or the Glam), Empathic Projection (Influence) and Energy Draining (the Drain).

When a Succubus has sex with a man, his climax causes an automatic reaction in the Succubus. She drains his life energy by about 75%, which puts him into an immediate stupor until his energy levels can recharge. This cannot be blocked by mental shielding. Evidence exists that this effect is enhanced by a reaction to chemicals in the man's semen, as wearing a condom cuts the energy drain to about 60%.

Notes on Kashani (Succubus) Gift: Limited evidence indicates that certain other Talents are strongly tied to the Succubus gene, indicating an interrelated gene complex - full Neural disruption, Empathic Projection, Electrokinesis, Orgonekinesis, and Energy Draining have been found in all Succubi tested. It also has been found that carriers of the S-gene, both men and women, manifest the same Gift/Talent complex as full Succubi, with the exception of the Succubus Gift.

Made in United States
Troutdale, OR
10/14/2023

13715515R00166